Publisher's Note:

Thank you for purchasing this book. It began as an idea, was shaped by the creativity of its talented author, and was subsequently molded into the book you have before you by a team of editors and designers.

Like all EDGE books, this book is the result of the creative talents of a dedicated team of individuals who all believe that books (whether in print or pixels) have the magical ability to take you on an adventure to new and wondrous places powered by the author's imagination.

As EDGE's publisher, I hope that you enjoy this book. It is a part of our ongoing quest to discover talented authors and to make their creative writing available to you.

We also hope that you will share your discovery and enjoyment of this anthology on social media through Facebook, Twitter, Goodreads, Pinterest, etc., and by posting your opinions and/or reviews on Amazon and other review sites and blogs. By doing so, others will be able to share your discovery and passion for this book.

Brian Hades, publisher

FANTASTIC TRAINS

AN ANTHOLOGY OF
PHANTASMAGORICAL ENGINES AND RAIL RIDERS

STORIES SELECTED BY
NEIL ENOCK

EDGE SCIENCE FICTION AND FANTASY PUBLISHING
An Imprint of HADES PUBLICATIONS, INC.
CALGARY

Fantastic Trains
An Anthology of Phantasmagorical Engines and Rail Riders

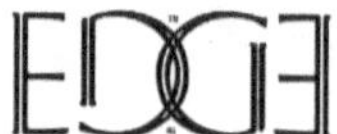

EDGE SCIENCE FICTION AND FANTASY PUBLISHING
An Imprint of HADES PUBLICATIONS, INC.
P.O. Box 1714, Calgary, Alberta, T2P 2L7, Canada

The EDGE Team:
Producer: Brian Hades
Acquisitions Editor: Michelle Heumann
Edited by: Heather Manuel
Cover Design: 100covers

ISBN: 978-1-77053-201-4

EDGE Science Fiction and Fantasy Publishing and Hades Publications, Inc. acknowledges the ongoing support of the Alberta Foundation for the Arts and the Canada Council for the Arts for our publishing programme.

Library and Archives Canada Cataloguing in Publication
CIP Data on file with the National Library of Canada
ISBN: 978-1-77053-201-4
(e-Book ISBN: 978-1-77053-200-7)

FIRST EDITION
(20190730)
Printed in USA
www.edgewebsite.com

Contents

Soul Train

Gavin Bradley

The train waited impatiently to depart the platform. It was a nightmarish mechanism straight from one of Dante's worst nightmares; made almost entirely of black metal, with joints held together with blood-spattered bones, flesh, and other fortunately unidentifiable gristle. The station was nothing more than a huge, prehistoric cave, its dark corners illuminated by dim torches and the beady eyes of flitting, formless creatures. An eye-watering, acrid stench completed the general "damned for eternity" motif.

Rooted to the spot on a rusted platform stood a short, plump man in a yellow anorak. He clutched a thermos of tea, his eyes wide.

"Toll!" yelled Charon, appearing from a nearby cabin. The little man gripped his thermos more tightly, staring at the train.

Charon sighed. He strode down onto the platform, stopping to loom over the man. The ferryman's skeletal body was interwoven with blue flames that some Ancient Greek poet had considered suitably occult for a vase. He wore a pair of blue and white striped overalls, a matching conductor's hat, and a badge saying: "Hello! My name is Charon and I give a Damn about good service!"

He sometimes wondered if the badge undid all the work of the blue flames.

Charon looked at the little man with bemused concern; it was like seeing a teddy bear front and center at an Iron Maiden concert. Another screamer, he thought wearily.

"Do you have your toll?" he asked.

"Erm, pardon?" said the man, peeling his eyes away from the train and seemingly noticing the enormous, combustible skeleton for the first time.

Charon groaned. He hated having to do this.

"Hark cowering spirit! I am Charon, Ferryman of the Dead, entrusted by the eternals to give passage to all damned souls of the earth to their place of eternal torment," he said in the joyless tones of somebody for whom the phrase "I'm getting too old for this shit" would be the understatement of the millennium. "As each man must payeth his passage in life, so be it in death, and I, Charon, am burdened to collect or cast ye into the pit!"

"Payeth?" said the man.

"Pay, then!" said Charon testily. "If I don't say it word for word, I get a pretty pointed memo from Inhuman Resources."

"Inhuman Resources?"

Charon waved a hand dismissively. "Health and Safety meetings on a Saturday, emails about the coffee machine with the word 'respect' underlined, 'team building' exercises pushing some bloody boulder up a hill. Inhuman, get it?"

"Oh, I suppose," replied the man.

"Listen," said Charon, with the almost endless patience of a skeleton, "I need your toll for the train, right? Two pennies. Very reasonable. It's the only rate that hasn't gone up with inflation. Head office doesn't think it's worth it to price people out of a ticket I guess."

The little man looked blank.

"Don't tell me you haven't got it?" asked Charon, rising to his full, imperious height.

The little man patted his pockets theatrically, in the universal gesture of all those who have discovered, lo and behold, that they have misplaced their wallet, only after ordering ten drinks at the bar (this is usually followed by a bartender looking toward the bouncers and making the universal gesture for "take them into the alleyway and, lo and behold, kick them repeatedly in the crotch").

"I'm afraid I don't have any change," he said, "but do you take transit cards?"

"Transit cards!" laughed the ferryman. "I am Charon! I have taken your greatest kings and lowest monsters across the river! I am trusted by the King of Hell himself, and you want to know if I take transit cards?"

"Well, do you?" persisted the man politely.

Charon turned away briefly, pulled a small handbook out of his overalls, and ran a bony finger down a page. "Unbelievable," he muttered to himself.

"Well, as a matter of fact, we do," he admitted. "But," he waved his hand in the air and a little card machine appeared, "we might not have done!" He sighed again. "Swipe here, please."

The little man swiped, but made no movement toward the train, instead returning to gaze at the horrifying steam engine before him.

"Look," said Charon, "what's your name?"

"Name? Erm, Henry," said Henry.

"Well, Henry, it's really not that bad. Mostly for show, see? Head office thought that ferrying people four at a time was an 'improper use of resources'," he continued, spitting the phrase out like bad wine. "Not to mention, people kept pushing me over the side and legging it back up the hill. Bloody Orpheus."

"Not that bad?" said Henry dreamily.

"That's right," said Charon encouragingly. "If it helps, think of it as a big prop."

"Not bad?!" repeated the man.

Charon hesitated. There was something different in the small, chubby man's eyes. They were twinkling.

"It's the most marvelous thing I've ever seen!" Henry yelled.

"Wait … what?" said Charon, but the little man had already scampered excitedly into the closest compartment.

"Wait 'til I tell our Marnie!" echoed Henry from inside the train.

"Come back here!" yelled Charon, striding arthritically after him. The whistle was blowing.

Inside, Henry was flitting excitedly from one part of the compartment to the other, running his hands down the brass rails, the black, mahogany paneling inlaid with bones and teeth, staring open-mouthed and occasionally unscrewing the lid of his thermos to take a nervous swig. "And I thought the 2:13 from Portsmouth to Weymouth was good! Wait 'til I tell our Marnie; she won't believe me!"

"Will you please take your seat," pleaded Charon, grabbing Henry by the arm. "We're leaving!"

"Sit? How can I sit? Look at this thing! It's incredible!" He shook free of the conductor's grip and scampered off to the far end of the cab, toward the other passengers.

Oh, Hades, thought Charon. Not another one. Over the millennia he'd had screamers, gigglers, cacklers, and for some had even had to venture to the supplies cupboard for a mop and bucket, but there was nothing like a hobbyist to take all the fun out of eternal damnation. What if Prometheus, chained to his mountain, had turned around and said, "Oh my! The quite rare, exceedingly vicious Aegean eagle! I must tell our Marnie!" There wasn't a special circle of hell reserved for people who traveled the world to take pictures of roundabouts or who spent hours, years, and marriages building scale replicas of naval ships from popsicle sticks in their basements, but, thought Charon, there really should be. The man who will spend a small fortune on a misprinted stamp is a man to be kept away from any metal cutlery.

"Just sit down would you?" he hissed.

"I couldn't possibly! Do you know where we are?" asked Henry.

"Do you know where we're going?" replied Charon, incredulous.

"Like that matters!" said Henry, waving a hand. "We're sitting inside Bar Car 3674!"

"Well actually, there's a lot more than three thousand, believe me."

"No, Bar Car 3674! Agatha Christie? Murder on the Orient Express?" He waited expectantly.

"Christie, Christie..." mused Charon. "The name rings a bell. You wouldn't happen to know if she was a cat person, would you?"

"Cats? I don't know," replied Henry. "Is that important?"

"I should say so! The boss is very keen on cats. Says if he spent the rest of eternity, he couldn't come up with a more naturally malevolent creature. You don't know how many people have booked their ticket on this train because of a stray kick to one of the little bastards," said Charon, whose own feelings toward felines were somewhat jaded by their prevalence to use his legs as scratching posts and, occasionally, toilets.

"Well, I don't really know about that," admitted Henry, "but Old Aggie certainly knew her trains. That's why she was our Marnie's favorite."

"Aggie!" Charon clicked his fingers, something which comes naturally to a skeleton. "Short lady? Curly hair? Always scribbling?" he asked.

"That sounds right. Did you know her?"

"Know her? She's given us some of our best ideas!" enthused Charon. "Only been down here forty-five years, but that woman's moving down in the world, believe me! The things I could tell you…"

But Henry had stopped listening. In fact, he was not even in the same compartment.

"The rest of the train is even older!" he yelled from the next carriage, which was packed with the type of people you wouldn't want to meet on a sunny day at the beach, never mind in a dark alley. Oblivious to the glares, grumbles, and growls of the other passengers, Henry continued to inspect the roof, windows and seats, vibrating with excitement and occasionally murmuring, "Wait 'til I tell our Marnie!"

He began to speak to the other passengers. "Excuse me, would you fellows mind moving out of the way? I really would like to see what you've got under there!"

Charon grabbed Henry and yanked him out of the carriage just as the first knife buried itself in the wall behind him. He was dead already, of course, but souls tend to remember things like: "a knife in the head really hurts."

"Why did you do that?" protested Henry.

"Not everyone appreciates being here as much as you do," said Charon.

"Oh, you think so?" said Henry, disappointed. "Well, trains can't be everybody's idea of a good time I suppose."

"That's true," agreed the skeleton, who knew that for many of the passengers a good time involved a pair of garden shears and a game of "Find the Fingers."

Henry brightened. "Perhaps if I just had a little chat..."

But Charon was ready for this, and before Henry could move toward the door he had a bony hand on the little man's shoulder, holding him back. The conductor could see the other passengers through the window and was grateful that they were only staring daggers. He looked down at Henry with exasperation. Suddenly two pennies per ticket and free rail travel didn't seem worth it. He decided to try reason.

"Listen, Henry," he said, "you do understand that this is the train to Hell, right? Eternal damnation, demons, pitchforks, bagpipers, lakes of fire, all that?"

"Yes, you mentioned that," replied Henry, smiling happily.

"And you're okay with that?"

"Well, it's not ideal, but Marnie always says: 'It's not where you're going, but how you get there.' And just look at this thing — it's amazing! It's like the grandfather of all trains!"

"That may be, but we can't have people running around enjoying themselves, got it? It's bad for morale. Well," Charon conceded, "it's good for morale, which is bad for morale, you see?"

"Not really," admitted Henry.

"What I'm trying to say is..." Charon hadn't slept in over three millennia, but suddenly he felt very, very tired. "What will it take for you to just sit down?"

"Well ... if it's not too much bother, I would like to see the engine room?" ventured Henry.

"Bother? Of course not! I wouldn't want you to feel as if you're imposing..." said Charon bitterly.

"Thank you, it's very kind of you."

"Lower your voice, would you?" hushed Charon, looking around nervously.

He clicked his fingers and, in an instant, they were standing in the train's engineer cab, with a great medieval mess of a boiler in front of them. Behind the firebox door, flames roared over sulfuric coal, bones, teeth, and other fossil fuels. Above them crisscrossed a maze of release valves and pipes, creaking and groaning with the pressure from the steam that leaked out of every joint.

"Amazing!" exclaimed Henry.

Charon looked down immodestly at his fingers. "Well, I have been doing this a long time…"

"What? Oh, I suppose that was a nice trick, but I was talking about the boiler. And couldn't we have just walked?"

"It's a long train," said Charon defensively. "And an even longer walk without it," he hinted.

"But we could have stopped to look at…"

"Exactly," cut in Charon.

"Who's there?" said a haggard voice from somewhere around the back of the boiler. "I'm warnin' you, I've a shovel here! It's not very sharp, but I can use it to stoke the boiler with the bones of you thieving basta— Oh, it's you Charon." A face (by technical definition) appeared. Exposed bone with some defiant fragments of skin and flesh clinging here and there gave the impression that the skull had been dunked in superglue and rolled around in some grizzly arts and crafts supplies. The supporting body made Charon look positively plump, and bore the tattered remains of a brown suit that had presumably gone out of fashion with the Victorians. Its occupant was obviously, undeniably, and pungently, dead.

"Who's this with you then?" asked the walking corpse. "Not giving tours again, are we Charon? Remember Orpheus?"

"Don't remind me Gresley. You know the Harpies won't let me forget that one."

"Won't stop harping on about it, eh?" There was a sound from Gresley, as he nudged a bare elbow into Charon's ribs, which could have been either laughter or tuberculosis.

"Did you say Gresley?" asked Henry. "Not Herbert Gresley?"

"That's right," said Gresley, tightening his grip on the shovel. "I don't owe you money, do I?"

"Every Raily knows Herbert Gresley!"

"Really?" asked Charon, surprised.

"No — Raily!" There was that small, embarrassed silence that is the natural successor to all really terrible puns. Charon, despite being the ferryman of the dead for millennia, had never actually taken a life, but he found himself seriously reconsidering this stance.

"Sorry, just our little joke," said Henry, nervously sipping from his thermos. "I suppose I'm just a bit giddy — this is the Herbert Gresley! The Flying Scotsman!"

"So?" asked Charon, who was really more of a boat man. "Anyone could push a Scot over a…"

"No, no," interrupted Henry. "The Flying Scotsman was a train. Probably the greatest one ever built! It could travel from Edinburgh to London in just over four hours, which was unheard of at the time! Just wait 'til I tell our Marnie!"

"Is that true Gresley?" asked Charon with polite interest.

The decaying face wrinkled into something, which, in some German impressionist's painting, could be deemed a smile. "Well, in my day, I was known for being a bit of a deft hand around a steam engine. The Flying Scotsman was my crowning achievement, before this of course." He waved a hand to indicate the train.

"You designed this?" asked Henry. "No wonder it's so … incredible!"

"You think so?" asked Gresley, giving Charon a slow "Is he for real?" look, to which the skeleton gave a weary nod.

"Of course I do! It's beautiful!" enthused Henry, his plump, earnest little face beaming.

"Thank you, that's very kind," said Gresley, and Charon groaned. "The guidelines for décor were a little strict, obviously, but it has become a bit of a passion project for me."

"You should be proud!" said Henry encouragingly. "So much power up front, carrying so much elegance behind — it's never been done before, I'm sure of it. If people up top saw this, they wouldn't believe their eyes!"

"That's certainly true," muttered Charon, and Gresley glared at him.

"Well, thank you…" began the engineer.

"Henry," said Henry.

"Thank you Henry. It's not often you get that type of appreciation down here." He shot an accusing glance toward Charon. "Tell you what," he continued, with an attempt at a conspiratorial smile that simply served to shift the remaining skin from one side of the mouth to the other. "How would you like to have a go on the controls?"

Charon, who had been pleasantly drifting off into a personal fantasy that didn't involve trains or little, fat, cheerful men in coats, was startled back to reality. "Now wait a moment Gresley, we can't just…"

Gresley waved him away before he could finish. "Oh don't be such a bag of old bones Charon." He ushered Henry over to a small control panel beside the firebox. "I mean there's not really much to do since we modernized the control panel. You just need to work this lever forward and back, and as long as you don't— Hey wait!"

But it was too late.

Henry had already leaped forward in uncontrollable excitement, grabbing hold of the large lever and pushing it forward until it hammered into the control board. The train lurched backward momentarily, and then shot forward angrily, speeding up with every second, and throwing Charon and Gresley to the floor of the cab.

"AMAZING!" shouted Henry, over the din of the blazing firebox and the yells of his two passengers. Steam erupted furiously out of the chimney, as the train continued to speed up; some even billowed in through the windows, creating a sulfurous sauna of heat and fog. Henry was almost entirely horizontal, and only a desperate grip on the lever prevented him from flying, as it were, entirely off the handle. Over the whines of the protesting engine and the screech of the wheels grinding against the track, Charon could swear he heard the words "wait", "tell" and "Marnie!" He had to stop this before they derailed. He was fairly certain he couldn't die, but it would take all the king's hell hounds and all the king's demons to piece him back together again.

Across the compartment, Gresley was frantically scrabbling on the floor, attempting to toss flaming pieces of coal back in through the flung-open firebox door, while trying not to follow them. Charon threw an errant lump at the engineer, and Gresley risked a glance up from his desperate task. Charon called out, but realizing it was pointless in the clamor, tried to convey the best "How the Hell do we stop this thing?"

look that his smooth, featureless skull could muster. Gresley, with the telepathy of the nearly skeletal, nodded toward a small chain in the corner of the panel closest to Charon.

Struggling to find his feet, he hauled himself upright on the side door. Outside he could see the blur of red, orange and black as lakes of fire, bottomless pits, and caves of unspeakable horror whirled past, so nauseatingly quick that he was suddenly glad he didn't have a stomach. For one sickening moment, as they sped around a hairpin bend, the whole train lurched to one side, and he realized they were traveling on one set of wheels. To his left, he could hear the sheer, unbridled, joyous laughter of Henry at the controls. Mad cackles he could handle, and bellowing, villainous chuckles practically qualified as white noise in Hell, but there was something unsettling about the pleasant man in the jacket's exuberant little giggle as the train plowed headlong toward the abyss.

At last, Charon reached the chain and pulled down hard. There was a hideous screech as the brakes made desperate contact with the tracks; sparks flew up outside the side door, inches from the skeleton's face. Almost as suddenly as it had accelerated, the train shuddered to a halt, sending Charon to the floor once more. Slowly, carefully, he picked himself up. He could hear the growls and groans of the passengers in the cars behind as they no doubt did the same. There wasn't an overabundance of teeth as it was, but after that, there was probably a pretty competitive game of "pin the molar on the gum" going on back there.

The cab was silent except for the occasional whimper from the cooling engine, and the hiss of the steam as it escaped the pipes and snaked out of the windows.

Gresley spoke. "Of course," he said, "she goes a little bit faster than the Scotsman."

"You think?" said Charon, barely controlling his anger.

"I think it was incredible!" chirped Henry, infuriatingly happy.

There was an almost audible "twang" as Charon snapped.

"Incredible? Incredible?!" he yelled. "We nearly went off the bloody track! Do you know the punishment I'd get for crashing this thing? Do you know the trouble I'd get into? Do you know," he said, with extra venom, "the damn paperwork they'd make me fill out?"

"I'm sorry, I didn't mean…"

"Of course you didn't, you stupid little man! You don't have a mean bone in your body, do you?" He threw his hands in the air. "You show up here, in Hell, with your stupid jacket and your stupid thermos, and your stupid smile and start saying how amazing everything is. It's not supposed to be amazing! It's supposed to be, well … hellish! I bet if they threw you into the lake of fire you'd say, 'Thanks very much, it's been awhile since I've had a hot bath!'"

Henry gave a little chuckle. "Well, Marnie did always used to say that I could find the pound in a jar of pennies."

"Shut up! Shut up! Shut up!" screamed Charon, striding over and picking Henry up by the lapel of his coat. "Listen, everything is not roses. It's fertilizer. This is the train to Hell, but I bet if the boss himself showed up, you'd shake him by the hoof, tell him how much you enjoyed the ride and say 'Wait 'til I tell our Martha!'"

"Marnie," corrected Henry.

"What?" barked Charon, momentarily snapped out of his possibly soul-icidal rage.

"The name is Marnie, not Martha," said Henry stoically. "I'd appreciate it if you got it right."

"Marnie then, whatever," said the skeleton, releasing Henry. "Who is that anyway — part of your little train group? Sad little fat men in rain jackets with hobbies so boring that they make Sisyphus's afternoon look like a day at the races." Behind him, Gresley cleared his throat unusually loudly for someone who didn't have much of one left, but tact was never really first nature to Charon. "No, I've got it! A cat! Marnie's a cat, right? Probably the only thing on the planet that could stand you!"

"She was my wife."

"Probably another little twerp in a— What? Oh. Well." The conductor stuttered, derailed. "You know in Ancient Greek 'twerp' really translates as…"

"We met at Charring Cross station," said Henry. "I'd forgotten my thermos, and she offered me a sip of hers. It was blueberry tea." He continued with a sad little smile,

"Then we just sat and watched all the trains come in, until it was just us left in the station. She passed last year."

Charon stared. The little man was staring straight ahead. It was the first time the ferryman had seen him without a smile on his face.

"Why are you here?" asked Charon softly.

"Well there was a train coming into the station and I just sort of … tripped, you know?"

"No, no." Charon waved a hand dismissively. "That doesn't matter. I mean, what did you do? Why are you on this train?" He clicked his fingers again. Gresley and the wreck of the engine room disappeared and they were once more inside the main compartment, surrounded by the other passengers. None of them were paying the pair any attention. The train shuddering to a halt had had the same effect as, say, the saloon doors swinging, the jukebox cutting out and a pool cue being swung at the bartender.

"Do you see him?" Charon put a bony hand on Henry's shoulder and pointed at a man with a murderous smile of sharp, metal teeth, who was making an industrious effort to bite his way through another man's leg. "High-level assassin with some country or other. Very troubled man. Hundreds of successful missions, until he was scheduled to kill a man during an MRI. Always mean to cats; I don't think he's even a dog person." He spun Henry around to a woman wearing a charred gray jumpsuit, who was whispering to some unseen figure beside her. "And her? Set more fires than the whole of the Grecian army. Burned hospitals, schools, but should have avoided the petrol stations."

"And him?" asked Henry, pointing to a nondescript man in a charcoal suit and tie, complete with round, gold glasses and a briefcase.

Charon gave the man a look of deep distaste and said, "Investment banker."

Henry nodded in understanding. "I think I see what you mean," he said, "but why are you telling me?"

"These are all bad people, not little men with thermoses who 'tripped' in front of an incoming from Dartmouth."

"Weymouth," corrected Henry.

"Whatever," snapped Charon. "The point is that all of them did something to get here, something terrible. Don't spread it around, but it's actually pretty hard to get a ticket these days. Now, why are you here?"

"Well I, erm, I was in another place, a lot brighter than this, no offence of course, and I asked if there were any trains nearby and the man, or at least I think he was a man, he had a sort of dress on, said that people didn't need to take trains because everybody flew and I said, 'well air travel's all very well and good but you can't beat some steam and a track to really see the country,' but he didn't really seem to come around at all, and actually got a bit testy, although I suppose he's under a lot of stress with all those people in line and everything, but eventually he said he knew a place with a great big train and I could go see it if I, erm, darned well pleased — only he didn't say 'darned' you know, which I thought was a little unprofessional. So, I said, 'yes please,' and the next moment I was here."

There was silence as Charon tried to pluck the salvageable pieces of information from the slew of words, like the last edible parts of a Thanksgiving turkey. "Did you say bright?" he managed finally.

"Yes. Very," replied Henry.

"And robes, something about robes?"

"That's right."

"And ... flying?"

"Oh yes. They were very keen on it."

"Bastards!"

"I'm sorry?"

"So am I." Charon grabbed Henry by the scruff of the neck and dragged him by his side.

"Stand still, got it?"

"Erm, yes, but listen I don't mean to be any bother," said Henry, but Charon wasn't listening.

His eyes glowed red as he muttered to himself. "Bloody harp and dresses brigade. I'm sick of them throwing their trash down here! Well I'm not going to stand for it anymore!"

"Exactly what are we doing?" asked Henry nervously.

Charon looked down. "Listen," he said, "you obviously don't belong here, but I doubt they'll let you back upstairs. Take it from me; they can hold a grudge for a hell of a long time. But I think I know just the place."

"Oh. I don't suppose… Are there any trains?"

Charon's natural grin got even wider. "You'll see."

He clicked his fingers.

———— «» ————

"Passengers please step away from the platform. Apologies for the delay, but the next train is not in service and won't be taking passengers at this time. We appreciate your patience and will notify you on the updated schedule as soon as possible."

A loudspeaker shrilled overhead with the kind of nasal, monotonous voice that derives a sadistic satisfaction from phrases such as "please stay on the line" and "your call is important to us."

"Thank you again for choosing Purgatory, and have a nice eternity."

"Welcome to Purgatory," announced Charon with a theatrical sweep of his skeletal hand.

"Purgatory? But it's a…"

"Train station?" interrupted Charon. "Yes, I thought it might be, for you anyway. And luckily the trains are impossible to catch here, because they don't really go anywhere. It's all about the waiting I believe. For some people, it's outside the principal's office, others a hospital room. For most people, it's an airport; Heathrow I think, which I always thought was a little mean. That's more like something our lot would think up."

All around them people were pacing on the platforms, staring at watches, tapping their feet, waiting without much optimism by empty baggage carts and flicking through coffee kiosk magazines that didn't appear to be from this decade. Steam trains rolled into the station, paused for what seemed like only seconds, and then disappeared to be replaced by others.

"It's the most marvelous place I've ever seen," whispered Henry. "At least twice the size of St. Pancras." He stopped his wide-eyed staring for a moment and turned to Charon. "But won't you get in trouble for doing this?"

"Me?" said Charon, surprised. "I imagine not. The man downstairs will like that I took the initiative; he's very big on that sort of thing. We have meetings on it and everything," he continued with the best indignant eye roll his sockets could manage. "Besides, he'll probably insist on sending a couple up the other way, just to even things up."

"But you can't stay?" asked Henry.

"Oh Hades, no! I've got a train to repair thanks to you," said Charon.

"Sorry about that."

"Well," shrugged the conductor, "you know where to find me."

"But I don't think I do…" began Henry.

"That's right," Charon hurriedly cut in. "Anyway, I don't think you'll need the company." He nodded behind the little man, clicked his fingers, and vanished once more.

"I wonder what he meant by that?" said Henry.

"Hello, love," said a quiet voice from behind him.

Henry turned around, slowly.

In front of him stood a small, rosy cheeked woman smiling apologetically in a yellow anorak, with mousy brown curls escaping out from under a matching hat.

"I forgot my thermos," she said.

Henry smiled back and handed her the flask in his hand. "It's blueberry," he said. "I hope you don't mind."

——— «》 ———

On a bench in Purgatory, the odd little couple sat down wordlessly, sipping blueberry tea and watching the trains arrive and depart.

Eternity began.

——— « O » ———

Gavin Bradley

Gavin Bradley is an Irish writer living in Canada, and has published short stories in *Glass Buffalo* literary magazine, and the anthologies, *Frozen Fairy Tales*, Dark Lane's: *Weird Tales 3*, *Ignis Fatuus*, and *Tesseracts 21*, amongst others. He has also published poetry in magazines and collections on both sides of the Atlantic and was selected for the Irish Times: 'New Irish Writing' award.

A Wish of Childhood

Melodie Leclerc

A train. I'd always wanted to ride on a train. Not one at a park, not a subway or an LRT, but an actual train with passenger cars, dining cars, sleeping cars... The whole package.

Sad that it had taken so long for me to finally manifest that wish. Out of the corner of my eye, I watched my fiancé speaking to a man loading a large crate. I vaguely remembered something about the special cargo she needed to bring home with her, but I couldn't find the memory that would have told me what it was. Most people would likely have just asked but she was always accusing me of not listening to her and we'd already had a serious fight; adding to it wouldn't be the smartest move I could make. How hard could it really be to figure out on my own anyway?

The train caught my attention again and I felt a little giddy, like a kid with a bag of Halloween candy. I could see they were already boarding passengers, and I turned back to where my fiancé had been, to find that her and the crate were no longer there. She had probably boarded without me — likely still angry about the fight we'd had. I couldn't even remember what it had been about. Which usually meant that it hadn't really been important. We were going to have to sort it out, but perhaps delaying that discussion wouldn't be ill advised. We both had long-burning tempers — time or physical exertion was usually necessary in order for a more coolheaded and rational solution to prevail.

Trying not to lose the good feeling I had, I got on the train. I wasn't quite sure where my seat was or if I had a place in a sleeping compartment. Well, it would come to me or I'd find my fiancé.

In the first car, I started to make my way down the aisle.

"We'll be rich!" a gentleman at the far end shouted excitedly, almost coming to his feet before his companion shushed him, firmly holding him in his seat while speaking quickly and earnestly.

Sensing that my attention or interest was likely unwanted, I did my best to focus on the design of the car, the smell of leather, machinery, and people, and the noise of other conversations and work being done. It was actually pretty easy to do, and I moved past them and into the next car without incident.

A quick scan of the few passengers in the seats showed a distinct lack of the woman I planned to marry. Focused as much as I was on trying to find her familiar features among the faces in the seats, I almost tripped over a young boy playing in the aisle right in front of me. Thankfully my reflexes were good enough that I managed to catch the corner of a seat and prevent myself from landing on him.

His big blue eyes peered up at me through a strip of black cloth that had holes cut out for his eyes. A messy blond mop of hair floated above the dark mask almost like a glowing halo and, of course, he had on a blue and red cape to finish off the look. His face split into a cheeky grin that displayed dimples. He couldn't have been more than six years old. "Hey mister, do you need help?"

Smiling back was instinctual. "No, I'm fine. Thanks for the offer though. You should be careful. Being in the middle of the aisle could cause an accident."

At once the innocent smile turned serious and he jumped onto the seat closest to him. "Right. It's a superhero's job to stop accidents and bad guys. I'm gonna be the best superhero in the world and beat up the bad guys and save people."

Nodding at him, I tried to show that I took what he said seriously. "That is a very noble cause, young man. Work hard and I know you'll succeed. Good luck."

"Thanks mister! Be careful, and if you need my help beating up bad people let me know. I'm a ninja you know."

"I will. My thanks." I turned quickly to hide my smile as I moved down the car. I was almost at the other end when an older woman, looking a bit frazzled, stumbled in.

"Excuse me, have you seen a young superhero around by chance? My grandson..."

Pointing back the way I'd come, I shifted so she had a good view of who she was looking for. She let out a heavy sigh. "Thanks. I've never actually got to meet him until now. You'd think that after raising my own children a grandchild would be like getting back on a bicycle. But that isn't so. I'd better get to him and have a bit of a talk... His parents are counting on me to take good care of him until they're able to join us and that could take a while. Thanks again."

Not bothering to watch them reunite I kept going, only to find myself in the dining car, where I finally spotted my fiancé. She was sitting near the window, a wistful smile on her face as the train finally started to move. She seemed so sad, even lost... If I could just remember why we'd fought, there might be a chance for me to help replace that forlorn look with one of her soft "you're ridiculous, but you're my ridiculous" smirks. Perhaps, if I could find out what was in the crate, maybe it could jog my memory... But how to do it while avoiding making her feel worse...

I made my way over to her table and sat in the chair opposite her, following her gaze out the window. "Thank you for this. I know you would have preferred to fly because it would have been quicker. It means a lot to me."

Her smile seemed to become a bit less sad and more wistful. Her voice soft, barely a whisper, she said, "We should have done this sooner."

"All that really matters is that we did it."

We fell into silence as we both watched the scenery pass by.

———— «◊» ————

Walking up to our table, a waiter asked if he could get anything. I shook my head but she ordered a ginger ale, casually mentioning that her stomach was a little queasy. I was about to ask if there was something I could do but she abruptly went back to staring out the window, and the words stuck in my throat.

I had learned long before that trying to force a conversation when she wasn't interested or ready for one would only lead to a more difficult situation for both of us. We both had a lot of emotion and, sadly, emotion was far from logical. She needed time to process what she was feeling so she could deal with it more rationally, and I usually did too. If I could just remember what our fight was about ... or what was in that crate...

"Look honey, I want to get a better look at the train. How about I meet you where we'll be spending the trip? Do you have our seat locations?"

She sighed slightly before slowly moving her ticket from where it had been hidden by her purse and arm. The black color of her dress made her skin seem much paler than it actually was. She took a sip of her drink as I leaned over to gently kiss her cheek. She shivered at the contact.

"I'll see you soon darling. Make sure to put on a sweater if you find yourself cold. Maybe try to get some rest." A soft smile tugged at the corner of her mouth, and her fingers gently touched her cheek.

Satisfied, I slipped out ahead of a train conductor making his way slowly through the dining section checking tickets, and I continued on to the end of the car, opposite the way I had come.

The next two cars were for passengers so there was no crate in sight. It was likely something she had to transfer due to her job at the museum. Possibly an artifact of some value but not so expensive or delicate that it needed a special or armed transport. If that was the case, though, something should spring to mind. Some fragment of memory tantalizingly close to the surface. Still, there was nothing, despite my inner peace needing to know the answer. If I couldn't remember before I found it, I might have to open it when I got there... Unless there was a really descriptive shipping label on it somewhere, maybe a manifest.

I stopped at an open seat and sat down for a second to look outside at the world racing by. It seemed as though that crate and what was in it was making me a little obsessed. Why did I believe so strongly that the answers to what I'd forgotten, the fight we'd had, the tension I felt, the sadness on my love's face, even the train ride itself, were inside?

Truth was, I didn't have a real answer, just a strong feeling and an overwhelming urge to find out, that only intensified the longer it took.

"Sir? Is there anything I can help you with?"

Glancing up, I found a young woman, blond hair in a braid, wearing a conductor's uniform.

I smiled slightly at her, though it likely looked rather crooked considering she'd surprised me. Almost as if she'd appeared out of nowhere. That and she was an entirely different conductor than the one I'd seen in the dining car.

"Is it that obvious?"

Her wide eyes held sympathy. "Sort of comes with the job. When you deal with people on a regular basis, in a more intimate way, well, you develop a knack for reading situations and individuals' souls fairly accurately. My offer stands, of course. Do you need any help?"

"Well, my fiancé and I have a large crate traveling with the cargo. I just want to make sure it's okay. Do you think you could take me to it? Just so I can have peace of mind?"

"It's not something we do regularly, but I was about to go check on that car anyway. Having a little company on the way there wouldn't be a bad thing. Is this your first time traveling by train?" She moved a step back so that I could get up.

"Yes actually. Something I've wanted to do since I was a young child but never had a chance. You know how life sometimes gets away from you; you keep putting your 'wants' aside to get done the things that take care of your needs or the needs of those you love. Sometimes it seems like five years — even if they were filled with happiness and love — goes by in the blink of an eye. That's sort of what happened to me, just really never got around to it until now, you know?"

She nodded slightly and moved in front of me, leading the way. "I hear that often, sir. It's a sentiment that many I've met seem to share."

We naturally fell silent as we walked.

As we were transitioning to the next car, we had to hug the wall to let another man pass. The man was grinning with an excitement I hadn't seen often — pure joy, as he stopped briefly beside me. "Isn't this wonderful? Not only a great mystery answered but an awfully big adventure as well. They might not think us fortunate or lucky but it's them I feel sorry for."

Just as quickly as he came, he was gone. The train conductor acted as if she hadn't heard anything and kept moving forward. I followed without asking her what she had thought he was talking about. After all, I couldn't risk the chance to see the crate for myself.

He was one of the most intriguing passengers I'd run into. Tied with him were the grandmother and her grandson. Still, there was something else about them that stuck out to me, something they shared, somehow, with the train conductor I was following. What it was eluded me, however.

"Next one is cargo, sir."

The second she said it my throat went dry and my feet seemed to turn to cement blocks. It wasn't rational, but I was suddenly afraid of what I was going to find out. It was just a large wooden box — nothing dangerous or scary. My fiancé wasn't fond of anything that was life-threatening or scared her, so why...

"Truth..."

"What?" I stared at the conductor, wide-eyed.

"I was just saying, truth is, we don't have a lot of time for this, so I hope you're ready to find what you were looking for." Without hesitating, she led the way into the cargo area.

For some reason the lights seemed brighter once she moved further inside, and I was blinded for a few seconds, blinking quickly to try to see through the dots dancing in my vision. A part of me must have thought that I would have a hard time finding the crate, but I didn't. It was right there in the middle of the car, as if it had been waiting for me the entire time. Creepy was an understatement; I wanted to run from the room and forget all about my unease and questions, but I was pulled toward it and couldn't stop myself until I was directly next to it. Slowly, I put my hands on the rough wood.

Without moving the crate's lid, somehow I could see what was inside, as if I had x-ray vision… Past the wooden top was the shiny, dark cherry red cover of a coffin. As I stared down at it, I knew, beyond a doubt, that my answers were nestled within. But my heart, mind and body froze, unwilling to see what I needed to.

The truth could only be put off for so long though, and soon I was looking down through the layers of wood and fabric, to my own face, held in a single moment in time. Me and yet not — just a vessel, like an empty shell I had shed because it was no longer able to contain me. I was no longer alive in the way that term had been defined all my life. That was the truth, and then I remembered.

─────── «» ───────

We'd been walking together. My love had told me we were expecting a child earlier in the day, and we were having a heated debate over names. Not unusual since our life together had always been filled with passion and testing each other's limits. It seemed the names we'd both loved since childhood were the exact ones the other couldn't stand. Such a trivial thing since it was the new life that was important, a gift. A name, whatever name we chose, was insignificant in comparison to that.

She had started to cross the road at the cross walk, more focused on the conversation than the street. What the driver of the car was most focused on, I have no idea, but the car didn't slow down as it was supposed to.

I didn't think, just moved, somehow finding the speed and strength to get to her side. I spun her around in my arms as if we were dancing, my eyes never leaving her face as I pushed her forcefully back toward the sidewalk. Watching the confusion in her eyes turn to horror as she processed what was happening. It was slow motion — so much happened in such a short time, seconds really.

There was no fear in my heart in that moment, only love. Love for her, for our unborn child.

I remember trying to tell her I loved her and that my lips moved, but I had no idea if she'd heard the words — all I could hope was that she could see all the love I felt showing in my eyes as I held her gaze. Just a brief moment in time, but it held everything within it.

The pain never touched me.

— «›» —

Peering up at the train conductor, things seemed to click into place. "You aren't really what you appear to be, are you?"

Her face seemed far more androgynous than I remembered it, as her lips curved slightly into a semblance of a smile that never touched the sorrow in her eyes. "No. Much is not as it appears to be — both in life and in death."

"Am I really on a train with her?" My fingers turned white on the edge of the crate as a tightness took hold of my chest.

"Yes and no. You now exist in separate planes but in the same place and time."

"She can't see or hear me, can she?"

A slight shaking of the blond head was the only response.

"But the others..." That was when I fully understood. The others I had interacted with were dead, like I was. The grandmother who'd only just met her grandson, the boy who wanted to be a superhero, the man on his greatest adventure — for what greater adventure or mystery was there than death? Perhaps even the two men who were trying to change their financial future... My fiancé hadn't actually spoken to me; at most I might have been able to claim that she had spoken at me. Not once had she even looked directly at me. And what about the baby...?

"She'll have a healthy baby boy. He'll be born on your birthday, and she will name him Leonidas for the love and sacrifice you showed that day. Leonidas as the great Spartan king who died so his people might live. Leonidas Alexander after his father who saved him. He will be a great man one day, and he'll never forget that you loved him and his mother."

"I wanted to be there for him." My heart ached and my voice cracked.

She laid a hand on my arm and I met her eyes. "You were."

———— « o » ————

Melodie Leclerc

Melodie Leclerc is an aspiring author hoping to make her mark on the world. She was born and raised in Langruth, Manitoba and graduated from the University of Alberta with a BA in English before teaching English in South Korea for two years. She is married and had three children — although her first son passed away, her remaining daughter and son continue to bring joy into her life.

Beg A Little Changeling Boy

Laura VanArendonk Baugh

This time, I'm going to tell you a story of the old days. Not the Oldest of Days, because I wasn't around then, but the days when steam engines pulled carriages of passengers and cargo into the West which was Indiana. This particular day, the engine pulled a carriage of children.

I wasn't worried about the infants and toddlers. No one was going to take them for cheap labor; they were a costly investment in money and time, and they would go only to those who truly wanted children.

The older children were old enough to be useful and young enough to be cute, and they were equally attractive to parents in need of a child and laborers in need of an apprentice. But the local committees generally did a decent job of evaluating potential homes.

The boys and girls in their teens faced the toughest odds. They weren't chubby-cheeked and adorable like the little ones, and they were suspected of carrying their bad habits west with them. They were old enough to look like hired help instead of the children they were, or should have been if they hadn't been aged so quickly on the streets of New York City.

It was not merely my duty to observe, it was my pleasure as well. It is perhaps the only advantage to being a half-breed freak of nature, the privilege of remaining in the human world and moving among the children the Fae can so rarely have. There are more than enough corresponding disadvantages. Still, my loyalty is to the Queen, wherever I am, and so I was here.

Already the crowd assembled at the platform was *awing* and pointing and enthusing over the various children available. *"Just look at those eyes!" "Those are some curls on that one, to be sure." "I'll bet he's a firecracker!"*

The younger children stared back, thumbs in mouths or fingers in hair, statue-still or twisting where they stood. It was a lot for a child to comprehend, traveling to a new state to find a new home and a new chance at life.

The older boys descended from the train carriage all in a group, clinging to the vestige of the gangs they might have known. They played it cool. They had learned to expect nothing, but had not yet mastered the ability to wish nothing.

I saw the moment he recognized the danger. I did not know what danger he sensed, but there was no mistaking the quick flare of his pupils, the defensive twitch of his arms to his torso, the step back into the shallow group as if to fade into the sea of humanity available in New York City. This was not a casual alarm, not for a boy who'd survived on city streets.

I scanned the crowd nearest him but saw no weapon, no particular leer, nothing which suggested a threat. Just two men whose smiles were a little more pleased than welcoming — a subtle distinction, but there's a lot of subtlety in my work, and I was looking for it.

Reverend Shapes and Sister Charity herded the children into a more-or-less organized mass and followed the beaming mayor down the street.

It's easy both to romanticize and to criticize what are now called the Orphan Trains, but look, none of you were there. You live in a world with Medicaid and OSHA, where children come home from mandatory school to play video games while parents work in safe cubicles or unionized trades. You might look at things differently if you saw children in dangerous factories or street gangs by day and sleeping on corners by night, if one in twenty residents of your own city was a homeless child begging or thieving or worse. "Oh, what a wonderful thing for children!" and "Oh, they should have done much better!" are equally mistaken views, luxuries of thought available only to those a century or more removed.

I was there. And children are my oath-sworn duty.

Back then, they weren't generally called Orphan Trains, and no one thought ill of a family expecting a child to work a farm alongside adults — all farmers' children did. And many of the children sent west weren't teens fit for physical labor, but young children abandoned by impoverished parents, rescued from slums where parents had died of disease or addiction, or surrendered to churches by parents who either had not wanted them or wanted them to have a better life.

As I said, I generally wasn't worried about these. East coast cities suffered tens of thousands of homeless children, but orphanages were scarcer in the west. A family wanting to adopt had little option but the out-placement children arriving on the train, and competition could be fierce.

We arrived at a restaurant which had been cleared of tables to make room. Reverend Shapes and Sister Charity sorted the children and asked them to please stand still and talk to the nice ladies and gentlemen, and stop chewing your hair, Agatha.

A woman in a pale dress, clearly her Sunday best for this occasion, kneeled on the swept floor to address this Agatha, with a man looking stoically hopeful close behind her. "We've waited ever so long for God to bring us a child. Would you like to come and be our little girl?"

She nodded, hair still in her mouth but smiling now, and the woman enfolded her into a warm embrace, squeezing her eyes against tears.

At least, I'm pretty sure that's what happened, as the sight was a little blurry for me, too. As I said, children are my duty, charged by the Queen herself. My task is to protect human children from human threats. I have enough Fae blood, too, that it's more than just duty.

I slipped down the line to where the male youths were clustered, trying to look detached and pleasant and unconcerned and useful all at once. The two pleased men were there, too, watching from a distance. I stepped up to the boys and put out my hand to the one who had scented danger on the platform. "Welcome to Indiana. I'm Robin Archer."

"Hello, sir." He hesitated, just for an instant — clever lad — but did not say more.

I gave him a secret smile to acknowledge that he was right to hesitate. This would be simpler if he trusted me. "Who are they?"

"Who?" he said, too quickly.

Well, I suppose he wouldn't trust me so quickly. "The two men, the ones you recognized on the platform."

His eyes widened. "You — you know, too?"

"I know nothing except that you know them, and would rather not."

He shook his head. "There's nothing going on, sir."

This wasn't going to be as easy as I'd hoped. "Let me know if you need a friend. Good luck to you all, boys."

A beefy farmer walked up; his face solemn. "Good afternoon, boys. I'll be honest, I'm looking for farm help. I lost my oldest son last year, and it's hard keeping up. I've got two younger sons and a daughter, and my wife's a true angel, but there's just so much to farming and I need the hands. It's hard work, but it's honest and I'll pay you a fair wage, and you'll live like one of the family."

One of the New York boys sniffed a derisive laugh, but another lifted his chin and said, "I appreciate your honesty, sir, and I'd be glad of a chance to try your work. I figure if a fight with the Plug-Uglies can't scare me, there's not much to your farm work which can."

The farmer's tanned face creased into a grin. "We'll see if you still talk that way when you got a sore cow that needs milking." He put out a hand. "I'm Sam Miller."

"Davey Cotters, sir."

I drifted back, watching the other children and prospective homes. It wasn't common here, but every water hole could draw predators, so it was good to keep an eye open.

A young boy pointed giddily to a couple in the crowd. "Are you Red Indians?" he demanded.

Look, it was a different time. He was a street child from an east-coast city of mostly European immigrants where the native populations had long gone, and the West was hardly more than the fantastic stuff of adventure stories. He would learn better. You would have done no differently in his place.

The couple laughed, and the man turned to the boy. "I'm not, but my wife is half, and some of our neighbors are Miami. One of them gave me this for our new son." He drew off the bow and arrow, tucked into a small quiver, which had caught the child's eye.

It was a real bow, unstrung and somewhat downsized, and the boy's eyes were saucer-wide as he reached to touch it. "Wow," he breathed.

The couple exchanged glances, and the wife stepped forward. "Would you like to talk a while?" she invited.

I left them to their introductions and walked on, scanning the crowd and watching the children. They were mostly starting to relax, giggling and talking with the anxious would-be parents.

"I don't see Greenly anywhere," someone was saying quietly to the mayor. "I think he stayed out of town today."

"Good, good." The mayor nodded. "I didn't want to have to order him out. Poor man. We all felt bad denying him, but I told him we just can't entrust a child to a man who hasn't got that drink under control."

I joined them. "Pardon me, sirs."

"I'm Mayor Landa. Pleased to meet you."

"Robin Archer, thank you. Pardon me, but did those men apply to your committee?" I indicated the two who had smiled on the platform.

The businessmen frowned. "I don't know that I've seen those men before. Are they local fellows?"

"I think they're here for a boy."

The mayor straightened with importance. "Not without approval from the committee. We have a responsibility."

So did I, and those men made the boy uncomfortable, which made me uncomfortable.

Sam Miller and Davey Cotters were waiting to speak to Reverend Shapes, and I took the opportunity. "Davey," I said, "my name is Robin Archer. What can you tell me about that boy?"

He followed my eyes. "Who, Harry? We knew each other before. Before the train, I mean. What do you want to know?"

"How does he know the men watching him?"

"What men?"

To be fair, Davey had his own concerns today. "Did Harry have any kind of trouble which could follow him out here?"

Davey shrugged. "His dad's in prison. Harry wasn't a part of that, don't be scared of him, sir."

"No worry there, Davey. Thank you."

The initial rush around the children had slowed, and now Sister Charity was introducing them and prompting each to say hello. I saw the pleased men slip toward the rear door, and I rushed for the front. I eased around the corner, between the two buildings, and paused just at the rear corner, where I could hear voices and the splash of liquid against the planking. Smell it, too. Disgusting.

"What if he doesn't want to tell us where it is?"

"Give me an hour with that boy, he'll want to tell every secret he ever had."

"He was doing okay for himself after Big Harry got picked up. He might be a bit of a scrapper."

"Not tied to a chair, he ain't. And nobody's enough of a scrapper to stand up to what I've been thinking. We start by smashing one toe, see, and move through every bone of the foot one at a time, just one foot, and then up, and then—"

"Shut up, I don't wanna hear about it. I don't want any part of that."

"You won't be so squeamish when we get our hands on that money. You'll want a piece of it, then."

"I was a part of that job too. That money's part mine already. Don't try to cut me out of this."

"It was Big Harry who cut us out. Only fair that his boy make it right."

There was a rustle of cloth as they repackaged themselves, and then the squeak of hinges.

It was a jaded story, asking a child about a father's hidden loot, but criminals never tired of cliché. Though Harry wouldn't see the weariness of it if these two got hold of him.

I circled the building and returned through the front door. I worked my way back to Harry, leaning against the wall with his arms crossed. I leaned beside him and propped a heel on the wall. "They knew your father?"

He scowled. "I knew you were lying."

"No, I didn't know when I asked. I know now, just as I know they plan to take you and make you tell where the money is hidden."

"And I suppose you want to help."

"I'd like to."

He laughed. "I'm not so dumb. Oldest touch in the book, to set up the threat and then pose someone as the angel to get you out, only the angel is part of the same gang. But usually they don't dress up an actual woman as the angel."

"I'm not a woman," I said with a sigh.

He gave me a skeptical look.

"Nor a man, either," I agreed.

His skepticism turned to a confused frown.

"And I'm not an angel, real or false. I'm something else entirely. And my task, whether you believe me or not, is to keep you and the others who came on the train safe."

He snorted. "Sounds like an angel to me."

"I don't need you to believe in me, Harry. Only to believe me." I flicked my eyes to the two men, now at the far side of the room. "Don't go with them, no matter what they offer you."

"Not likely."

"Good." I started away.

"Hey."

I turned back.

"I don't know where it is."

"I don't care," I answered. "That's not what I'm here for."

He blinked once, and I walked away.

The little boy was now clutching the Miami quiver to his chest with one hand, hugging it like another child might hug a doll, and grinning fiercely as he held the wife's hand with the other. It looked like that had ended well.

I saw Mayor Landa and one of the two men in close conversation across the room. The mayor looked uncomfortable. I started toward them.

"Sir, this is irregular, and we have the children's welfare to consider—"

"You got no reason to think I won't take excellent care of that boy," the man said. "You got nothing bad said against me."

"I don't have much good said for you either, Mr. Smith, and I don't know you well enough to hand a child over to you."

"That's no child, that's nearly a man, and he's been handling himself all right in a New York street gang, so what do you think he's got to fear from me? Ain't I got a right to adopt same as any other citizen?"

Mayor Landa caught sight of me behind Smith and seemed to remember his declaration. "The same as any other approved citizen, yes, and you haven't been approved. If you want to apply to the committee, sir, that's fine, and there'll be another train along—"

"I don't want to wait that long!" snapped Smith — if that was his real name. "I want that boy, today."

"I'm afraid that's impossible, Mr. Smith," said the mayor firmly.

"See if you get re-elected," growled Smith, turning away.

I followed him at a distance and worked my way to the rear of the crowd, edging closer to Smith and his companion. It was hard to pick out their whispers over the happy chatter.

"…not gonna work."

"What if we just follow home whoever adopts him? Take him from there?"

"Only if he ain't adopted here, he gets back on the train, and we have to…"

They pushed their heads closer together, and I couldn't hear more.

Well, now there were more people at risk than just Harry, which was bad enough. I worked my way back to Mayor Landa. "Excuse me, Mayor, but do you have a sheriff here?"

"Sure, Sheriff Tillerson. Why?"

"Call him here, and I'll explain."

"He's probably around, it being such a big day." The mayor turned to scan the crowd, and I turned with him.

Which is why neither of us were prepared for Smith to jump forward and pistol-whip Harry solidly in the face. Scrapper or not, Harry wasn't expecting a sucker punch with the butt of a revolver, and he was staggered.

Smith grabbed the stunned boy and pulled him around between himself and the startled onlookers. "I'll be taking this one with me," he said, leveling the gun and swinging it slowly back and forth to cover the room. "Looks like none of you had your heart particularly set on him, so I guess you won't mind much." He started for the door, pulling Harry with him. The boy's face was bleeding and he wasn't recovered enough yet to fight back.

Normally I carried a Colt 1877 Thunderer, which would have been enough to end the situation promptly. Smith was looking back and forth over the whole room, leaving small openings, and if you know anything about me or my kind, you know a quick shot over a slouching boy would have been simplicity itself. But the M1877 had a delicate temperament and was at this moment deposited with a gunsmith for yet another repair on the trigger spring. I had only my bare hands for stopping Smith.

Harry blinked and tried to rub blood from his eye, and Smith gave him a little shake. "Nothing funny, boy, or I'll lay you another," he warned.

Harry's eyes caught mine, and everything he'd protested was vaporized in his pain and fear. His voice was small but clear. "Help."

Smith snatched up Harry and bolted out the door, jerking it shut behind him. By the time we had it open again and pushed the crowd of us through, they were on a bay horse. Smith had Harry half in front of him, still using him as a shield as he turned the horse up the main road.

"Stop him!" cried Reverend Shapes. "Don't let him take him!"

"That's my horse!" shouted someone else. "He stole my horse!"

"Somebody has to have a gun!"

"Don't shoot! You'll hit the boy!"

Smith spurred the startled horse past the crowd and pulled Harry around to cover his back.

The young boy who was going to live near the Miami was gaping beside me, and I snatched his precious new bow and braced it to string. It wasn't a heavy draw. There was only one arrow, but then, there was only one abductor.

Mayor Landa saw me and pointed, as if I could have missed the object of all our consternation. "Stop them! Shoot the horse!"

I nocked the arrow, sighted on the galloping figures, adjusted for distance and wind and speed and the horse's rocking stride. I released.

Portals to the Twilight Land are brutally difficult for me. I cannot charm humans into cheerful cooperation. I cannot sing to shame the birds, I cannot craft magic armor, I cannot give golden coins which turn in the morning to twigs and leaves. My one true inheritance is the special gift of projectiles beyond human skill. I prefer the firearm, as you know today, but I am capable with a bow.

The arrow sped, arced, and plunged over Harry's wide-eyed stare into Smith's neck. He convulsed, and the horse balked at the cruel yank on the reins. Smith and Harry tumbled to the dirt, where Smith kicked one leg and reached uselessly for the arrow.

"You shot him!" gasped Mayor Landa.

"Of course," I said. "The horse didn't do anything."

I started at a run. Harry rolled and began to crawl away. I ignored the high-tailed horse as it circled, going directly to Smith and bending to jerk the arrow free. He screamed and choked. I didn't much care. "Shove a bandana or something in that if you want to live," I suggested.

I turned to see a man closing on us with a Remington in his hands. "You must be Sheriff Tillerson," I said. "Better arrest him quick."

"And what about you, mister?" he said. "We all just watched you shoot a man."

"To save a life," I said. I reached out and caught the collar of Harry's shirt as he stood, half-restraining and half-supporting him. "Ask young Harry here, and I think he'll tell you this so-called Smith is wanted for robbery. Part of his gang is already in prison. There might be a bounty on him."

Harry nodded shakily. "That's true. All of it. He helped steal fifty thousand dollars two years ago, down in Indianapolis. Killed a teller. And Smith is his real name."

Well, even I can be surprised.

The sheriff trained his gun on the downed Smith. "I'd be obliged if one of you would fetch me the doctor and my handcuffs."

I pulled Harry close and we started walking back to the crowd of people surging toward us. We didn't have much time. "You didn't want anyone to know about your father being in prison."

He grunted. "I know how it is out here," he said. "They think we don't, but we do. They don't want a kid they think is going to be trouble. They already know we're street kids, gang members. When they find my dad's in prison for robbing and killing—"

"Reverend Brace set up out-placement because he believes blood doesn't breed true," I interrupted. "He thinks the eugenics men are wrong. He thinks if you take a child out of the trap of poverty and crime, he can learn something other than poverty and crime. That's the reason behind these trains in the first place. The question is, do you agree with him?"

Harry shook his head. "No, the question is, do these people agree with him?"

"Indianapolis just opened free kindergarten for both white and colored children. Look how many of these folk showed up for you, even knowing what you just said about streets and gangs. And look at me. These kids left on church doorsteps — I was one of those, with a note asking them to bury me when I died. Things like me don't usually live."

He looked up at me, blood glistening on his face.

"I didn't die, and I never really fit in, not in the human world or the Twilight Lands. But I've found this to be a good place anyway."

Mayor Landa and the group surrounded us, gushing horror and enthusiasm and praise and concern. I bent close to Harry's ear. "Maybe if you want them to give you a chance, you should give them a chance."

I squeezed his shoulder and then turned to the boy whose bow and arrow I'd borrowed. "Here you go. Thanks for their use. Mind the blood."

He stared open-mouthed at the blood clinging to the head and then looked up at me, beaming. "Indiana is great!"

"It sure is," I agreed, ignoring the horror on his new mother's face.

We passed on the sheriff's request for a physician and his handcuffs. After a moment, I worked my way out of the group and followed the man who had started away down the street, the only one not focused on the downed outlaw or the rescued boy. I called to him. "Wait a moment. We need to talk."

He whirled, gun drawn, and I shook my head. "Just talk."

He hesitated. He was scared, and shooting me would draw everyone's attention to his quiet escape. "What do you want?"

"You didn't want to be part of torturing a kid. That saved your life today."

He blanched. He probably thought I was reading his mind.

"But you might want to think about your life and how it came to this. Maybe think about how it could go in another direction after this."

"Mister, trust me, I'm already thinking," he said. "Things just haven't gone right for the last three years, but I couldn't get out. They said they'd kill me if I left, as I could testify."

"Looks like you're out now."

"And much obliged. My sister married a preacher out on the frontier; I figure I can get out from under the warrant out there while they set me straight."

I didn't much care where he got it worked out as long as he did. "Good luck."

He holstered the gun, nodded his head, and we went our separate ways.

I didn't much want to stay around for the sheriff's questions. Smith could take care of himself, and Harry had more information than I did. I was halfway to the train station when I heard his voice. "Hey!"

I turned around and saw Harry watching me. "Yes?"

"That's it? Are you just — leaving?"

"Seems like it."

"But — I mean, you didn't even ask me."

"About what?"

"About what? About the money!"

"I told you, I don't care," I said. "And you told me you didn't know where it was."

"I lied," he said.

"I didn't," I answered.

He stared at me.

"But," I said, "if you want, we can return it. That might make things easier on the community."

He hesitated and then nodded. "It's not far. I can show you."

As I said, I don't have the trick of giving out money which turns to sticks and leaves. It would be handy, but my screwed-up heritage didn't include that bonus. So I had to manually collect sticks and leaves in a bag for our excursion.

Harry said there was one robber left, he didn't know where, who might come back for the buried treasure. So we loaded the coin and cash onto the mule we'd brought and reburied the strong box, now filled with twigs and dead leaves. It's the nearest I'll ever be to the money trick, and I drew a sad, bitter pleasure from it.

Harry and I asked to meet privately with the bank president and returned the money on the condition that the details of its recovery be kept quiet, to protect Harry's new family, and that he not complain about the one thousand dollars I reserved for Harry's future college education.

Harry graduated from the fledgling Indiana Law School and later was instrumental in lobbying the Indiana General Assembly to fund free kindergartens. I went on doing what I do by order of the Fairy Queen, which is generally less recorded in media of the time.

But I do it still, just the same.

——— « O » ———

Laura VanArendonk Baugh

Laura VanArendonk Baugh loves both train travel and writing fantasy of many flavors, as well as other genres and non-fiction. Her novel *The Songweaver's Vow* won the 2018 Realm Award for Best Fantasy. She lives in Indiana, where Robin Archer's tales are rooted in local flavor and history, and enjoys Dobermans, travel, chocolate, and making her imaginary friends fight one another for imaginary reasons. Find her new novels and more at www.LauraVAB.com.

Destination 1945

Rachel Leidenfrost

1985

"Take a ride to the past! Like no experience you've ever had!"

Isabelle turned and looked at the man, his loud bellow startling her. His top hat and tails looked out of place in this neon-and-pastel sweater vest world. A bead of sweat rolled down the side of his face. It had been an unusually warm fall, especially for Philadelphia.

She disregarded the man, focused on the headline in front of her: *Nine thousand people killed in Mexico City quake.*

The world seemed so aggressive to her. People killing people. Pirates. Guns. Even the planet wanted to kill them. She pushed her light hair back, wishing for a moment it wasn't sprayed so solidly in place. It itched. Damn fashion. Lately, she didn't even know why she bothered trying to fit in. She'd never found her spot in the world and she'd begun to believe that she never would, that someday her tombstone would read 'cast' or 'dutiful daughter.' She wanted to be the heroine in her own story, but the older she got the dimmer her future seemed.

The pair came from out of nowhere. Loud and boisterous, they rolled down the street like characters from *Charlie and the Chocolate Factory.*

"What's this? A reenactment you say? Where does it go? What will we see?" The woman had dark, perfectly coiffed hair and demanded the attention of everyone around her. A rotund boy of about ten whom she tugged at her side pulled gum out of his mouth and stretched it between his fingers as far as it would go before getting bored and shoving it back in.

"I don't want to do a reenactment, Mom!"

"Young man, this is no mere reenactment. This is your chance to see history come to life. Located over a genuine wormhole, this is a real-life train ride through history!" The eager salesman turned to the mother, his black and silver suspenders shining in the sun. "And as for what you'll see — who knows? Every day is different. You may see lovers wandering through the Central Terminal, the most beautiful dresses and hats you can imagine, handsome soldiers departing, maybe even some soldiers lucky enough to be coming home." He wiggled his eyebrows, leaning in closer to the mother, who blushed.

Isabelle realized she had dropped her paper. She took a couple of halting steps and found herself in the middle of the small group. She pulled out her wallet. "How much?"

The merchant smiled, his teeth shining like Chiclets. "Twenty dollars per person."

Isabelle pulled out a twenty-dollar bill and handed it over, her palms sweaty. The past had a strong pull on her, tugging her like a tether — or maybe an anchor. She reached up and touched the locket at her neck, distracted.

The mother frowned. "That seems like an awful lot for a reenactment."

"Not a reenactment, *ma Cherie*. A peek at history. And you can enjoy our family rate. Just thirty dollars." He leaned in closer and the woman reached for her purse.

——— «» ———

Isabelle crossed the square, following the ticket seller's directions to a small street a block away, the entrance hidden behind two tall, narrow buildings. She'd been this way many times and had never noticed the road. She made the turn and stopped abruptly, surprised to see a large train dominating the small space. The steam locomotive shone in the sunlight, the black steel polished to a high gloss and trimmed with a vibrant orange. Wisps of steam puffed out of the smokestack as the engine heated up for the journey.

Isabelle looked down the track. There were seven passenger cars. She was a little disappointed to see there wasn't an open-air caboose at the end. Outside one of the cars, the salesman was helping a smattering of passengers onto the train.

She haltingly joined them, twisting the ticket in her hand nervously while she waited.

The man gave her a hand as she stepped on to the block and then the train itself. He was chattering at her, but she didn't notice. She was distracted. Onboard, she was surprised to feel the hum of the engine vibrate through her shoes even though they hadn't yet disembarked.

Isabelle fell onto the old leather bench seat, the battered brown material crackling as she settled in. She fiddled with the locket at her neck, her mind lost in the past. Her father had fought in World War II. Her mother had talked of little else for years on end. He never made it home. Isabelle herself never met him. She was born in 1944, shortly after her father shipped out.

The war had casualties people never thought about. Her mom never recovered. Her dad infused every moment of their lives from her mother's refusal to date, to simple things like what they ate for dinner each night, to Isabelle's frowned upon choice to be a nurse. Her father liked meat and potatoes after all, and as for nursing, her mom reminded her constantly that you "can't save everyone."

Isabelle had enough insight to know that she was quiet, and she didn't necessarily endear others; she understood her upbringing may have something to do with that. But, inside, she felt like a whole different person was hidden, just waiting to be released. It was as if she herself had spent a lifetime waiting for a lost love to come home from the war. She often wondered how her life would have been different if her dad had come home, or if her mom had stopped waiting.

She opened the locket and looked at the two pictures. Her mom's Alzheimer's had made the truth even more clear. She never stopped thinking about Richard Maxwell and hoping for his return. Her entire world began and ended with him. At the end, Isabelle wasn't sure if she even remembered having a daughter.

"All aboard!"

The loud announcement from outside shook Isabelle loose. She peered out the window to see one last couple making a dash for the door. Moments later, the salesman stowed the box and climbed on board. He was the only attendant in the passenger cars.

He picked up a bulky microphone and smoothly dived into his routine.

"Ladies and gentlemen, boys and girls, my name is Harvey H. Heartcrest, and I'm pleased to welcome you on today's ride! Are you ready for the experience of a lifetime? To find the thrill of discovery? To take a peek at history? Next stop: 1945!" He held a large wooden whistle up to his lips and blew hard, his rosy cheeks bellowing out. *Choo! Choo!*

The handful of people on the train clapped politely, most eyes directed out the windows.

Isabelle let her attention wander, checking out her fellow travelers.

There was the dominant mom and whiny son. The young couple who dashed to the train at the last moment nestled closely together in the last seat. A grandmotherly-looking woman sat alone a few rows back; she looked emotional. Isabelle briefly thought of joining her but checked the impulse. She wasn't in the mood for company.

Another half a dozen people were in the compartment, making it a third full. She peeked down the aisle and saw a similar number of people in the adjoining compartment. The end of the car was chained off with a velvet rope. She briefly wondered what they did with the remaining cars.

The train set off with a slight jerk before settling into a steady rhythm. Isabelle looked out the window.

Philadelphia was a bustling city. Mid-day brought a mix of characters. Men in baggy coats and women with big hair rushed from place to place while others relaxed along fountains and park benches, eating lunch, chatting and smoking. A dozen children played in Great Bell Park as they swung by.

Isabelle wondered where the reenactment was. She didn't remember any large open areas through here. In fact, she would swear they were headed toward the harbor.

She jumped when Harvey blared into his mic once more. "Are you ready for a glimpse at history? This is it!"

All eyes were drawn to him. Outside the train, the world went gray as they rode through a bank of fog. Moments later, in the wake of his announcement, every eye turned toward the window.

"Oh my God."

"How lifelike…"

"Look, that actress is crying."

Isabelle stared out the window in shock. In the blink of an eye they'd entered another world. She twisted around to peer out the window behind her but saw nothing.

In front of her, the world of 1945 came alive. The women wore high-necked stiffly suited dresses and soft ruffled shirts, tied at the throat. The look was topped by perfect little hats and pairs of heels. Little girls mirrored their mothers and little boys wore short pants and argyle sweaters. She saw very few men. Those she did see were old or infirm, moving with difficulty, though that didn't stop them from opening a door or doffing their hat for a passing lady.

The train moved more slowly and Isabelle soaked it all in. She could just see the edge of the harbor and those waiting by the first two docks. Her eyes were drawn continually to the same woman. She had light blond hair, perfectly coiffed, and gently rocked a pram. But she didn't look at the baby. Her attention was riveted on the docks, her eyes bouncing anxiously from one area to another, dissecting the space before moving on. Occasionally, she brought a handkerchief to her eyes and dabbed, but Isabelle wasn't sure if she was aware of it. She looked haunted.

"And I hope you enjoyed your glimpse of history today!"

Isabelle glanced at the attendant, startled, as he began sharing facts about 1945 through the sound system. In the moment that she'd turned from the window, she missed the transition again. When she looked out the window, she saw only gray mist.

Very tricky, she thought. He times it perfectly so that you can't see where or how you get into the reenactment. For surely it had to be a reenactment.

Isabelle paused for a moment, reflecting on the look on the woman's face. Her acting was superior.

For the rest of the ride, Isabelle fiddled with her locket and thought about what might have been. She fought off waves of loneliness and settled into the feeling of melancholy. It was getting harder and harder to find a spark of interest, to pull herself back. She thought of the gray mist.

When they pulled up to the train station in modern day Philadelphia, Isabelle disembarked and resolved to put it out of her mind. She didn't need this kind of stress.

------ «» ------

But she couldn't forget…

She kept dreaming about the woman pushing the pram at the harbor. And in her dreams, the waiting woman had her mother's face. The more she thought about it, the more determined she felt that it was her mom. But was that wishful thinking? Was her mind projecting what she wanted to see? Or, did this alleged wormhole show each of them a slice of their own past?

A few days later, Isabelle found herself again in the city center, buying a ticket, boarding the train. She was determined to see everything — not to be fooled by the salesman's clever timing.

The train departed and Isabelle gazed out the window.

She was looking as they passed into and out of the gray fog, though she still couldn't see how it might be produced.

When they made the transition, the weather was stark. They'd gone from a sunny day to rain. People on board *oh'd* and *ah'd* in appreciation. Isabelle immediately craned her neck, seeking the harbor.

Finally, she saw her. It was definitely the same woman. Her clothes were slightly different but the haunted look on her face was the same. She stood there, pushing the pram and staring at the docks, oblivious to the rain running down her face.

Isabelle twisted and turned, trying to get a better look at the woman's features. The hair was the correct color and the petite nose could be right, but she just couldn't tell at this distance.

She stood up, determined to walk farther down the train, maybe find a window that opened. But Harvey was there.

"Where do you think you're going, young lady?" He smiled at her, but she saw the steel in his eyes. She hated fake charm. She was forty-one years old and she knew she looked it.

She stared at him. "Just going to see if there was a bathroom on this train."

"Ah, I'm sorry to say that you wouldn't like the bathrooms of 1945." A chuckle. "But, we'll be back in our time in just a few minutes and you'll be able to go."

Isabelle recognized a battle she couldn't win. She sat back down.

As they passed back into the mist her mind spun, thinking of everything she knew about the 1940s.

———— «» ————

Isabelle spent days at the public library, pouring over books about the past. She'd always been a history buff — interested in peoples and places of the past — and the 40s came alive in her mind as she flipped through the books.

The more she read, the more excited she became, thinking about the classic films, groundbreaking novels, and the simpler way of life of the 1940s and beyond.

The next time she rode the train, she was ready. She wore sturdy shoes and her locket. The super-sized purse she carried was full — of items both useful and sentimental. She'd given away her few plants and her goldfish in case her plan worked.

When she boarded, she took the car to the left — despite Harvey's wave to the right — and settled into the last seat, hoping the adage "out of sight, out of mind" held true.

He picked up the microphone in the other car and started going through his spiel. When he began talking about the history of steam locomotives, Isabelle rose and quietly made her way to the bathroom.

She locked the door and waited. Harvey's voice sounded muffled and unclear through the door. A small dingy window showed the outside world. Her eyes darted from the window to the floor and back. She didn't know what would happen when they switched over to 1945. But she was ready. She had her feet braced along either wall. Would the floor drop out? Did the wormhole pull people through the toilet bowl?

She waited patiently, enjoying the vibration of the train through the soles of her shoes.

Suddenly the scene through the window changed to the now familiar glimpse of history. She looked at the walls in surprise. They remained the same. So did the floor. She delicately pressed one foot to it. Firm. Even the toilet looked exactly the same. Why did Harvey say she wouldn't like the restrooms in 1945?

Too late, she thought of the window; it was awfully small, but it was private. Isabelle pushed on the latch with all her might, the metal groaning. Finally unlatched, she pushed up on the frame, but it wouldn't budge. Layers of thick paint cemented it in place. She furiously dug through her purse, grabbing a nail file. She hacked and sliced at the paint, strips of it tearing off at a time. She gasped when she saw fog trailing in front of the window.

Isabelle sat down on the floor and cried. She felt so lonely. Would it be so much to ask to have someone close to her? Someone to hold her when she cried? To feel like she belonged?

Banging on the door roused her. Someone twisted on the handle, yanking on the sturdy metal.

"I know you're in there, lady! Everyone else has exited."

Harvey. Isabelle ignored him, hoping if she stayed perfectly silent, he'd go away.

"I'm not going away either. Don't make me break this door down."

She sighed, standing up, and unlocked the door. She tried her best to look dignified, but she must have looked a mess. Harvey's face softened when he saw her; she saw a glimmer of sympathy in his eyes before his jaw tightened.

"Listen, I don't know what your problem is, but I'm running a business, and I can't have people misbehaving or trying to disappear. You can't come on the train anymore."

Isabelle felt conflicted. She certainly didn't want to hurt someone's business...

But it sounded like Harvey had implied that it might just be possible to disappear.

———— «·» ————

She tried to do the right thing. She really did. But all she could think about was 1945. The woman at the harbor who looked like her mom. The well-behaved kids running around the parks. She'd spent so many years giving everything to her mom, and her life had only gotten narrower, more limited in the last three years as her mom's dementia took over. She had no life or family of her own, only regrets. She'd rarely found the time to date and, if she was completely honest with herself, men hadn't exactly lined up to ask her. None of her relationships had ever even been serious enough to talk about kids.

That was what brought her to the train station in the dead of the night, a crowbar and lock cutters in hand. In the dark, the train looked menacing. The hard, cold steel mingled with the shadows, creating a snake of darkness; she had to squint to find the steps up and to count the cars. It was nothing like the gleaming, gorgeous train of daylight hours.

Isabelle found the last car and hoisted herself up onto the stairs. The pocket door looked like it sealed entirely — maybe with some sort of internal latch. There was no padlock and no window to lever. She peered into the darkness but could only see the vaguest of shapes. She stood there for a moment hoisting the crowbar, but ultimately couldn't bring herself to break a window on the majestic train. She hopped down and made her way to the next car. Same result.

She stood there, looking at the train and knowing there had to be an easier place to get on. She put one hand on the side of the train and started counting. When she reached the cars they used for passengers, she pulled herself up to the platform again. It was the same pocket door — maybe a bit more used — but still inaccessible.

She had one more place to try before she gave in and broke a window.

She made her way up to the caboose. A single step hugged the bottom of the door — clearly something the professionals used, not the passengers. She put her tools in her bag, strapped it across her body, and jumped for the train.

Isabelle cracked her face against a hard piece of metal alongside the door, but she managed to wrap the fingers of her right hand around something tubular. Her right shoulder screamed in protest and her feet thrashed as she struggled to find purchase. Finally, her left foot found a scrap of metal and she took a bit of the weight off her shoulder.

For the first time, she wished she'd brought a flashlight, though it was probably best that she hadn't. She'd die before she spent the next few years locked in a jail for breaking and entering.

She pulled herself up to the single step, squeezing both feet onto the metal platform, and there it was, the only item shining in the dark, the hint of silver making it easy to pick out. The padlock appeared to be attached to a hand-built hasp, and Isabelle was sure the original lock had been more elegant — probably with a beautifully wrought cast iron key. She pulled out the lock cutters she'd bought that morning and positioned them on the lock. She pushed the handles with all her might and the snick of the blades cutting through the metal echoed in the night.

She held herself still for a long minute. Her heartbeat sounded like a drum, and she was sure that someone would have heard her by now.

Finally, she moved, allowing her spine to relax. She took the two pieces of the lock and threw them as hard as she could into the adjacent trees. A broken lock would mean an intruder, but she hoped a missing lock might be chalked up to forgetfulness.

She pulled open the door and entered the caboose.

——— «» ———

Isabelle couldn't help herself. She spent a minute in the caboose, checking out the equipment and peering out the front window. Amongst the equipment she found a flashlight. She debated for a moment before taking it — she'd already broken into the train. She promised herself she'd leave it behind.

The first three cars were passenger cars, identical to what she'd traveled in previously. The fourth car was a canteen; Isabelle wondered why Harvey didn't have it open on their journeys to the past. She looked behind the register and saw bags of chips and pretzels, gum, and candy bars. Even wooden train whistles were available for sale.

Junk filled the fifth car. Broken machinery, engine parts, tools, a mechanic's bench, and lots of extra coal. She spied a small cot in the back of the cart, coated in oil but soft looking.

Isabelle felt shocked when she saw what the sixth car held. A vast number of square shapes covered in sheets filled the space. A walkway was just barely visible down the center of the car. She pulled off one sheet to find an antique china cabinet. Another sheet hid a plain trunk. When she opened it, she found stacks of old stock certificates — Wells Fargo from the 1800s, Ford from 1956, even a brittle piece of paper stamped *East India Company*. Under a third sheet she found an old table with a suitcase on top of it. The suitcase held a uniform from the Civil War. All the items were antique … and valuable. She re-covered them, her heart pounding. She didn't want to get involved in whatever was going on here.

It might be perfectly legitimate — purchasing, storing and transporting antiques. But her heart told her the items must come from the past. Her palms felt moist; her body trembled. A new start was just a train ride away.

Isabelle was tiptoeing toward car seven when she heard the noise. *Hump-phhh. Hump-phhh.* She held her breath and listened. The rhythmic sound went in and out. She wondered if it might be some sort of machinery, but that didn't make any sense. She gasped and took a step back when she figured it out. Someone slept on this train.

She'd started with the seventh car when she tried breaking in, reasoning that it would be less obvious since it wasn't used every day. If she had been successful… She wondered if it was Harvey, another employee, or a vagabond like her.

She took a step closer and peered in. The interesting shapes she'd seen from outside were gone and it took her a moment to realize a curtain covered the window. Definitely living quarters then and not a vagabond.

Isabelle quietly traveled back to the fifth car. She pulled the cot behind a large bench full of equipment, put a pair of clean overalls on top of the oily mattress and laid down.

«»

When she woke, the train was alive. People in vests and engineer hats shouted to each other down the length of the train. She heard footsteps coming her way, followed by a yell.

"Come on, Jim. Hop to. I need that coal. What did I hire you for?"

A man stopped on the other side of the bench, his dirty brown hair curling out from under his hat. Sweat beaded his upper lip.

"Coal. Got to get the coal," he muttered to himself, throwing bag after bag of coal onto a hand truck. Isabelle willed her body to shrink and to remain perfectly still. She held her breath, her lungs beginning to burn and her head to spin.

Finally, Jim was gone. Isabelle got up and removed the evidence of her night on the cot. She looked at her watch. She had an hour until the train departed for 1945.

She walked carefully through the car, gently trying every window she came to. They were all painted shut. She took a screwdriver from the bench and ran it along the seams of one, trying the window again. She couldn't get it loose.

Isabelle peered down the row of cars, looking for Harvey. If he followed his normal pattern, he should be in the square selling tickets right now.

She crept down the aisle, finally arriving at the door to car seven. She tried the handle. Locked. She took off her sweater and wrapped the crowbar in it. She looked down the aisle, saw nobody, and bashed the crowbar against the doorknob. The muffled noise sounded incredibly loud to her, but nobody came to investigate. The knob hung limply against the door. She entered a room unlike any she had ever seen.

A huge four-post bed draped in gold dominated the space, but there was still room for an antique chest of drawers, framed artwork, and a writing desk from what must have been the 1700s. Hanging over the desk was a death mask from ancient Egypt she would swear looked authentic. The room overflowed with treasures.

She took another look at her watch and moved to the windows. They opened and closed with relative ease. She smiled for the first time in weeks. This would be how she made her escape.

She returned to car six and closed the door to Harvey's car. She positioned the knob the best she could. With any luck, he wouldn't return to his room between selling tickets and the train ride.

———— «» ————

The train would depart in ten minutes and Isabelle was twitchy.

Just a minute ago, Harvey had come barreling down the aisle with something dark and heavy in his hand as he headed for his room. He'd only been stopped by the walkie talkie at his belt.

"Four more coming in from the station, boss."

"Damn it. Fine. I'm on my way." He took the item he held and shoved it under a sheet. He rushed back down the aisle.

Isabelle had made up her mind. She had to look. Something about the shape and sound of the object when he set it down seemed too familiar. She just had to work up her courage.

She crept over to the table and raised the sheet. Laying on top of the antique table was a gun, tucked into a holster with a heavy belt coiled around it. She stared at the item, afraid to touch it but afraid to leave it too. Finally, she grabbed the gun, dropping the sheet back in place. She had no idea if it was an antique or new.

She didn't want to take it, but also didn't want it accessible while she tried to escape. She tucked the gun into the suitcase with the Civil War uniform.

The train began to hum under her feet as the engine built up a head of steam.

The five minutes before she heard the telltale "all aboard" from outside seemed never-ending. She knew Harvey would go straight to the microphone. She should be safe.

Finally, the train began moving. Isabelle couldn't hear Harvey's announcement from this distance and couldn't miss the transition. She needed all the time she could get. She glanced rapidly back and forth between the aisle — looking for danger — and the window — looking for the telltale fog.

When they passed through the gray fog, she made her move. She grabbed her bag and rushed to the door of

Harvey's chambers. She got the door open and headed in, closing it behind her. The broken knob fell to the ground, clanging loudly.

She held her breath for a moment, reasoning it wouldn't be heard five cars away. What she hadn't counted on was the straight sight lines on a train.

Harvey saw her enter his chamber and boiled over with rage. He threw the microphone down without a word, the feedback causing a loud squeal. He took off at a run down the aisle.

In the sixth car, he slid his hand under a sheet, reaching for his new gun. He was outraged to realize it was missing. He threw open the door to his chamber and saw her at the window.

Isabelle struggled to open the window. The motion of the train made it more difficult, and she cursed herself for closing it earlier.

"Stop!" The loud roar made her jump. She spun around to see Harvey standing in the doorway.

She turned back to the window, earnestly tugging at the metal frame. It inched up but it wasn't enough. Harvey was there. He swung a bat at her, and she noticed vaguely that it was covered with signatures. It connected with her left shoulder, and pain shot up and down her arm.

She reached into her bag for the crowbar and pulled it out. He stopped for a moment, surprise on his face, and she swung with all her might. She connected with the side of his head and time stopped for a heartbeat, before he crumpled to the ground. Isabelle turned around and smashed the window with the crowbar, desperate to escape into the past before the wormhole closed and they returned to 1985.

She put one leg over the sill and then the other. She jumped.

⸺ «» ⸺

Harvey came to a minute later. He could feel a pounding in his head, and worse, he saw the broken window and knew what it meant.

Boots pounded down the aisle and moments later two of his staff were there. He waved them away.

Harvey looked out the window with regret, watching the troublemaker push through the crowd. She'd ruined a great setup for him.

He sighed and took a notepad out of his pocket. He flipped to the third page. Every line except one was crossed off. It said "1945." He took out a pen and drew a thick black line through the date.

———— «〉 ————

Isabelle had made it! She was in 1945. She struggled through the crowd, eager to get to the harbor or at least to get out of sight of the train. When she worked up the courage to turn around, the train was gone.

She reached the edge of the harbor and saw the woman with the pram and the hair of spun gold. She fingered the locket at her throat as she got closer. The woman's profile came into fine focus and Isabelle's heart beat faster.

She thought about all the proof in her purse. The photo albums, the death certificate, the holiday photos that didn't include Richard Maxwell. If this was her, did she stand a chance of convincing her to truly live?

She approached, her heart in her hand. The woman looked up.

Isabelle swallowed.

"Mom?"

———— « O » ————

Rachel Leidenfrost

Rachel Leidenfrost writes fantasy and science fiction stories for both adults and children. An avid reader, she's inspired by classic and contemporary works as well as the quirky and unusual. By day she is a marketing and communications executive, by night an author; this is her third published short story. Follow her on Twitter. (@ RLeidenfrost)

Steampunks needed to make steam boiler survival soup

A little recognized use of steam power is its use for cooking, especially in times of famine.

Learning to cook with a pressurized steam vessel (aka a pressure cooker) is one of the most important skills a survivalist can ever learn. With a pressure cooker, gathered and scavenged food sources can be made edible, palatable and safe. You can use the pressure vessel to preserve food by canning. Under intense steam pressure harmful bacteria and viruses are killed. Not only is the food sterilized but so is the liquid, during a time when clean water can be scarce.

The survival benefits of cooking with pressurized steam are so valuable that during the Great Depression, the US government encouraged its use. Steam cooking and canning schools were sponsored by the Civilian Conservation Corps. These schools demonstrated cooking and canning techniques. Steam pressure cooking was credited with saving thousands from starving during the Great Depression.

The greatest example of utilizing steam pressure vessel cooking for survival can be found in the history of WWII. During the height of the war much of Holland was engulfed in famine when the occupying Nazi army implemented a food embargo on the rebellious Dutch people.

To the rescue came stationary steam boiler engineers, who converted their stationary steam heating boilers into massive pressure cookers. With the help of citizens who scavenged, gathered and hunted every possible food source, the engineers produced what was called "survival soup". After being cooked and sterilized, it would be transported in milk cans and barrels by trucks that had been converted from petrol to wood burning steam power, to soup kitchens across the Dutch nation.

Popular ingredients in the survival soup were tulip bulbs, songbirds, beets and rodents. It would contain rawhide and animal-based wallpaper glue as well. Under a policy of "don't ask, just eat," millions of people avoided mass starvation.

Hopefully, for the sake of survival, your steam mechanic skills will never vanish. You steampunks could be the saviors of the future.

Cursed

Kendall Eifler

Orilly flinched as the Yellow Guard snapped the handcuffs harshly shut over her outstretched wrists and splayed fingers. They were bulky but light, the metal cinching as the plates clicked into place one after the other, adjusting to the exact measurements of her hands, until they fit like gloves. There was no way to use a curse without moving your hands and the guards knew it. She had never used her curse at all until today. She had always been so careful. But now here she was, stuffed into the backseat of the Yellow's vehicle in front of the school. She was being taken, most likely, to the Crucible, somewhere from which, the rumors had it, you never came back.

However, Orilly had other plans. It was a risk, but it had been time to take one. Orilly had decided to see if the rumors were true; the Cursed disappearing off trains, whispers of the Resistance growing stronger. If they were, and she was clever enough, she just might accomplish what she had been dreaming of for a long time. She drew in a deep breath and clenched her jaw. Was all this really worth it? She would have to make sure it was. She needed to find the Resistance, she needed to get them to trust her, and she needed to do it fast.

It was a short cruiser ride to the station. She watched from the slowing guard cruiser as the maglev train station came into view. The maglev trains were the only way between the domes since the air was so contaminated from the Final War. This meant that for the Yellow Guards to transport her, the next step was the train ride.

The train before them was at least as beautiful as it was functional. The blue, silver, and black swirls that accentuated the streamlined cars came to a point at the needle-like nose, mixing into a sky of metallic blue. It hovered steadily over the track beneath it, patiently waiting to weave itself along the way to the next dome and further. It looked so perfectly formed, she could imagine it speeding around the world, never stopping, just doing what it was clearly born to do.

Soon they were seated in the first passenger car of the maglev. She barely noticed when the train began to move; it was so smooth, not a bump at all. She leaned back against the plush cushion of her seat and took in her surroundings. It was almost time to execute her plan. Orilly always had a plan. She had her sources and there had been talk for a few days now that the Dimes, a faction of the Resistance — so called because, before curses were illegal, people would often pay a dime to see someone use theirs — were in the area. She was taking a chance, acting on uncertain information. Rumor had it that if the Dimes were here, there was a good chance they had a train-op going strong.

It wasn't so unusual for a cursed person to get caught accidentally using their curse. What was unusual about Orilly was that she had gotten caught on purpose. She needed to get to the Resistance, and this was the best idea she had to get them to trust her.

Hopefully a member of the Dimes would have noticed her being walked in by the two Yellows. It was hard to miss their neon-plated armor. But she had to be sure. So Orilly looked around. She needed to find something that would work. Then she noticed the earrings on a frumpy-looking old lady who sat next to a bored child across the aisle from her. Perfect. There was no way she could actually get her curse to work while being gloved, but she just might be able to do enough.

Orilly concentrated hard on the earrings; she imagined her fingers moving to pull them and twist them open and out of the old lady's ears. Nothing happened. She tried again, concentrating harder. *Beep! Beep! Beep!* Her insert began to set off its alarm. It echoed down the car and along the train just as she had hoped it would do. At once the guards seized her hands and her concentration broke.

"Prisoner, cease that immediately," said the guard to her left, holding his baton out threateningly in the direction of her face. The alarm trailed off. Was it enough? The glaring Yellows made her hope it had been.

Once the guards had released her, the second step was getting to the train's bathrooms. They were the only place she could think of to be alone. Orilly waited for the people in the car to settle. A fair amount of them had gathered their things and left the car, clearly perturbed by recent events. That was fine with Orilly; it just made her job easier. After a few moments, she decided it was time to act.

"Um," she said, trying awkwardly to look into the masked eyes of the Yellow that sat opposite from her. "Um, I need to use the bathroom." The guard stared at her. She tried not to stare back. She had to appear weak or they would never let her go. "Can I just use the bathroom? I'll be quick, I promise." Nothing.

The other guard, the one sitting next to her, kicked out his neon yellow plated boot, connecting with the taller guard's shin. He jostled as if he had been asleep and muttered, "What?"

She tried again. "I need to use the bathroom, uh, sir. I'll go quickly, but I really need to go." The taller guard, who, by the markings on his chest, was vastly more experienced than the short, thin one, nodded and stood up. He grabbed her roughly by the upper arm and lifted her as if she were a puppy, placing her in front of him. The smaller Yellow went to stand up, presumably to help, but the plump guard simply planted his oversized gloved hand on the Yellow's helmet and pushed him back down to his seat like a cork in a wine bottle.

"I've got this one, Topher. Back in the day, the up-and-ups trusted us enough to put just one of us with a prisoner. Those of us with any shred of self-respect are still perfectly capable."

Once they reached the bathrooms, and the door clicked behind her, Orilly inspected the room around her. She looked around for possible exits. There was a drain in the center of the floor, much too small. And the small circular air unit on the ceiling didn't seem to hold any hope of a way out. She was stuck. This was the end of her plan. She heard the Yellow knock on the door. "Just a minute!" She was starting to panic. This was where her information ended. Make it to the bathroom. If you make it to the bathroom, rumor had it that there was some way to escape, but no one ever said how. She needed to concentrate.

Orilly sat down on the closed toilet and tried to take deep breaths. There was so much riding on this moment, and it was disappearing faster than she knew how to handle. She felt so unprepared. Up until now, she had known what to do, had had a plan. From this point on she would have to rely on herself. She began to inspect the room around her again. The walls were metal and arched over her head into a rounded ceiling. The floor was… Her thoughts trailed off. She leaned closer to the wall opposite her. She ran her incapacitated finger along a thin ridge she had thought was just part of the design of the wall. She gave it a tentative push. Nothing. She had to try to pry at the crack. It was so frustrating to not be able to use her curse the one time she actually needed it to survive. What could she use? There was barely anything in the bathroom, let alone something thin and metal. She clasped her hands over her face in frustration. "Ow." Some of the scale-like handcuffs scratched her face.

That was it! If she could just bend out one of the rounded pieces of her handcuffs, she could make a sort of lever to pry open the panel. She bent awkwardly so that she could place her hands on the floor. Then she wedged the corner of her shoe's heel between two plates and stamped down with all her might. It worked. Now one of the pieces of metal stuck out at an odd angle. Quickly she jammed it into the crack and jerked. A plate of silver tiles ripped backward off the wall. With no time to think, Orilly bent it as far as it would go and squeezed into the small space behind the wall, pulling the sheet of metal back behind her and pushing the edges into place.

Then she looked around. The same tiny room, silver tiled walls and matching floor drain, but this time she stood face to face with a urinal. Just perfect. She had hoped to be somewhere like a storage room or a closet, but no. She was in, of all places, another bathroom. Of course she should have put that together. The men's room had been directly to the right of the women's when she had entered. She was out of ideas. She leaned against the side of the bathroom, the cool of the metal barely a comfort to her.

Suddenly, she felt the surface she was leaning against bend and warp beneath her weight. She jumped away.

Orilly's heart skipped a beat as she stared at what was most certainly a large bubble forming in the wall directly in front of her. Frozen, she watched the thick metal bend and sway like jello right before her eyes. She backed up against the back wall of the unit, as a tiny dark-skinned hand emerged, appearing to come right through the metal. And almost as soon as she had caught her breath, the bulge pulled away and in front of her, having emerged entirely now from the stainless-steel protrusion, was a small, grinning boy who couldn't have been older than twelve.

The boy stuck out his hand, the same one that had pushed its way unnaturally through what Orilly had previously assumed to be an impenetrable wall. "I'm Sam, or at least that's what you can call me. I'm with the Resistance." He was still grinning, proud of his unexpected entrance. "I'd explain more, but we've got to get going. Don't worry, it's all safe."

And with that, he stretched his hand out in front of him, grabbed Orilly's forearm, and she found herself following him through the wall. It was a very strange feeling, walking through the bending and bulging metal, as if she were forcing herself through a thick sheet of cold glue.

She was pulled sharply until, with a pop, she found herself in yet another bathroom. Sam let go of her arm and started digging through his pockets, leaving Orilly to stare at him in amazement. Clearly this kid had a powerful curse. She had watched him wave his hand delicately in front of them, solid metal bending completely to his will. Her heart began to pump with a new cautious excitement. So, this was what the rumors had been about. But her train of thought was interrupted as Sam delightedly pulled something from the depths of one of his pockets. He held it out toward her and smiled widely again, the creases of his grin nearly reaching the edges of his cheeks.

Orilly couldn't hold in her gasp as she realized what he had. He was holding a magnet. Magnets were strictly forbidden. People even said that owning one could give a plain child a curse, that they might even be the source of curses. They said that if you were found with one the Yellows would burn your entire house down to the ground, that the demonic little pieces of metal could drive an adult mad. Instinctively she backed away — as much as she could, anyway, seeing as the bathroom they inhabited barely left the two room to move at all.

"Watch this." Sam's voice broke her from her thoughts. He used one hand to grab her wrist and the other to run the magnet back and forth against her handcuffs. Slowly, as if gently urged by an invisible force, the plates of the handcuffs began to loosen from her outstretched hands. Barely thirty seconds had passed when she could wriggle her fingers; another ten and Sam was able to pull them off with ease. As if he had practiced it a thousand times, the small boy rolled them up into a ball with the ease of a real Yellow and stuffed them into one of his pockets, the bulging fabric leading Orilly to wonder what else could be hiding in there.

"Don't worry about the Yellows. They can search the train all they want; they've never found me in the place I'm apt to take you — if you pass the test."

"What test?" Orilly glanced suspiciously at Sam.

"Well, you have to show me your gift... I mean curse, sorry, force of habit. That way I'll know I can trust you. I've already shown you mine, so we'll be even. It's part of how it works. Don't blame me, this comes from higher up. I'm just doing my civic duty, plucking Cursed off trains and getting them to safety."

Orilly folded her arms. "You'll have to do something about my implant then, unless you'd like the whole train to know we're in the staff bathroom." As a little girl, her implant had gone off when she had accidently used her curse, and the blaring siren and flashing blue light it made was the opposite of what she needed right now. Everything had to go perfectly. This kid was clearly well trained by the Resistance, so he was vital to her if she wanted to do what she had set out to this morning.

"That's easy," said Sam. He whipped out the same magnet he had just used. He dug into another one of his bulging pockets and pulled out a small roll of tape. "Here, just tape this to your skin above it and you'll be fine. I'll need it back eventually."

Orilly took a deep breath and sighed. No getting out of this one. But maybe she could keep her curse a little bit obscure. She had to find something to do that would make it look weaker than it really was. That was the safest way. So, she went over to the sink and placed her hands just above the hot and cold knobs. She made herself look as though she was concentrating very hard, much harder than she really was, and slowly turned the handles without touching them, until a thin stream of water trickled out of the spout. She turned them back and turned around, crossing her arms over her fast-beating heart. Sam was smiling enthusiastically.

"There," she said. "Now can we get to this safe place before someone figures out to look in here?"

Sam began to pull brown cloth out of his left back pocket. "I've got this for you. Nothing special, but it has a hood, so it should give us cover at least for a few minutes. That will hopefully be long enough for us to get to the storage car at the end of the train. Come on, put it on." Orilly pulled the brown cloak over her school uniform and Sam reached over and tugged the hood snugly over her head. The staff bathroom led out, not to the same waiting area as the men's and women's rooms, but into a sort of staff lounge. Luckily it was entirely empty.

Somehow, Sam and Orilly managed to walk through all the cars without anyone uttering a word. When they reached the last car, Sam breathed a sigh of relief and threw open the door, ushering Orilly in behind him. On each side of the car, top to bottom, were rows of black, shiny safes. They varied in size from as small as saltshakers, to large enough to fit a few people inside. And then she knew what he was going to do. Orilly did not like tight spaces. But soon she and Sam were stuffed rather uncomfortably into one of the largest safes.

"I haven't even had the chance to ask your name yet," she heard Sam remark.

"Orilly."

"Well, Orilly, welcome to the Resistance."

After what felt like forever, the two sardines began to feel the train slow. "It's just about time," said Sam. "There's a panel here that I'll pop off so we can both roll out."

"Okay," said Orilly, who, at this point, was becoming unfazed with Sam's ludicrous suggestions.

The train had slowed to almost a stop when Sam pushed open the swinging panel and they both rolled out onto the packed earth next to the tracks. Sam jumped up just in time to whack the panel back into place. They were barely yards from the station, but since they were on the back side of the train, there was no one around to see them escape.

Seconds later, Sam was across the tracks and off into the crowd. He was yelling for her to follow him. She darted between people and suitcases and clouds of dust. Suddenly it seemed like there were Yellow Guards everywhere. They must have reported her missing. She'd been expecting it. But this was real. Squad hovercrafts and cars had pulled up around the train station. And then she saw him. A Red Guard. She had never seen one before. And the moments it took her to look around were enough to lose Sam.

She tried to push through the crowd; maybe she could find somewhere higher up, easier to see from. There: the platform. She had to get there. Pushing in that direction, a man barreled right into her and she collapsed into the sandy ground. Her arm seared with pain. It took all her strength to try to force herself up against the people moving over her. She was going to be trampled. More legs hurried past and Orilly was knocked this way and that as she tried to get up. Then she felt a hand on her arm. She jerked in fear, trying to pull away. But it wasn't a Yellow at all; it was a young man, thick as a barrel. "Careful," was all he said, his voice echoing the rumble of the train that was now pulling away from the station only a few yards away. By the time she regained her balance, the man had disappeared back into the crowd.

Orilly shook her head, trying to clear her mind. She needed to focus. If she was to have any hope at all, she had to find Sam. The platform — that was where she had to go.

She hardened herself with new, panicked resolve and began to weave her way through the mob of people hurrying in varying directions. She managed to pull herself up on the platform, but she wasn't tall enough to see over the people around her. Then she saw it. It was a risk, a huge risk, but it might be her only hope. Leaping, she grabbed hold of the closest LED orb's post and began to climb. Finally, she could see everyone around her. Scanning the crowd, something caught her eye. There, maybe ten yards away, was Sam, circling behind the station. But no sooner had she caught sight of him than someone shouted, "Hey, there she is!"

Orilly looked down to catch sight of a Yellow roughly pushing people out of the way, making a direct beeline for her. She stuffed down a yelp and jumped down from the post, running in the direction she had seen Sam disappear.

She whipped through a large family, knocking over a pile of luggage as she ran.

"Sorry," she said as she flew past. It was like a puzzle. She looked for openings and zigzagged through them, progressing toward the back of the station.

Then, out of nowhere, her arm jerked back, almost pulled from its socket. A neon yellow plated glove dug into the skin of her forearm, and she lurched backward, adrenaline pumping hard. The other yellow arm swooped out toward her, trying to find its mark. She wouldn't be taken down like this. Orilly dropped all her weight to the ground, dragging the Yellow off balance. As he wobbled, she shot up again, her elbow bent like a weapon above her head, catching the guard right between his chin plate and chest plate. She felt the sickly squish of the connection. There was no time to see how badly she'd hurt him. She used the seconds he grabbed his own neck to flee.

Rounding the corner of the building, she saw him. There was no time to talk; they just nodded at one another and took off, Sam in the lead. They ran down alley after alley, changing direction so often that she had no idea where she was. But they weren't alone. A few turns in, she heard the shouts of Yellows. Their lead began to diminish. And the occasional flash of red among the yellow was making her stomach turn.

Just as her legs were beginning to give out, her breath stinging in her chest with every pace, the pair darted around a corner into another alleyway and Sam grabbed her arm, forcing her to stop in the center of the alley. Sam dragged her over to an old rusty metal door in the side of a large building.

"In here." He beckoned to her and she squeezed in behind him.

Closing themselves in, they realized they were in some sort of supply closet, filled with brooms, buckets, and spray bottles of various chemicals. The two stood next to each other, breathing heavily with their hands on their thighs. There was a white door with a portal-like window on the far wall. Gathering up her courage, Orilly peered through. A market. Cleanly dressed hawkers stood at rounded desks topped with holograms of various wares: cords of wire varying in thickness and color, bot parts, and metalworking tools. Clearly, they had stumbled upon the dome's metals market and it was busier than Orilly had ever seen the one back in her dome.

"We have to get to the other side," Sam said. "We can't go back the way we came, or we'll get caught."

"But there are guards everywhere," she replied. "We've got to think of a better way, and fast."

Orilly concentrated. She had to put her mind into gear like she did in Calculus, when a particularly difficult problem was given. She scanned her environment. The cleaning chemicals, the mops and brooms, the bin of rags, a few yellow contamination suits. That was it. She knew what they had to do. So she gritted her teeth and started grabbing an armful of brooms and mops.

"What are you doing?" Sam was watching her in utter confusion.

"Plugging the aeration modules."

Sam's eyes widened as he started to catch on to her plan. This building had a complicated aeration system with tubes that spilled air from the filtration plant, where outside air was sucked in to fill the domes. That meant that it got air not from the purified air already inside the dome, but from the contaminated air outside. It was an antiquated system that was being phased out. In an air emergency in a building like this one, everyone would have to clear the building until the breach of the system was inspected by officials and cleared. It happened every once in a while, so it wouldn't be too suspicious, and it was the one emergency a Yellow wasn't cleared to address. Orilly grabbed up some of the cleaning chemicals and began to spray them into the aeration holes, then re-plug the holes with the handles of brooms and mops. No sooner had she plugged the last one than the contamination sirens began to wail.

"Hurry," yelled Sam over the noise, "we don't have much time."

Orilly grabbed for the doorknob into the market. "Oh no." It was locked. As she dropped her hand, Sam's replaced hers in trying desperately to wrench open the door, but to no effect.

"My curse won't work," said Sam. "This door is made out of solid wood."

But Orilly already knew what had to be done. She couldn't give herself time to think it through. She would have to reveal more of her curse. There were no two ways around it. Concentrating, she felt in the air as if the doorknob was in her empty hand. She pushed and pulled, frustrated, for what felt like forever, feeling the metal bits inside the lock begin to line up. Then, finally, the door flew open and, with Sam behind her, she raced through the now-empty metals market.

"Oh my God, I can't believe I just did that," she said.

"That was awesome!" Sam said. "Right, just follow me. There's a safe place I'm supposed to take you to for the night. Then we can get farther away from here in the morning."

"Are you sure that's a good idea? Won't the Yellows search the entire dome?"

"I'm sure."

And he looked it, so as he took off, she followed.

Just as she felt like she couldn't run any longer, Sam pulled up in front of a corner pub with a neon LED sign that blinked out the name *Old Frog Pub and Lodgings*. Sam whispered something into the com by the door, and gears of green, black, and silver creaked to slide open the circular door.

Sam dragged Orilly through benches and tables full of rambunctious customers and the thick smell of alcohol. A quick nod to the bartender and he started up the spiral staircase. At the top was a door with a locking panel. The door scanned Sam's hand as he pressed it against the screen.

"I wish I could stay longer," he said, opening the door to the first room on the left and gesturing to her to head inside, "but I've got to be somewhere. Make yourself comfortable. And get some sleep. This place will be safe for the night, but we'll have to clear out in the morning."

Orilly was about to ask exactly what they were going to do in the morning, hoping he meant to take her somewhere even higher up in Resistance secrecy, but he dashed off before she could get out the words, the door locking behind him.

Orilly looked around the small room Sam had left her in. Three sets of bunk beds and a few floating shelves were her only company. She was finally alone. For the first time since those handcuffs had clicked down on her wrists, she let out a sigh of relief and a grin. She flopped down on the bed's neon blue sleep sack and let her aching body relax. She had them just where she wanted them. It had almost been too easy. She felt against her calf for the gun she had hidden in its holster, even though she knew it was still there. Just like she knew her knives were still sheathed in the lining of her boots. She only allowed herself a short while to bask in a job well done. She had found the Resistance, but that also meant that her infiltration had only just begun.

——— « O » ———

Kendall Eifler

Kendall Eifler lives in a cottage on Cape Cod with her partner and two cats. She majored in counseling psychology at Lesley University, where she also took writing classes. She enjoys drawing, reading, and nature. Born in Boston and raised in West Concord, MA, Kendall has been telling stories since she can remember.

Twitter handle: @KendallEifler

Website: https://kendalleifler.wixsite.com/home

Devil on the Night Train

Samuel Marzioli

A broiling summer day and sporadic rains turned the house into a sauna. Maja and her grandfather Esidro paid their dues by resting on the front porch step, waiting for a touch of cold that only night would bring. While she read, he soaked his old bones in the quiet, gobs of smoke spewing from the fat cigar trapped between his lips — a smell like earth and wood and spices.

"I finished another scary book yesterday," Maja said when the light began to fail. She crimped a page to mark her place and set her book aside.

"Oh?" Esidro said, tapping an inch of ash into his ashtray.

"Yeah. This one was about a clown who lives in the sewers and feeds off the fears of children."

"Clowns aren't scary. What did he do? Pop a balloon and make the children cry?"

Maja had to lean in close to understand him. Not because his accent broke syllables into separate words. It was the way he sometimes let his voice lapse, a thin reed of sound that wavered with a tired flourish.

"Oh, Grandpa," she said, when she finally caught his meaning. "I guess you'd have to read it to understand." And then, "Do you have any stories for me today?"

"Filipino stories? Or monster stories?"

"Both."

"Maybe. Did I ever tell you about Ongloc, who hunts bad children and turns them into coconuts?"

"And eats the coconuts with his razor-sharp teeth whenever he's hungry? Yeah."

"What about the aswang, who can transform into an animal and suck a baby right out of their mother's stomach?"

"The shape-shifting, blood-sucking human eater? Yeah, that too."

"Then maybe it's time you heard about the Devil Man."

"Who's that?"

"There are many versions of the story, but the one I know is this: they say he drives a train around on the darkest nights, searching the world for a victim. Once he finds one, he kills them, leaving their souls trapped in the passenger cars forever."

Maja pursed her lips, sucking on the taste of indecision. "I guess that's kind of creepy."

Esidro *humphed*. "You guess?" he asked, and diverted his attention to the sky.

Maja followed his gaze. The sun had dragged the clouds along its westward path, leaving a full moon and ample stars, their soft light glinting in the smear of gray above them. Night had come, and — Maja knew — so had bedtime.

"It's getting late. You should go inside," said Esidro.

"How about one more story. Please?"

"No."

"Fine," said Maja, slapping her knees and standing. "But you should know I won this round. My story is definitely scarier."

She waited by the doorway for a hug, but Esidro didn't rise, didn't say goodnight, didn't even turn to face her. When she at last picked up on his sulking mood, she rolled her eyes and sighed, letting the front door bang shut behind her.

——— «» ———

Maja barely slept that night. A black train invaded her dreams, its polished dome cover glinting in the moonlight, its endless cars grinding, clacking, squealing on phantom rails. The dead pressed up against the windows as they hurtled down her street, staring through the open curtains of her bedroom, to her dream-self sleeping oblivious within. Worse, she realized her grandfather had been a passenger. Huddled in his chair, his expression wasn't simply sad, but lost, defeated.

That image of her grandfather stayed with her long after she woke. The diversion of a school day helped, but it was never far outside her mind, and filled her with thoughts of death and pain and misery. Only six years had passed since she'd lost her parents, but her memories of them were too distant to be real. The idea of losing her grandfather — the only family she could truly remember — made her feel sick, a profound ache beyond the reach of any words she could muster.

She did her best to cheer herself up during the bus ride home and as she whittled the day away playing on her computer. She pictured the Devil Man's train painted all the colors of a rainbow, spewing cotton-candy clouds, with zoo animals sitting in the passenger cars like humans. The idea made her smile, but wasn't strong enough to calm her. By the time she and her grandfather went outside, to enjoy the final dregs of light, she could no longer hold it in.

"Grandpa. Remember what you said about the Devil Man last night?"

"Yes."

"That wasn't real, right? It can't be."

"What makes you say that?"

"Because it doesn't make any sense. How would a devil get a train or know how to drive it? Also, trains aren't exactly quiet. Why couldn't someone hear it coming from a mile away and run in the opposite direction?"

Esidro tapped his cigar's ash against his shoe, watching the swirling nimbus of gray smoke suspended above him. "I don't know."

"So it was just a story!"

"I didn't say that. While growing up in the Philippines, I saw and heard many strange things, but none as peculiar as the Devil Man. Do you remember when I told you about my experiences during World War Two?"

She shrugged. "Kind of."

"I only shared part of what happened. Never this. After the Japanese attacked the Philippines, I had nightmares of a shadow man piloting a plane over my home, the symbol of the rising sun emblazoned on its wings. When the Japanese occupation forces arrived, I had nightmares of that same phantom pilot. Only now he drove a tank that cruised the city streets, the barrel of its gun pointed at buildings and the helpless citizens cowering within.

"Once I came to the United States, his tank became a boat. I traveled across the continent, from New York to Oregon, and the boat became a train. So no, I don't know how he gets these things, or whether they're real or some kind of illusion. But I believe them to be the Devil Man's way of taking my greatest joys and deepest fears and using them against me. Does that make sense?"

Not wanting to upset him by admitting it did not, she nodded slowly, and then changed the subject. "I noticed you have two cigars tonight. Is one meant for me?"

He answered her grin with a patient smile. "As it so happens, almost fifty years have passed since the liberation of the Philippines." He lifted the second cigar from his shirt pocket and exposed its chipped and peeling wrapper. "Sad as it is, this one means a great deal to me. I'm saving it, for when the mood for celebration strikes."

Tonight his smoke smelled sweet, with just a hint of nuts and pepper. She satisfied herself by taking gulps of air into her mouth, hoping she could collect enough smoke to blow rings like he did. He in turn *humphed*, and held his cigar's trail of smoke as far away as possible.

Maja yawned. "I'm going to bed."

"Sweet dreams."

"Goodnight Grandpa."

They hugged and she went inside, leaving him lost beneath an ample cloud of smoke and reverie.

———— «» ————

Maja had another night of troubled sleep. In her dreams, she crawled out of bed in a stupor, crouched by her window, and watched the black train chuff into the small confines of her front yard. Three figures staggered down the steps from the murk of the first passenger car. They lined up side by side on the low grass, their limbs held stiff, bodies swaying with intoxication — or so she thought, before the interior of the train flared, and the truth revealed itself more clearly.

They weren't drunk, they were dead. Light threaded through their wounds, accentuating every opening with a sickly yellow glow. The man on the left watched her from a pale crater in his forehead. The man in the middle smiled from the broad glimmer of his throat. The man on the right beckoned to her, his finger framed between the puckered flesh that was his headless neck. She gasped. As if triggered by the sound, the light blinked off, smothering the men again in darkness.

Maja sunk below the window frame. Only the chattering of her teeth alerted her that she wasn't sleeping anymore. So then, what part of what she'd seen had been real? She couldn't bring herself to guess, didn't dare peek up over the windowsill to find out for herself, merely pushed in closer to the wall, and waited.

An answer came sooner than she expected. It started with a rapping at the front door. She heard a tap coming from the window of her grandfather's room, followed by a bang against the bathroom's outside wall, and then a voice flitted in from some unknown distance, attended by the steady drum of footsteps. Waves of cold enfolded her, sunk like needles into her skin. Whatever ounce of courage her uncertainty had offered vanished.

"*Esidro. Nasaan ka, Esidro?*" said a man's voice, his gravel baritone sweetened by the honey of its timbre.

"*Esidro, nandito ang mga kaibigan mo. Lumabas ka at kausapin mo sila. Naaalala ka nila.*"

She knew the language was Tagalog, but she'd never learned, couldn't recognize a word apart from her grandfather's name. At first the voice veered away, but then it scuttled closer, as if its owner had circled the house and was now rounding back on her position. She swallowed hard, the wet grinding of her throat exploding in her ears.

"Perhaps you'll only answer if I speak English? It tastes like burning charcoal on my tongue, but I'll use it if you insist."

The footsteps and voice converged on her. Her window screen crackled, followed by a deep, harsh sniffing mere inches from her head.

"I can smell you Esidro, can smell the stink of flesh rotting on your bones. Why hide? Why make this difficult when you're so close to death already?"

Maja had to run, had to get help, but her legs were slender lengths of rope that couldn't possibly support her. Her only chance was to wait it out. Maybe if she didn't move, didn't make a sound, he wouldn't notice her. Wouldn't know that she was—

"Little girl?"

She held her breath.

The voice, now stern, continued. "Little girl. Didn't your grandfather teach you manners? When the Devil speaks, you answer."

The cry that escaped her throat endured long after the Devil Man left and her grandfather stormed the room, accompanied by the modest reassurance of her lights. When white spots twinkled in her vision, and her lungs reversed from want of air, she settled into a whimper. Her grandfather held her for an hour. But nothing, not even his crushing hugs and his promise of "it's okay," could restore her to her senses.

Esidro fell asleep on her bed. For the remainder of the night, she cuddled close to him. Weariness clawed at her, dragged her eyelids down. But she didn't bother going back to sleep. As far as she was concerned, she'd never sleep again.

———— «» ————

Maja dressed and caught the morning school bus. Usually her grandfather accompanied her to the bus stop, but he'd looked so frail in his exhaustion she couldn't bear to wake him. At school, she kept to herself, barely listening when her friends or teachers spoke to her. She prayed the Devil Man was only a dream. But her mind rebelled against such a convenient notion, piling memories into a wall of evidence before her. At recess, she sat beneath the shade of the breezeway, rocking back and forth, inhaling the scent of fresh-cut grass to calm her. So many thoughts of the night before crammed her mind; she had no room left for new ones.

After school, her grandfather met her in the entryway. She could tell something had upset him. His eyes, normally so calm and passive, darted inside the thin cover of their lids, as if searching the house for latent signs of danger.

"Are you ready to talk?" he asked.

"Yes."

"Good. Follow me."

He led her outside. As they passed through their neighborhood, it bothered her how complacent everything appeared. Children gamboled through the streets, and adults worked in garages, or managed the chaos of their front lawns. She couldn't find a trace of wayward shadow or a crack in reality's veneer, just a bright, suburban stretch that knew its limits, and didn't as much as creep an inch out of place. It wasn't right, wasn't fair. A devil had violated her sense of what was normal, and now nothing had a right to feel sane.

Once they reached the corner park, they found an isolated bench and sat. The stifling heat made her armpits damp and her face drip with sweat, but she didn't care, barely noticed.

"A long-dead friend visited me last night," he said, wiping his forehead with the back of his hand. "I could hear him calling through my window. 'Come outside Esidro. Let's talk beneath the stars like we used to.' Judging by your screams, I take it someone visited you as well?"

She nodded.

"Which means he has come back."

She nodded again.

"I thought he'd forgotten about me. I'm sorry, Maja. I didn't mean to get you involved."

"But why? What did you do to make him hate you so much?"

He *humphed*, hands turning purple from the strain of his clenching fingers.

"You say that like this is one of your books or movies. As if I'd robbed a grave or broke a Bulul statue and am now being punished for my sins."

"I'm sorry," she said, brushing his arm. "I didn't mean to blame you. But what did happen, Grandpa? I need to know."

His apprehension made him stiffen. The momentary flexing of his muscles filled his sagging clothes so that he seemed much younger, much stronger than before. But he sighed, shrunk down again, as if the burden of her question or the memories it summoned had deflated him, aging him back into himself.

"I'll tell you what I can remember."

———— «◊» ————

This was after the initial blitz, when Japanese war planes ripped into our cities, killing many of my friends and family, including my mother. It was after invasion forces landed on our shores and the evacuation of our cities and towns to the hope of someplace safer. It was also after the Bataan Death March where ten thousand prisoners of war, including my father, were killed during a sixty-mile trek into captivity.

I was a teenager, not yet a man, when my little sister and I returned home to meet the inevitability of an occupation. We quickly learned to live with our enemies, adapting to their rules, their curfews, their violence. To be honest, it wasn't hard. To disobey meant death. We wanted to live so we simply didn't disobey.

Beyond that, the Japanese fully intended to turn the Philippines into a proper possession. They made allowances, to keep the civil peace. During that time, they let us grow gardens, clear roads, and repair damaged buildings. Weekly swap meets were instituted where we could trade for food and clothes. They even let us gather and play games, albeit under their unwavering vigilance.

My friends and I never cared for sports. Instead, we took the opportunity to smoke cigars, mostly the ones left in my father's private collection. The four of us would meet by the edge of town. There we would speak nonsense, tell stories, or make crude jokes that only young boys would find amusing.

The Japanese didn't care what we did so long as we didn't appear to be colluding. We also shared cigars with them from time to time, a goodwill gesture meant to win us more freedom. Because of this, we thought nothing when a stranger appeared in our midst, asking if he could have a cigar. A wide-brimmed straw hat threw a deep shadow across his face. We assumed from his strange accent that he was a Japanese soldier, though he didn't wear a uniform or carry a gun.

From that day forward, he visited every time we met. He never showed his face and never spoke, only puffed on his cigar and listened. Were it up to me, we would have put up with his unwelcome presence for as long as it lasted. We were nobodies, meant nothing, and it wouldn't have taken much for someone to convince the men in charge to shoot us. But Lorenzo, the boldest of my friends, soon grew annoyed by the stranger's constant beggaring.

"We don't have any more cigars to give. Maybe you can ask your Japanese friends if they will share their cigarettes."

The stranger shook his head. "No. I only want Filipino leaf, not that Japanese poison."

"I'm sorry. What little we have is ours."

Lorenzo turned his back on him. The rest of us began to do the same when the stranger made a noise, something like a growl. He snatched his hat from off his head, and for the first time we saw what was hiding beneath the shadow of the brim. His face was smooth and white. Though he had no eyes, he tracked us all the same, sneering from a little crumpled hole that passed for a mouth. We were wrong before. He wasn't Japanese, Filipino, or even a man. He was a devil.

"You think war is hell?" the devil said. "This is only a taste of what is waiting on the other side." He put his hat on, this time turning his back on us. "We'll meet again, when the time is right. Maybe then you will realize a cigar is a small price to pay for my good favor."

He left. We were too stunned to speak, to make sense of what we'd seen or heard, so we left too, each to our separate houses. The devil's words began to work their evil magic that very night. We discovered Lorenzo the next day, lying by his front door with his throat slit. Soon after, the Japanese took my friend Manual and his family, and beheaded them for suspicions of collaborating with the resistance. Lastly, an officer shot Aurelio because "he didn't bow to a superior like he was supposed to."

Once soldiers kidnapped my sister and forced her to work as a prostitute in a comfort station, I had no reason left to stay. Home wasn't home without my friends and family. I waited for the cover of darkness, gathered as much as I could cram into my pockets, and fled into the jungle. Eventually, I was found and taken in by a Filipino guerrilla unit.

The war truly started for me right then. I had no time to worry about devils or curses any longer. For a time, I even managed to convince myself that he was a figment of my imagination, created to explain all the pain and death and suffering around me. But I heard stories — on long days waiting for the raids at night, or long nights waiting for sleep to find me — and they were always the same: refuse to give the devil-man a smoke and he'll drag you down to hell.

When General MacArthur returned and helped liberate the Philippines, I left my country behind, thinking I could escape my curse by hiding far away. It seemed to work. Despite bad dreams and omens, the passing years made the devil's words feel like empty threats. But I was wrong again; there is no escape. The Devil Man has found me, and he won't stop until he has collected my body and soul, just like my friends before me.

———— «» ————

Dinner was a solemn hour. Maja's fear inhabited the house like a living thing, its presence filling up the rooms, threatening to suck the air right out of them. Every so often, an unexpected noise presented itself — the yowling of a cat or the scuffling of a branch against the windowpane — and she would tense, waiting for the intrusion to succumb to the greater pull of silence. Esidro was of a different mind. He eventually flipped on the TV and watched a sitcom while they ate, his rasping titters dwarfed by a chorus of the show's canned laughter.

Maja was astonished by the pretense of his composure. With sunlight fading, it wouldn't be long before shadows spawned and broke into the silhouettes of dead men and a monster. The first time had been a warning, meant to frighten them — of that, she had no doubt. So, what would happen the next time the Devil Man appeared?

She pushed food into her mouth, let the scrap roll across her tongue. It was the only thing she could do to keep herself from crying.

———— «» ————

The goodnights Maja traded with her grandfather felt more like goodbyes. Before he closed his door, he begged her to stay inside the house, to promise that she wouldn't interfere no matter what she saw and heard. She promised, but she regretted her decision as soon as she cut her bedroom lights.

Her only option now was to stay awake, to support her grandfather with nothing but good thoughts and best wishes. A sense of disconnect pervaded her while she lay in bed, as if she were in two places at once, the real her watching with frustration from the corner of the room.

She tried to pass the time by praying. But as her vigil lurched into the dark of morning hours, Heaven's only answer was a stubborn disregard. She fell asleep still muttering at her ceiling and the vast expanse of stars she imagined far above it.

She only snapped awake again when the front door groaned and the wall shuddered at its closing.

"Oh God," she said, throwing herself from the bed.

Through the window, she saw her grandfather standing in the modest strip of their front yard, still wearing a long, white t-shirt and jeans. He stuffed something into the waistband at the small of his back that she couldn't see in that insufficient light. The world faltered. In the stillness that followed, the black train appeared, a blur gliding through the muted streets, the vagueness of its details clarifying with every forward thrust. Once it eased onto the outer edge of their property, the Devil Man descended from the engine.

"Esidro," he said, arms held wide as if intending to embrace him. "I thought I'd find you hiding beneath your covers or cowering behind your granddaughter again. I thought it'd take at least a dozen more visits before you met me face to face. But here you are, the very second I arrive. Could it be you missed me as much as I missed you?"

"Don't talk to me like that," said Esidro. "I'm not here to make friends, but to end this."

"I agree. The time is finally right. Take your place inside my train, among your friends, and this will finally be over."

Esidro *humphed*. "It won't be that easy. First agree to leave my granddaughter alone. Promise me you won't hurt her or let her come to harm and maybe I'll go with you."

The Devil Man laughed. "Don't forget your place, old man. I came out of respect for our history together, but if I had wanted to, I could have coaxed someone to cut your neck while you slept, or a drunk to take a detour through your bedroom wall. Your choice isn't if you'll come, but when."

He motioned, a subtle nod in Maja's direction.

Maja heard a noise behind her, like the parting of wet lips, and swiveled around to find the dead men standing in her bedroom. At first they stared, inanimate like statues, like a company of marionettes left slumped against their strings. But then they twitched, energized, imbued with life.

"Grandpa!"

Despite the swollen volume of her scream, she could still hear the Devil Man's gloating.

"Your friends are meeting your granddaughter. Better hurry. It won't be long before they rip her apart."

The dead men trudged forward in synchronous strides. Maja threw herself against the window screen, knocking it loose. But with a sudden burst of speed, they encircled her, seizing her in the meat shackles of their hands. She snarled in savage fury, twisted to free herself from fingers pressing purple bruises into her skin.

"Grandpa, help!"

"Board the train," said the Devil Man, "and I promise this will all be over."

"No!" Esidro shouted.

He reached into the waistband at the small of his back and pulled the hidden object out. It was a pistol, its blue steel finish reflecting specks and streaks of light. With his hands wrapped around its grip, he let his eyes drift along the barrel and fired twice at the Devil Man.

"You should be ashamed of yourself," the Devil Man said, shaking his head. "Fifty years and this is the best you could come up with? You can't kill what doesn't live."

As if Esidro hadn't heard, he spun around, rushed toward Maja's bedroom, and ripped the dangling screen from off its perch. Maja did the best she could to sag and cup her ears. Her grandfather squeezed off three more rounds. The bullets slammed into the dead men, knocking them aside, loosening their grip enough for Maja to wrench herself free.

"Run!" Esidro yelled.

Maja did as commanded, retreated from her room, scrambled down the hallway, almost overcome by the raw terror sloshing through her insides. But once she reached the back door, a memory barreled through her mind and she froze in place. It was the image of her grandfather from her nightmares. He was seated on the Devil Man's train, his ashen face stricken of all its joy. If she left now, the Devil Man would take him. Her nightmares would become reality and she would have no one left. She loved him, needed him, too much to ever let that happen.

"Please," she whispered in the empty room. "Help me save him."

At once her thoughts returned to the stories her grandfather told her. If she'd learned anything, it was that Filipino monsters always had a weakness: raw rice to ward off the manananggal, salt to burn the aswang, a split coconut to trap Ongloc. Could it be the Devil Man had a weakness too? It seemed ridiculous to consider, more Dumbo's Magic Feather than a stake through a vampire's heart. And yet, it was the only thing she had to go on.

An inkling of a plan blossomed inside her. She raced to the bookcase in the living room, tipped up the lid of her grandfather's humidor. To her relief, the chipped and peeling cigar he'd shown her was inside. First she cut the cap off and then waved a butane lighter beneath it — like she'd seen her grandfather do a hundred times before. Vague suspicion of its provenance seeded her with hope, but she didn't dare even think about them for fear of jinxing it.

By the time she ran outside, the Devil Man was already leading Esidro by the hand, the dead men flanking them on both sides.

"Wait!"

Esidro turned to her, shivering, his face streaked with tears. "I'm sorry, Maja, but I have to go with him. It's the only way to save you."

"But—"

"Remember your promise. Go inside. I don't want you to see what happens."

She held the cigar out, letting the red eye of its burning tip peer into the distance. "I brought something for the Devil Man."

The Devil Man chuckled, but then sniffed at the air. "It can't be." His earnest strides slowed into an amble. "That's impossible."

Throwing Esidro's hand aside, he bounded straight for Maja. The urge to flee roiled up inside her, but she couldn't move, felt like an animal trapped in the hypnotic lull of headlights. He plucked the cigar from her hands and her skin began to twinge, as if desperately trying to peel away from the spot where he'd made contact. But that was nothing compared to when he removed his hat. At the sight of his round and swollen face, she thought of seeping wounds, of the pale borders of deep gashes and the white rims of ulcerations. She almost vomited, but turned away in time to keep the sick from rising up.

"Ah, vintage Filipino leaf," he said. "Brings back memories." He took a deep puff, held it in for minutes before releasing the smoke in a long, contented sigh. "Was that so hard, Esidro? You could learn a thing or two from your granddaughter."

Maja swallowed, barely daring to look up. "I gave you what you wanted. Now will you leave my grandpa alone?"

The Devil Man stepped closer, the threat of his proximity nearly shoving her back. He studied her. Something like a smile pulled the muscles of his cheeks before he set his hat upon his head, shrouding his face again in darkness.

"As I said to your grandfather before, a cigar is a small price to pay for my good favor. Keep him if you want him. A bag of skin and bones would make a sad addition to my collection anyway."

He took another earnest puff and withdrew back to his train, ascending to the engine. The dead men trailed after him, boarding just as a whistle blew a harsh, enduring, suffocating note. With that, the black train plunged into the ground, dragging the stiff segments of its passenger cars like a snake sliding into a burrow.

Esidro staggered over to Maja and latched onto her shoulder, his profound exhaustion matched only by his stupefied expression. "How did you know that would work?"

"I didn't, but I hoped," she said.

Together, they scanned the space the black train had occupied, half expecting it to reverse, for the Devil Man to return and claim his prize. But as if to prove the world had resumed its proper course, a police siren wailed, announcing its approach, winds blew and the branches of tall trees began to sway again. Whatever had occurred was finally over.

"Do you think he'll keep his word?" asked Maja.

"Who can say for sure? But let's act as if he will and trust in God to make it so."

"Grandpa."

"Yes?"

"I'm sorry."

"For what?" he said, cradling her face, brushing the hair out of her eyes. "After all you've done for me, what could you possibly have to be sorry for?"

"You won. You were right before. The Devil Man is scarier."

Esidro grinned and wrapped his arms around her. Maja cried, remembering that image from her nightmares and realizing she'd never expected to see him smile again. With a squeal of brakes and throbbing lights, the police arrived. Soon they would ask their questions about gunfire, and screams over dead men, and a monster that had left no evidence behind. But Maja couldn't find the strength to care. She hugged her grandfather close, pressing hard against his chest, too numb to feel anything but the stinging of her tears and the solace of his living, breathing, still-warm body.

—— « O » ——

Samuel Marzioli

Samuel Marzioli is an Italian-Filipino of mostly dark fiction. His work has appeared in numerous publications and podcasts, including *The Best of Apex Magazine* (2016), *Shock Totem*, *InterGalactic Medicine Show*, *Tales From the Lake vol. 5*, and *LeVar Burton Reads*. You can read more information about his work at marzioli.blogspot.com.

Where All Roads End

Jason Lane

There were three bullets. One was silver, one was lead, and one was iron. Raymond Stenson picked them up and one by one slotted them into the old colt revolver. He spun the chambers, listened to them clicking. Slowing. Stopped. He checked the clock over the mantle. 11:50. No more time.

He stood, slowly. Stowed the colt in his jacket pocket where it made a dead weight. He paused by the mantle and adjusted the folded note there, then went down the steps.

On the ground floor lay the shop. Antique clocks and bric-a-brac lying in unsteady shadows. Strange forms of gutted machinery and forgotten workings. He passed them by, out into the night, took out the key, thought better of it, and left the door unlocked.

There was only one street. It ran from the station down between the houses and shops before fading away into the plains. Every window was dark and closed. Every door locked. Every curtain drawn. No one would risk being about on the night of August 12. There was Finnigan's parlor where he sold ice cream and the few groceries the town sustained itself on. There Milton's bookshop, the covers of the latest thrillers posing behind the glass. All waiting for the train to stop, the passengers to disperse while it refueled, and investigate a town that had grown merely because here was where the line paused for water, wood and coal. Buy, depart, never thinking of it again. The water tower made a fat shape on spindly legs in the moonlight. A town without a name and merely a single road that went nowhere. Customers, produce, everything borne in on the rails.

Raymond touched the colt in his pocket, reminding himself it was there. Remembering another late August night. Remembering Abigail. A flutter of yellow sundress and a smile. Hair the color of autumn leaves and skin kissed golden by the sun. His heart beat heavily. He clutched his shirt.

He came up to the platform. No one was about. No trains ran at midnight. But everyone knew better. Knew one train did come in once a year, steady as clockwork. Coming since the rails were first laid.

He found a seat and waited. Checked his watch. 11:55. He shouldn't have started so early. Gave him too much time. But maybe remembering was good. It would inspire him. He didn't know if he could shoot when he saw that face. Not the six times, playing roulette for whichever bullet might end it. If any did. He found he wasn't afraid of dying, or whatever might happen. He focused on the memory and hoped the anger would come.

They'd all grown up by the rails. The hum of the passing trains like old friends. Watch them. Listen. Know their individual cries of steam and thrums of pistons.

Abigail had known them. Could name them from a mile off. They would sit on the cords of wood and watch the smoke billow in the distance. Sometimes, race along them when they first arrived. Whooping and shouting. Wondering the who, the where, the why. She knew the schedules perfectly. Had it etched on her mind. Her father was the station agent and always carried the lantern that glowed like a single red eye.

"Here comes the 11:10 to Chicago. The 4:15 to Brenswick," she would say, her voice soft and her lips painting a smile. She knew them all. And a few times he would wake in the dead of an August night to the soft whistle and the thrum of the rails. Hear her stir across the bed. Sense her lips move through the dark. A whisper. "12:00 to where? To where?"

That was how he knew. When he heard the longing. The allure of mystery for the train that never showed up on any schedule the station received. He'd fear for her then. He'd been right to.

Wait. What was that? He stood up. Looked down the tracks. There! The eye. A stabbing glow of white. Wait. Listen. There! The whistle. It screeched a banshee wail through the dark. The gritted iron teeth of a cowcatcher flashed. His hands were sweaty. Listen! The thrum of engines. The beat of pistons.

It came. A dark bulk. It flashed by, whistle screaming again. Here! Here! The rush of air tore his hat off and sent it flying away. Pulled at his clothes with ghostly fingers. It slowed, all black. He scanned the windows of the cars but saw no one. But *he* would be there. He was always there.

It rolled to a stop, brakes dragging against ties with a screech. Lighting sparked all down the way. The clock on the station front rang out. Twelve booming strokes.

Midnight.

The engine breathed white steam. Billowed it across the lonely platform and the dark. Raymond turned, watching.

A shape moved in it. Walked out of the whisking fog. The darkness resolved to a man in a stiff-brimmed and flat-topped hat. A travel case swung at his side, its silver lettering spelling R.M.C. The man stopped. The hiss of steam sang through the night.

Raymond touched his pocket. Felt the colt. Felt that grim weight.

The man moved. He put down his case and from a pocket brought out a wooden square. He unfolded it. Again. Again. The square grew wide, stretched the man's arms. He held it out and legs extended with a clack, and he set the table down. He thumped its top and a small sign fell down its front. He spread his hands, took a deep breath, and spoke.

"Welcome! Anyone! Come one and all! The Royal Montague Company is proud to present the finest of wares! What you need is what we have! In my bag I carry wonders! Gathered from all the parts of this fine world and brought to you today! From the Orient to the inland Ivory Coast! From treasure ships tossed on Tierra del Fuego to the unknown wastes of the northern pole! From the heart of India and the shores of the Bering Sea! We bring with us things no one else can provide. Catch lightning in a jar! Have your fortune told! What you want we have to give! The love of your life will be yours! The kink in your back shall be cured! All of it here! Come! Come! Come and see!"

The town was quiet. The words rang down the empty streets. A voice that tapped on windows shut tight. Shook doorways and rattled locks. The town held its breath. Waited.

Raymond stepped forward.

The man behind the table turned his way. "You sir! And what might I interest you in today? I have something for every man and woman! For every need, a cure! Bad dreams chased away? This eye, the prize of a Chinese emperor and which it's said can see through lies? Perhaps a coin which shall always bring you good luck?"

The wares danced in the man's hands. Picked from the case, spun about. Revealed, returned in favor of the next.

"No," Raymond said, unmoved, unfazed by the dancing menagerie of treasures. "I have a question."

"Ah! You'd like a fortune then? Here we are, here are the cards." A deck with a checkered back came to his hands. He shuffled, cards fluttering between his fingers like startled wings. "And what can I tell you my good man? Perhaps your destiny? The prospect of the heart? How you shall die in the years to come?"

Raymond drew the revolver. Held it at his side. The man's eyes flicked down to it. He didn't lose his smile or the rhythm of the cards. "Ah, a connoisseur I see. Well I should inform you that I give out my wares! No need to threaten I assure you, sir. Or perhaps you seek a bullet which cannot miss! A round that can kill anything it strikes?"

"What happened to Abigail?"

"Abigail?" The cards made a sound like leaves in autumn as he shuffled them. "Ah, a name I recall. From this very station, wasn't she?"

"What did you do with her?"

"Why, I gave her what she asked for. Something from my briefcase which would answer her dream!"

Raymond leveled the gun. "What?"

"A ticket, nothing more," the man said, grinning still. Grinning wide. Dancing the cards between his fingers. "A ticket to wherever she would like to go. To ride the rails until she was done. See the world my friend! Explore it all! Know it all! See it, then back aboard. Where to next! Who can say? Not even I will know where her whim will take her then. To the distant coasts of Bombay or the sands where the Caliphate held sway. The mystic East where sorcerers still fill forbidden courts. The heights of Europe's greatest cities and kingdoms! To meet kings and queens and emperors. Who can say!"

Raymond looked at the train.

"Not here my friend. No longer here. Let's see." He laid out the cards before him. Three, their backs glistening and waxy. "Here we are! A fortune for me to tell. Now let's see." He flipped over the first. "Ah! The Lover I espy. What a surprise! And here we see the Warrior! Are you then?"

"No."

"Pity. Pity. You carry his arms. Perhaps a scabbard which will keep you safe from any wound? No? And here! Why it's the Wanderer! Look at that! And so, your lady friend does. From station to station. Train to train. Escaping to the farthest reaches of the world. A fine thing. Fine indeed. Traveling like myself, a wandering salesman of the fantastic." He laughed. His eyes flashed and his smile grew strained. "In my case I hold the treasure of ages. And what would you like from it, sir? I have something for everyone."

"I want her back," Raymond said.

"Back? Back from wherever she goes? The adventures she takes? Back here where she escaped?"

"You took her!"

"Never take anyone, that I can say. I don't run the train. I just ride it. Just do my bit to the small places of the world. Small places where no palaces grow or buildings scrape the sky. Bring some wonder to the little peoples' lives. Little wonder. Little fine things. Treasures for those who will never see the things beyond the seas."

"What do you want? I'll pay it."

The man clucked his tongue, swept up the cards with a brush of his hand. "Everyone assumes a price. A soul perhaps, but I'm not like Him. Yes, of course, there is a price. Cannot get something for nothing you know. But never what you expect! Can a man with luck forever in his pocket know the thrill of the game again? Can a woman who travels the world settle down? Can a man who delivers wonders stay in one place? Who can say! It's how it is. But is the reward worth the price? That's for them to know. I cannot give that. But everyone assumed the worst of me. But it's my lot to seek them out. Delivering hope and fortune and adventure to those who take it."

Raymond cocked the revolver. Silver. Lead. Iron. One would do it. One would have to do it, no matter what the man before him was. "Bring her back."

"And if she doesn't want to?"

"She would. She must! Why wouldn't she?"

"I couldn't say. But she left. Perhaps this little fellow might interest you?"

Raymond ignored the little windup toy soldier placed on the table, its key turning as it clattered about in circles. He stepped forward. Pressed the barrel of the revolver against the man's brow. "She wouldn't leave me."

"Did she leave you?"

"I…"

His voice faded as memories bled in. Her watching the trains come in and out. Sweeping down the iron highway to distant places. The names slotted in the timetable. How she listened. Poised. Her face uplifted, the whistle thrumming through her body as she stood at the kitchen sink. Looking out the window of the small shop where they lived. Watching the crowds disembark. Leaving a town where no tickets marked. A small place. Too small for a spirit like hers. The colt shook in his hand. The man watched him; eyes fixed down the barrel.

Raymond let the revolver fall. Hung it limply at his side.

The man picked up the table and the legs retreated. He folded the table into squares smaller and smaller, then stowed the smallest in his bag. Snapped it shut.

"It seems I have nothing in my case for you," he said. "No. Nothing for a man who seeks the woman he loves. And who goes who knows where."

"Nothing," Raymond repeated hollowly.

"But it should be said that the The Royal Montague Company always has something for every man with a wish. A desire he would pursue. We stake our pride on it you see! And never have I left a customer unsatisfied. So, to the man who would see his bride again, who would seek her out across the world, I do have one last offer in which to make. One way he might wander round the world and seek her out."

Raymond looked at him again. "Which is?"

The man in the flat-topped hat patted his case. "Nothing in my case…"

———— «» ————

The train pulled out as the clock rang out. Announcing the first hour of August 13. White steam swirled in its wake and faded away from the station, and the town seemed to exhale. Escaping another night.

A man walked down the street. He had dark hair and a mild smile. His hands were clasped behind his back, and as he walked, a trim neat jacket, the sort worn when the first winds of winter come down from the mountains, sank about his frame. Fitting him fine. Just fine. He went down the street going nowhere and rattled every door until he found the one unlocked. He passed inside, left a flat-topped hat hanging on a hook and observed the bric-a-brac of gutted antiques and lonely machinery.

"Always meant to learn a trade," he mused, and flashed a smile. He saw a note on the mantelpiece and plucked it off. Turned it over, then tore it up. He breathed in, letting the air of the shop fill him. Fit him. Take him in. He smiled, and the eyes that opened to the shop were warm and familiar. The sort you see in any nameless town settled off the rails.

"A fine town," he said, "to rest for a spell."

———— «» ————

And autumn came, leisurely stripping trees of all their leaves. Winter blanketed the world. Spring melted the snow and things bloomed. Summer lay thick and torpid, and through it all the trains ran with clockwork precision through the little town just off the side of the world. The years rolled in and out as they ever did. All things the same.

And then the wind grew cold and August came again. And on a certain day every house locked its doors and windows tight, as they always did. And when the clocks struck midnight there came a banshee wail. A streak of darkness and rain of sparks as a train drew up to the station all alone.

And in a shop a man raised his head from the guts of a clock and took off his glasses. He listened. Waited. And from the depths of night a man's voice rang out to rattle windows and doors.

"Welcome! Anyone! Come one and all! The Royal Montague Company is proud to present the finest of wares! What you need is what we have! In my bag I carry wonders! Gathered from all the parts of this fine world and brought to you today!"

And the man in the shop listened, and there came the light and joyful note of a woman's voice. "We bring with us things no one else can provide. Catch lightning in a jar! Have your fortune told! What you want we have to give! The love of your life will be yours! The kink in your back shall be cured! All of it here!"

And the man in the shop smiled and turned back to his work. And when he finished, the clock tolled one, and he listened to the train hiss and blow, and whistle as it vanished back down the rails.

—— « O » ——

Jason Lane

Jason Lane is an aspiring author from Whitehorse, Yukon. He was born, raised, and educated there with brief forays to the south where the weather is milder. He has a number of self published works and has been featured in numerous anthologies.

A Ring Around the World

Liam Hogan

"All aboard the train that never stops!" hollered the station master, as the locomotive clanked and grumbled, belching alternate clouds of smoke and steam.

Henson stifled a derisive sneer. It wasn't the Girdle trains that never stopped, uneasy as this one appeared to be at rest. There wouldn't be much point. Passengers had to board and passengers had to disembark and station masters had to wave their silly little flags.

And sometimes — often — they all had to wait for a delayed train coming the other way. The regularly spaced stations were the only places two trains could pass along the single track, their dance stuttering to a clumsy halt whenever repairs were needed.

Henson tucked his satchel in front of him as he clambered up the three steep steps and through the narrow carriage door. Somewhere behind him his trunk was being loaded into the luggage car. He put that out of his mind. There was no point in worrying; letting it out of his sight was distressing but unavoidable. The trunk was as secure as he could afford to make it.

Instead, he concentrated on the enigma that was the Girdle as he negotiated his way through the crowded carriage, the air thick with tobacco smoke and the fug of migrant workers.

No, it was the *track* that never ended. A Girdle train only traveled in one direction, either east or west, endlessly circumnavigating the world on a shiny metal ring fit snugly around its equator. Engineers liked to joke that their locomotives were built facing the way they would always travel, and couldn't ever be turned around.

Along the Girdle's leveled route, wherever the lay of the surrounding land allowed, communities bustled. North and south, the rest of the watery planet was uninhabited and would assuredly remain so, until some alternative means of transportation was invented.

Or *re*-invented, strictly.

The Girdle was artificial. Regular, and perfect, and hollow. A man-made strip of land, though man had obviously come a long way since; all of it down. No one was sure when it was built, and none could conceive how the Ancients had achieved this stunning feat of engineering. Even its name, *The Girdle*, suggested an impossible vision from somewhere high above. Somewhere the planetary curve could be seen, instead of the earthbound view: the distant vanishing point, two rails merging into the heat haze at the horizon.

The rails were a recent addition, running along the Girdle's upper surface. Threads of hard-earned metal sitting beneath the bright sun, steam trains hurtling in both directions. Completed barely two decades ago, it had been meant to bring order and prosperity, to unify the settlements.

Instead, it had devastated them, the inhabitants flocking to the bright lights of the six Solar Cities, with Girdle City the brightest light of all. All along the route rural stations lay neglected, forlorn, migrants demanding higher pay and leaving whole crops to wither at a capricious whim. Leaving hardened men to exploit what little was left.

If the fishermen deserted the seas, Henson grimly thought, the Cities would starve for sure.

Reaching the front of the passenger coaches, he pulled back a curtain and found himself in first class.

The seats, the luggage racks, the soot-speckled windows, all were the same either side of the arbitrary divide. The only difference — and what the higher fare paid for — was fewer people. First class meant not having to scrum with everyone else.

Owlish eyes stared up at him from the section's only occupant, a thick tome hiding half a round face, before dropping to reveal an inquisitive smile.

"I'm sorry," Henson said, turning to go.

"No, no, please, join me, sir."

Henson hovered, uncertain. There hadn't been a single available seat in the carriage he had just come through, people and luggage crowding even the thin central aisle between the wooden benches. "I don't have the right ticket," he admitted.

"Never mind that!" the owl replied. "If the inspector comes by, I'll gladly upgrade a fellow scholar of the line." He beamed, lowering the book to his lap.

Henson eyed him coolly. "What makes you think I'm a scholar?"

"Well now. The cut of your coat, dusty though it is. Girdle City tailoring, I'll warrant. And if not a scholar, at least an explorer, an adventurer, someone *interesting*? Plus, you have so little baggage — just that little satchel? Obviously not one of the usual farm workers."

The owl's tilted head, his close scrutiny, made Henson uneasy.

"You don't trust me, sir?" the owl continued. "The way you pat the gun at your hip… Reassured by its presence? No killer thankfully, otherwise I would not be so generous with my invite! If you were a killer, sir, you would not need to feel for your weapon. You'd *know* it was there and that thought alone would give you the reassurance you seek. So, yes, an adventurer. One not averse to traveling in dangerous lands?"

Henson half-considered joining the third-class passengers. There, people stood or squatted with their wares and even animals. Usually for only one stop. The people who traveled third class never had far to go.

Or perhaps he could share the steps with the ragtag urchins, his legs dangling out over the tracks as they clattered by, faces and clothes darkened by smuts.

But what harm could this softly spoken man do? Even if he was too damned inquisitive by half.

He stretched out a hand. "George Henson."

"Marcus Cairn. Um, *Professor* Marcus Cairn." The shake was limp, but at least it was dry.

"And what are you a professor of, Mr. Cairn?" Henson said, taking a seat across from him.

"Why, the Girdle, of course! What else is there to investigate?"

Henson looked out of the grimy window. They were on a stretch of the line with sea to either side, blue waters sparkling in the sun. When he turned back, his smile was firmly in place.

"What indeed."

"Have you ever been inside?" the professor asked.

Drumming his fingers on the wooden bench, Henson nodded. To admit he had would not be all that unusual. To suggest he hadn't would contrast too strongly with his appearance, the clues the professor had already picked up. It would peg him as a liar.

"Remarkable, is it not?" the professor said. "That tunnel, stretching into the distance, blacker than the blackest night. One wonders what the Ancients used it for."

Henson stared at him in genuine surprise. "Surely that is the least of its mysteries. The trains?"

"Ah yes, the trains that we have so clumsily replicated, that we have perched even more clumsily on top of *their* great structure, as if to claim it for our own." The owl looked wryly amused. "And yet their tunnels have no tracks and the carriages we find below have no wheels. Sparking dreams and myths of a cavern somewhere, a treasure trove of Ancient, pristine, everlasting wheels!"

Henson laughed uneasily. That had been the legend that had set him on his path; exploring the more remote stretches of the Girdle, looking for whatever could be removed, reused, sold. Which, it turned out, had been precious little.

The professor, his eyes magnified by the thick lenses in his glasses, scrutinized his fingertips, running a thumb along their edges. "There are those, this scholar included, who think the example set by those magical trains has skewed our redevelopment. The Girdle has thrown down a gauntlet.

Man might regress as far as basic agriculture, but by damn he won't forget the trains!

"It is a challenge we should not have risen to. We should be focused on better plows, not steam engines. Fishing boats, not rails. Nails, not guns, which require the scavenged tubes of the Ancients because we are incapable of metal work to that degree of sophistication. Even our trains depend upon Ancient vessels being converted into the boilers we cannot create ourselves."

"It's only a matter of time—"

"Is it?" the professor interrupted. "You think we can reclaim what has been lost? You assume the Ancients ran this planet as a self-sufficient settlement?"

Henson's stare widened. The academic licked his plump lips and continued. "There are those who think the underground, trackless railway is a mere by-product. That it was never intended as a means of daily transportation, as we use our steam trains. That it was merely a way of accessing the workings of the Girdle's true purpose: the second, thinner tunnel."

Henson felt bile rise in his parched throat. "Second?" he croaked.

"Yes." The professor nodded. "The second tunnel. Fewer people know about that one. But you do, don't you, Mr. Henson?"

"Another train track?" he asked, recovering.

"Too narrow for that. Too packed with machinery. Perhaps it is a good thing it is not so easily broached. It would be a shame for it to be torn apart by mere *scavengers* before we can attempt to understand what it is."

The professor inclined his head once again. Held out his hand. "May I see your weapon, Mr. Henson?"

Henson looked down to white knuckles clamped over his holster, fingers clipping and unclipping the leather fastener. He hadn't even realized he was doing it.

And now this scholar was asking him for his gun…

"Careful," he said, reluctantly handing it across the narrow divide. "It's loaded."

"Interesting…" muttered the professor, poring over the device, fingers carefully exploring every facet. "The trigger mechanism is your own design?"

Henson nodded. He'd paid a small fortune for the eight-inch length of smooth, Ancient pipe. Everything else — even the gunpowder — he'd had to learn to make himself.

It was the price of the indestructible metal barrels that meant such guns were few and far between. And would stay so, until they learned to work Ancient materials, or at the very least, dismantle their machines to liberate more of the precious tubes.

The professor handed the weapon back, casually, nonchalantly, as if it were no more than a plaything in which he had lost interest.

"So, the second tunnel. My own theory is that it — indeed the whole Girdle — is a scientific experiment. As big as the Ancients could possibly make it: the size of a whole planet. A gargantuan device powered by the Solar Cities."

"An experiment? To do what?"

The professor shrugged, his rounded shoulders hiccupping. "We lack the knowledge to even contemplate the workings of the machine, let alone what it was built to prove or disprove. And we may never know. You see, to understand their experiments we would have to *become* the Ancients. And I don't think they lived here."

"But ... where then? Are we not descended from them? And what about the City buildings, their homes, now ours?"

Another shrug. "Left behind. *Temporary* accommodation. As for us, well yes. Descended we must be. But from the scientists, or from the equally discarded workforce that constructed their device?"

The professor settled back into his seat, flipped out his bulky pocket watch, tapped the glass surface and peered out of the window, though there was nothing to see but the dazzling blue waters. "Either way, the Girdle is too big a thing for this planet, too big for the pitiful population the thin strip of land and adjoining islands can bear. So I think they set it up, left it running, and left our ancestors behind at the same time."

"The experiment is still running?"

"Probably not." He smiled. "Perhaps our ancestors weren't supposed to be here. Perhaps they — *we* — are not guardians but strays, here by accident. Either way, our scavenging down the years is likely to have disrupted the operation.

"But maybe it was only designed to run for a dozen, fifty, a hundred years. Who can tell?"

Henson sat mulling over the professor's words. The accusation of "scavenger" needled him, but was there any truth to the rest of it?

"An interesting hypothesis," he admitted. "But no more than that, surely? Do you have any proof? Is that why you have traveled so far from the cozy comfort of Girdle City's libraries, in search of verification?"

The barb wrought a sour look from the professor. "My own area of expertise is a little narrower than the entirety of the Girdle. And yes, Mr. Henson, I suppose it *is* just a theory. I'm particularly interested in Ancient tools. The off-cuts and spares — like those that form your gun — are limited and nearly depleted, though men such as yourself continue to search the length and narrow breadth of the Girdle for them.

"We know we cannot break down their devices; that no amount of force or fire seems to make the slightest dent on the metals they used. But we also know that the Ancients put them together. We think it is some sort of magnetic coupling. Finding a device that allows us to dismantle the Ancient machines… That would be very valuable indeed."

Professor Cairn checked his pocket watch again. "Well, Mr. Henson, it's been a pleasure, but I need to be ready for my departure."

Henson nodded, then frowned. "Girdle City won't be for another couple of hours yet."

"Indeed. However, there will be another stop before then."

"It's not scheduled—"

The wheels of the Girdle train shrieked demonically. Curses and luggage flew forward from the carriage behind, and Henson lurched in his seat. Professor Cairn, with his back pressed to the bench, watched indulgently.

"There. My stop."

Through the window, Henson caught a glimpse of a man carrying luggage. *His* luggage! That box was the fruit of nine months of hardship, of sacrifice. He sprang up, reaching for the pistol at his waist, then froze.

The professor's easy grin had slipped, and, in its place, a snub-nosed device had appeared in his pudgy hands. Something had hardened about him, as though he had dropped a mask.

"Please, take a seat, Mr. Henson. These men are friends of mine, and I'd rather you didn't do anything foolish."

Henson fought against the tension. Small though the gun was, it was pointed at him from barely an arm's length away. Impossible to miss. He considered making a grab for it, but that was an awfully desperate measure, a last ditched, life-already-forfeit action. Slowly, carefully, he sat, his hands raised in front of him, well away from his gun belt.

"Good, good. And now, if you please, slide your satchel toward me."

There seemed little point in arguing. Especially as he could hear shouts of protest from within the carriage, along with sudden gasps and yelps as that protest was roughly stifled.

He slid the satchel across the floor with an outstretched foot, eyes locked on the professor's. Waited until those eyes wandered, until a hand fumbled blindly for the strap.

But the owl's gimlet gaze — and aim — didn't wander.

Not until the curtain was tugged aside and a dust-streaked figure appeared, scarf wrapped around his — no, *her* — head. Professor Cairn — if that really was his name — pushed the satchel toward her. "Check it."

She hoisted it up, flipped it open and turned it upside down, resulting in a clatter of Henson's most precious possessions. Her booted foot rummaged through them, crushing the pages of his notebooks disparagingly, before she pounced on the dull gleam of a hip flask.

The professor shook his head. "Leave the man his liquor, Marie-Anne."

There was a fierce wordless battle, before she averted her eyes and tossed the flask through the air. Henson clumsily caught it, catching a scowl in the bargain.

"Ah," the professor said, nodding down the carriage. "Here comes the trunk."

Henson's heart sank as another ragged figure appeared. This one was a good foot taller than the woman, two feet taller than the professor. An ox of a man, carrying the heavy box on his own. Cringing second class passengers shrank away from him as he passed, cowered in fright as he dropped the trunk to the carriage floor.

Henson heard it crush the things that had once lived in his satchel and winced.

"Careful Sam!" the professor admonished. "What's in it?"

"Locked," Sam replied thickly.

The professor turned to the owner of the box. "Open it," he ordered.

Henson wavered, until the gun wagged. Reluctantly he fished the key from around his neck, slotted it into the lock, heard it click.

He was about to raise the lid when a slim boot slammed it back down, stopping him in his tracks. "Uh-uh," Marie-Anne said. "Back to your seat, mister."

He sat, cursing silently as the stout lid was swung open and the three of them crowded around, Marie-Anne on her knees as though praying before an altar. Even through the scarf Henson could tell she was beaming. "Pay dirt, Prof."

The professor gave a small bow. "I thank you for that, sir. I'd ask the source of such glorious bounty, but doubt you'd be willing to tell and time presses. Never mind. Our paths may cross again Mr. Henson, and if they do kindly show me the same respect I have shown you."

As he turned to leave Henson drew his pistol, hesitated for the briefest of moments as he tried to recall the last time he'd checked it was primed, before savagely pulling the trigger.

There was a flat clunk as something misfired. The steel wheel didn't spin, didn't strike the pyrite block, didn't send a shower of sparks leaping toward the powder charge. A flat clunk, with no explosion, no speeding bullet.

The professor looked balefully over his shoulder, his hand restraining his companions, holding back the anger in Marie-Anne's eyes, the dull hate in Sam's.

"I'm disappointed, Mr. Henson. And more than a little surprised. In the back as well! Perhaps you'll become a killer yet. But not today and not if you let an old fool tamper with your gun. Sam, take the box. Marie-Anne, relieve Mr. Henson of his weapon."

The girl stooped to the discarded satchel, seized the powder pouch, the spare musket balls, the bottle of oil, even his tinderbox, before triumphantly grabbing the precious gun from Henson's immobile hands. The rest, the notebooks, the hand drawn maps, she kicked savagely under the bench.

"My apologies, Mr. Henson," the professor said. "It is best not to upset Marie-Anne. Such a temper! Good day."

Slumped in his seat, Henson watched through the train window as they climbed down from the carriage and were joined by two more men, the five of them heading toward a waiting fishing boat, the professor walking sedately, the others giddy with excitement.

Some catch they'd landed today, he thought bitterly.

He leaned back on the hard wooden bench and sighed. Uncapped the returned hip flask and took a small sip, wetting his lips. He didn't drink deeply; it was too potent a brew for that. Whatever they had done to stop the Girdle train in its tracks, it might be a while before it started up again, especially if the repairs were more than the onboard engineer could manage. It could be a long wait.

The contents of the stolen trunk he'd found in a building buried by drifting sands, at the tip of a spit of land miles from the Girdle. More pieces of Ancient metalwork than he'd managed to scavenge over the preceding four years, a treasure that would be sorely missed. And yet...

His fingers fluttered to his inner pocket. He checked there was no audience, that the gang hadn't changed their mind and come back for more plunder, before extracting a gleaming tool, staring at it in wonder, still somehow miraculously his. It was this slim silver wrench that had allowed him to carry the piping away, the gentle *click* as it was applied to each section, releasing the locking mechanism within.

A device far more valuable than the simple pieces the professor had stolen.

Henson had thought to demonstrate the tool before the rich men and scientists of Girdle City, constructing and dismantling the parts in his trunk. Thought to auction it to the highest bidder, setting him up for life; no more scraping in the dust for things the Ancients had thrown away.

Such a foolish daydream. To swap *this* for a mere sack of coin? The professor had taught him a valuable lesson. Why, with this tool a man could build a new world! Build *and* rule. With all those Ancient treasures lying barely twenty feet below the endless train tracks, what couldn't he achieve?

He slipped the wrench back into his chest pocket where it nestled next to a heart gone cold with the grim determination to never let anyone stand in his way again.

———— « O » ————

Liam Hogan

Liam Hogan is an Oxford Physics graduate and award winning London based writer. His short story "Ana", appears in Best of British Science Fiction 2016 (NewCon Press) and his twisted fantasy collection, *Happy Ending Not Guaranteed*, is published by Arachne Press.

Web: http://happyendingnotguaranteed.blogspot.co.uk/
Twitter: @LiamJHogan

The Memory Glass

Laurie Stewart

Darynda P. Young was running late again. This time, it could cost her the opportunity of a lifetime.

Her wooden heels clicked sharply on the marble floor as she hurried for the Human sector. She'd spent way too much time in the Alien Sector buying art supplies. But how could she resist the paints and glitters available only there? Alien worlds birthed those incredible hues and textures, and she'd needed them the moment she saw them.

But now she had less than an hour to buy lunch and find her connecting mag-train. Which could be anywhere in this sector.

The Hub was a wonder of engineering, human and alien fused into a beautiful, flowing, almost surreal sensibility of stone, glass, polymers, and precious metals. There were fountains throwing glowing or colored liquid into the air, glass bubbles carrying exotic animals, fish, or aliens, each holding its own atmosphere, and carried along by whirring brass feet. Above her head was a fine web of pipes, fragile and sheer as spider silk.

A thousand ways to paint this place sprang to mind. From the clash of colors captured in abstract, to a small focused portrait in painstaking detail.

Darynda shook herself and determinedly looked away from the hypnotic dance of light and movement. She checked that her mechanical luggage was following properly and set off down the corridor to the nerve center of the Hub.

The luggage, looking more like a small brass fridge than a suitcase, trundled dutifully behind her.

The discovery of monopole magnetics had made space travel cheap, and it turned out habitable planets were plentiful. Now, sixty years after the first colony ship had left Earth, hundreds of planets had their own identity, their own culture, human, but no longer of Earth. The Hub was filled with people from every settled world and a few non-human worlds as well.

Her father had moved away from the poverty of the Earth cities when she was five. They had taken a mag-train to the Hub, then a colony ship to the Hoortan moon base. They said that life was better there, but everything seemed shades of gray. And she needed color!

The family was happy enough; her father was a minor executive at the mineral extraction plant, so they could afford a decent sized living unit. Like everything there, it was carved out of the rocky moon's surface and locked behind multiple airlocks. It was safe, but dull. Hazy memories of running through flowers in the open air haunted her and made her heart ache for more.

Looking up at the high, curved ceiling, she was drawn in by the clockwork miniatures of people and carts moving about their business. A tiny baggage cart crashed into what must be a food kiosk, starting a small fire. People crowded around, and a spray of fire retardant misted from a web of pipes that flew over to hang above the cart, putting the flames out almost instantly. How did they fake the fire?

Then her perception shifted, and she realized that there was no ceiling. The Hub was a sphere, she was standing on the inner curve on one side, and looking at the floor on the opposite side. Her mouth hung open and she prayed her connection wasn't all the way over there.

The mag-trains docked at airlocks set at specific points on the outside of the sphere, carried along with its spinning until they reached the entrance to the magnetic tunnels that wound to their destination. Missing that timing could mean spending days or weeks waiting for your mag-train station to line up with the right tunnel again.

Something new caught her eye, and she was distracted again. There was an ad for the Memory Glass Diamond Jubilee tour. They had fascinated her on her last visit to the modern art museum on Hoortan. Three large, slightly curved glass panels, each a different view of a garden, swaying gently back and forth in a gentle, silent wind, each of them a loop of reality taken from the artist's memory and embossed into living glass. If you stood close enough, it filled your vision, as real as if you were there. She loved the bees in the lilacs best. You could almost hear the buzzing and smell the flowers; they were so rich and lifelike.

She had been ridiculously delighted at seeing the name Pamela etched into the corner of each Glass in flowing script. Her own middle name, it seemed to connect Darynda to the art form, and it still fascinated and called her.

And now she had a chance to study with their creator! She'd been invited to get her Master's degree at the prestigious art school founded by Pamela herself. The artist must be nearly ninety, but Darynda had heard that she still picked the students herself, mentored them, and still worked with the Glass, the Master of the craft she had created.

Shaking herself, Darynda looked for a station map. She didn't dare be late this time. If she missed her mag-train, she would miss her chance to really study Memory Glass with the only teacher who mattered. She'd learned all she could at the colony's art school, and her attempts were ... disappointing. Even though the letter from the academy had praised them, and said they were the reason she'd been given a scholarship, she knew they would never extend the invitation a second time.

She found the map and tried to find the Earth hub. She ran her finger through the air above the map in an attempt to follow the path from the "you are here" light. She could just make it if she hurried a little more and stopped gawking at everything like a fool.

Then a shock passed through her as her finger paused over a large block in the hall outside the Earth hub. She couldn't believe it. A twenty Glass exhibit was just outside the Earth Station hub! Twenty! If she hurried, she'd have time to look at a few of them before boarding.

She turned to her luggage and touched the control for "high speed". Her luggage seemed to rev up, clanking and humming slightly. She was still thrilled with it, a gift from the whole art college in Hoortan base. They were so proud of her, the only colonist ever to get a scholarship to a real Earth school.

It used a combination of micro-electronics and molecular steam power to follow the radio signal in her bracelet. She could even program it to follow simple verbal directions, like "follow me." Her family had also given her a beautiful leather-bound art journal, with her initials and an embossed photo of her family layered onto the cover.

Darynda pulled out her passport, train ticket, and travel visa, sent by special mail from the Living Glass Academy, and raced straight for the Earth hub.

A moving slide-walk, an escalator, and a couple of corners later, she suddenly stopped, staring, and raced back around the corner. From the corner of her eye she'd seen a man with a gun. She huddled on the floor, heart pounding. After several minutes of silence, she peered around the corner. A man, dressed in heavily travel-stained clothing and carrying a handgun, stood several meters to her left. Her stomach clenched, and her lungs froze, her breath stopped in her throat. The man raised his pistol. There was no place to hide. There was no one nearby to help her.

There was a little old lady laughing at her.

She looked to her left again and saw the same man jump out from behind a partly collapsed building and fire at her. There was a hint of someone falling beside her, and then the scene reset itself.

It was the Memory Glass exhibit! She had made it on time! She looked around. Gone were the sleepy gardens and happy bees. The hallway was a terrifying look at the old Urban Wars on Earth — bombed buildings, shattered glass, broken bodies. Ten life-sized Glasses on either side, it stretched down the hall, all the way to the counter that marked the Earth Station check-in.

Darynda glanced at the old woman, a bit embarrassed to have reacted so obviously to the shooter. The woman waved her hand, gesturing for Darynda to come over.

"I'm sorry, I shouldn't have laughed at you for being scared."

"Startled. I was just startled," Darynda blurted, running a hand through her hair.

The woman patted the bench beside her. "Sit down, dear. You look like you need a minute."

Darynda sat, looking along the hallway again. "Why are there are so many Glasses about the war? Where are the lilacs?"

"Oh, I remember the lilacs. They were my favorite Glass." She smiled at Darynda. "How are you doing, dear? Is this your first trip to the Hub? No." She shook her head. "You've seen Glass before. This must be your second."

"No, this is my first. I've seen them in a museum. I was really looking forward to seeing more but these just aren't the same. They're so bleak and hopeless. I get enough of that at Hoorton."

"I didn't want to do so many; you know. But the Glass only takes strong, powerful memories. The gardens were from before the war. After ... I just couldn't..." She paused, drawing a deep breath. "The Urban War was a terrible thing. It was all over money, you know. There were so few jobs, so little housing you could afford. Then the farmers stopped bringing in food. People died by the thousands. Those that were left were never the same."

"You? You made all these? You're Pamela?"

She nodded, barely smiling at the awe in Darynda's voice. She gestured to the Glass that had startled Darynda. "That was the moment my first husband died. The love of my life, he was. We were trying to get a group of children out of the city. We were ... ambushed."

Darynda looked at the Glasses nearest them. In one, people scrounged for food in the bombed out remains of a grocery store. Their gaunt faces and dirty clothes spoke of a moment in time that had seemed like ancient history. In another, a small boy stared at the camera, his tear stained face a testimony to loss. Looking to the woman beside her, Darynda realized that the war hadn't been that long ago, less than twenty-five years before she was born.

The twenty Glasses told a story, lined up so that you seemed to pass through the war from the first bombs to the escape to the dirty gray shelters.

"We tried to help, but there were so many." Pamela's hand shook slightly as she reached up to check her hair.

The Glasses were all ugly, all violent. Such a contrast to her bright pink dress and jacket, and the jaunty little feathered hat perched on her snow-white bun.

"I'm Darynda. I'm going to Earth to study at your school." Darynda held out her hand.

"Darynda." The wrinkled cheeks instantly bracketed a wide, tremulous smile. "I haven't heard that name in ever so long. Since before the war. Maybe that's what struck me about your Glasses, Darynda written like a memory on the frame."

"I was named after my grandmother. My father never saw her again after the war children were taken by the government." Darynda withdrew her hand, slightly disappointed that the woman hadn't shaken it.

If she'd been waiting here ... and she'd recognized her name, mustn't Pamela be here to meet her? She looked at the woman's hands, so thin and white, the knuckles showing like knotted ropes. Arthritis? Maybe she couldn't shake hands.

The disappointment was short-lived. This frail, old woman was Pamela! The artist responsible for a whole new art form and the greatest Glass artist who ever lived. Darynda was practically bouncing in excitement. "Are you still doing Glasses? How do you get them so clear? I had so much trouble focusing; all my early ones were all fuzzy. I tried so hard to get my Glasses right. I'm a good painter, but the Glass is so different."

Pamela fanned herself, her face a bit flushed, and smiled crookedly. "We need to go, dear. You can't be late, mustn't miss the train this time."

Darynda glanced around for her luggage. It was hissing, seemingly impatiently, at the gate. She held out her hand, thrilled when Pamela used it to lever herself to her feet. She was surprisingly strong for such a bird-like thing.

Together, they presented their tickets at the counter. They were seated side by side! *Had Pamela planned it this way when she booked the tickets? Of course, she had to have. Then why did she seem so nervous?*

They were seated by a sour faced man in a metallic blue uniform. Everything on the train was metallic, the seats beneath their cushions, the walls, the luggage bins. It had to be for the magnets to work. But it wasn't as comfortable as she remembered. Nor as big. Now it seemed a bit shabby, and way more crowded.

She carefully aimed her luggage into the slot assigned to her, and after a few tries, got it in snugly enough not to fall over. Pamela handed her a small leather case, which she happily tucked in beside her own. Now they looked like they were traveling together. Darynda grinned.

As the mag-train hissed and popped, disconnecting from the space station's air and power supplies, it started to vibrate and change pitch. They were getting ready to be thrown from the magnetic locks. Darynda wished that there were windows on the mag-trains, but the pamphlets had been clear. Seeing the space distortions with the naked eye would drive sentient beings mad. Still, it would be so inspiring. She could have made a Glass about that; she was certain that she would never forget this trip.

Pamela handed her a large, dog-eared package. As she started to rise to put it, too, into the bin, a small gesture stopped her.

"Did you know there's a mathematical formula for figuring out how many rats you can keep in one cage? X many rats, everybody is fine and happy. X+1, they fight until only one is left alive. People too, it's what started the wars. Too many rats in too poor a cage."

"Has your art style changed again? From the war to something lighter, maybe? I would love to know…" Darynda's smile slipped. Was Pamela senile? She didn't seem to even hear her question.

"Time, it's running out, you know." Pamela's hand was shaky as she pointed to the clock over the door to the next car.

Darynda reached over to clutch at Pamela's hand, to make sure that she had the old woman's wandering attention; there was one question she just had to have answered.

"How did you discover how to put the memory loop into the Glass?"

Pamela pulled her hand away and looked at it, as if making sure it was still there.

"There was one on the ship; I pulled it apart to see. It's the magnets, I suppose. Every monopole ever found is on the mag-trains and the Hubs. Just imagine what they're doing to time and space, making it all bendy, and what if it ends up one too many rats?"

"What ship? What do monopoles and rats—"

"You must hurry. You can't be late this time. There's so much to tell you, so much I don't dare."

Darynda stared at her, worried. They were already on the train. "Are you all right?"

Pamela whispered, "Fading. No time, you must read page four right away. You must know…"

Her face was paler, even the pink of her dress seemed faded. Darynda looked around frantically, but everyone was buckled in for the departure, and the crew had vanished. No one met her frightened gaze. Something was wrong, she knew it.

Darynda reached for the bell-pull to call the conductor, but Pamela grabbed her hand, bony fingers like steel rods pulling her attention back to the old woman.

"Sit at the very back, the very last seat. Promise me. You'll be very early. You were always on time after this. Be brave."

"But…" Darynda was confused. She couldn't change seats now, the train was about to move, and Pamela was … Pamela was glaring at her with an almost feral grimace.

"Go!"

She glanced around; there was only one empty seat left, the one beside the luggage rack, the furthest rear seat on the mag-train.

Darynda hurriedly switched seats. Then, glancing back at the old woman, she angrily opened the package. She was pretty sure that Pamela would be furious, but so was she. *Sent to the back like a child.*

On the very top was a small Memory Glass of a man with a little boy, laughing at the viewer. And underneath, a journal of faded and worn leather, a fancy *D*, *P* and *Y* barely readable on the front cover. Like hers. One corner was stained dark. The stain also covered the corner of almost every page, like it had been dipped in brown ink. She flipped through the pages of tightly spaced writing.

Page four was an old news clipping, fragile and faded almost to sepia tones. Darynda lifted it, tilting it to catch the light.

It was of a woman standing in front of an old hospital, looking shaken and confused. She was clutching the arm of a man in police blues. The headline read *"Only survivor of mystery spaceship crash!"* She was wearing a modern dress, despite the obvious age of the clipping. Darynda squinted, bringing the clipping closer. It was ... her. In the dress she was wearing now.

She stared around her; she couldn't understand it. The clipping was dated sixty years ago. As the mag-train started away from the station, small bursts of white light on the magnetic rods covering the inside of the carriage showed the fields pulling the mag-train to the Earth system. Darynda looked back down at the journal page. It had a note written in the margin.

"Get under the luggage and hang on. And remember."

She stared at the shaky handwriting as a strange thrumming filled the carriage. The light flashes were speeding up and changing to blue. The mag-train began to shake as Darynda lurched for the luggage rack, still clutching the journal. Her stomach twisted, and everything went red.

———— « O » ————

Laurie Stewart

Laurie Stewart is a mobility-impaired woman, living outside of Ottawa. She has been published in several anthologies, mostly themed. She also has two published novels with Corvid Moon Publishing.

Special Delivery

Dwain Campbell

"Get your behind out of my face, you waddling old Jack." Unkind of me, because Salty comes by that belabored gait honestly.

"Get your ugly gob out of my keester, Flyboy." That stings. I used to be Clark Gable handsome, until that flash fire in my Wellington cockpit.

We are the has-been debris of the Hitler War. I suppose we should be grateful for this clerk job on the Railway Post Office. But this is the longest, darkest, most hellishly cold night of the year, and the frigging Christmas rush is off the charts. To make matters even worse, a wicked flu just one notch down from the Spanish influenza has this trip reduced to a skeleton crew of two.

"All aboard," shouts the conductor in a practiced Town Cryer voice. "All aboard the Ocean Limited, bound for Moncton, Sackville, Amherst, Springhill, Truro and Halifax." The conductor impatiently stamps his rubber galoshes on the platform and dolefully studies fat, mushy snowflakes parachuting to earth. It's the wee hours at a hick New Brunswick station with zero traffic, so plainly the passenger train is waiting on us. I get jazzed and pass up a slew of parcels too small for freight. Mostly filled with shortbread cookies and fruitcakes for sailors at the Halifax naval base, I guess. My stomach rumbles.

In short order, we are squared away, and the Ocean Limited heavily lurches into motion. The 4-8-4 Confederation

Locomotive is a real beast, power to spare. Salty and I curse our way into the Railway Post Office, or RPO for short. Normally she is a marvel of organizational efficiency and a vital keystone of Canadian civilization. Here, amid rows of canvas mail bags hung on metal racks and towering maple wood cabinets with hundreds of labeled letter slots, we sort and collate mail even as the Ocean Limited steams its way from Montreal to the Atlantic. But tonight, woefully shorthanded, the Halifax mail keeps piling up as we barely stay ahead of each impending whistle stop.

Our solution? Ignore the growing mountain and then work like Trojans once we're deep into Nova Scotia.

The RPO is a harum-scarum jumble that smells of ink pads, rubber bands, wet canvas, salami and mustard from our midnight snack — who has time to eat! — and twine that confines parcels wrapped in snowflake splotched butcher paper. I check the RPO mailbox, and sure enough there are three Christmas cards, all Halifax bound. I postmark each with an officious bang of my stamp.

December 21, 1944. Maybe there will be peace on Earth next year, though the current Jerry offensive in Belgium doesn't sound good.

The Ocean Limited rapidly accelerates into an endless wilderness of snowy spruce, fir and birch. For some reason, there is no caboose tonight. Just plain wrong, a grand old lady like the Ocean should not be shy her Tail Gun Charlie. Our RPO constitutes the rear, and I peer out hoar-frosted hind door windows into wintery blackness.

"God Almighty, it's so cold my fingers are pink," complains Salty. Did I mention that our tiny oil heater went kaput just as we cleared the St. Lawrence? This is the worst shift in my postal career. I think I would rather be skylarking over Germany.

"Carry on, Petty Officer," I quip as I unlock mail bags and spill contents into a wooden bin centrally located between sorting cabinets. We divvy the bundles and start sorting letters and cards with Moncton mail getting the priority.

"Aye, aye, Fight Lieutenant," he wisecracks. "Bombs away." With that, all is silent except the *thunk-thunk* of letters flying into rectangular cubbyholes and the *clack-clack* of steel wheels on cold Canadian National track.

Twenty minutes later, deep in our work, we hear three sharp whistles. *Toot-toot-toot.*

"The Arthur Road mail crane," cries an appalled Salty. Appalled, because bloody months can go by and never does a waiting mail sack appear on the crane stationed by this crossing, miles out in the sticks. However, three toots from the engineer means exactly that.

The Ocean Limited is a longish train. I have a few seconds but no more. Breathless, I leap like a white-tailed buck for the front door, bang through, and poise by the V-shaped catcher arm like a sprinter at the blocks. There are few mail cranes on the entire route, so I am terribly out of practice at this. However, my pilot reflexes come to play, and with lucky timing I swing out the hooked arm just right. It cleanly snags the sack off the crane, and, the train not slacking a beat, I triumphantly reenter the RPO with my prize.

Except, it isn't a sack. Well, it is, but not an official gray canvas Post Office sack closed by a metal padlock. It's a sack made out of moose hide, if I were to guess, and snugged at the top with yellow rawhide.

"What the hell?" exclaims Salty, swiveling in his chair for a look. "That Rural Route driver on the Arthur Road must be the Mad Trapper of Rat River. He's sending us mail in a woodsy sea bag."

I grunt agreement. The rawhide knot comes loose in a flick and I dump the contents. Content, I should amend. A single stone bottle bangs into the bin. No breakage, thank God, for that's a mile-long form to fill out.

Salty scuttles over on his chair. I should add that he never walks lest he has to. In '42 he was three decks below the waterline on HMCS Kingsport when a torpedo took her. The shock shattered both his ankles. He compounded the injury by clambering up several ladders in a successful bid to escape Davy Jones' Locker. Sheer terror lends wings to even broken feet. However, he never was the same in the hiking department. I expect it doesn't help that he's pudgy and rotund as Santa Claus, a squat 200 pounds at least.

More rawhide attaches a leathery envelope to the amphora-shaped, tawny bottle. On it is nothing but a single name written in bold flowing script.

Poseidon.

"No street address, no town, no postage. Undeliverable. It's a relic for the dead letter bin." Talk about strange.

"Open it up. Let's read it, Flyboy." His breath stands in the air; that's how cold it is in here. I sullenly kick the broken heater.

"Yeah, and lose my job."

"It's a prank, no mailman hung that satchel. I'll assume responsibility, like a good Petty Officer would."

I'm shocked, yet I hand it over to him, making myself complicit to the crime.

"Why, it is a card, neatly penned I must say. No backwoods hick wrote this." With ink stained fingers Salty adjusts owlish spectacles and reads.

Dearest Uncle, Lord of the Ocean Dominion,

Another turning of the year is upon us, and Olympians in exile from the cacophony of war in our homeland must make do in this New World. Hermes stubbornly remains about the Aegean, so I use mortal agency to deliver this solstice gift, this potent cordial, to soothe your troubled brow. Thunder and fire within your sacred depths: how dare the humans! This is a refreshing nectar, replete with subtle enchantments to quicken your godly blood. The ingredients were supplied by Circe; you know I am no vintner. This drink is much too fiery for the Nereids, your errant handmaidens, so do be careful in stowing the crock should you not partake in one sitting.

As for myself, I enjoy the hunt through these foreign snowy tracks, though the game be passingly strange. The ursine bruins are ebony and large, the wolves altogether savage, but these moose are fauna of an entirely different order. And this reprehensible rodent named a porcupine...

Your loving niece, Artemis, Huntress

"Huh," grunts Salty, slipping the card back into the (vellum?) envelope. "Artemis sure sounds like a Frenchy name. Some skirt is sending her man a crock of Maritime dirt road moonshine." He eyes the bottle thirstily.

"Or…" I'm nothing if not suspicious. "Or … Artemis and Poseidon are German code names, and you just read off a ream of Nazi gobbledygook code."

Salty belly-laughs. "A Nazi message from Arthur Road, ten miles past the end of nowhere? Get serious."

"Where better then, if you don't want the RCMP Special Branch on your arse? We'd better set it aside for the authorities."

That goes over like a lead balloon. "You kidding? It'll go straight to Undeliverable. Then on Christmas Eve some P8 Medically Unfit paperweight supervisor will snitch it and get merrily blotto." He stuffs cold fingers under his armpits. "It's 4:00am, and we need a medicinal if we're going to survive this shift."

"No way, Skipper. I aim to keep this position." As a former officer with two years at McGill, I could go far in the peacetime Post Office. Small town postmaster easy. I confiscate the stone bottle and card and put them beside the form that records our shift activities. "Look, I know this bloody car is an icebox, I wish I had my old bomber jacket. After Moncton, the dining car will send up hot tea and eats. That'll see us through."

He accedes with ill grace, for there are immediate worries. Registered mail. CODs. Torn and damaged parcels that need to be tagged. Small carry-bins chock full of Moncton bound parcels have to be positioned by the door beside the bulging letter sacks. Always a race against time as the Ocean Limited, with increasing frequency, roars out of woods to thread snow blanketed fields owned by Acadian farmers. This suggests we are out of the wilderness, rushing toward Moncton. A small city with lots of important offshoot routes — Prince Edward Island and Saint John in particular — Moncton is a crazy-as-all-get-out stop.

We manage Moncton, but only just. Salty and I are military men, though discharged from different services. The military and Post Office are not much different in operation. Peons are told when to pee, when to stop peeing, and what pot to pee in. Regimentation equals disciple equals getting the job done, on time. Adversity is not an excuse. In fact, there are no excuses.

As the Ocean Limited starts her last New Brunswick leg, we're both knackered. I'm a young buck, I can trudge through thick and thin, but Salty is nigh on sixty and not the dynamo he was on the good ol' Kingsport. And, at the end of the shift from Hell, all he has to look forward to is a lonely bed-sitting room above a Gottingen Street tattoo parlor. If he has a woman, or kids, I've not heard a word of them. He can hear the navy ships leaving dock, maybe even glimpse them through the dingy clapboard houses of Halifax, but perhaps that is a curse, no solace at all, to a Jack who will never go to sea again.

We cross the ice-clad Tantramar Marshes, next stop Amherst, Nova Scotia. Preoccupied, I fail to note how often Salty's squinty eyes are drawn to Poseidon's dram. Consequently, an hour later, after Springhill, I do a foolish thing.

"Salty old man, the dining car Joes are likely run ragged too. They're late with vitals. I'm going up ahead to the dining car to fetch our goodies." Honestly? My ears are so cold they feel like icicles. The dining car is the warmest coach on the train.

"Good idea, Looney-tenant. A cup of scalding tea would straighten me right out. I'll hold the fort."

I head forward, negotiating the rollicking and bouncing steps between cars with practiced ease. Thankfully, the passenger cars are tolerably warm, though fitfully sleeping passengers hug into voluminous winter coats and wish for quilts. It is a typical wartime crowd, with a good number being servicemen on the way to various camps or mighty Halifax, HQ for the fleet and staging port for huge transatlantic convoys. Too, lots of young women cradling cranky toddlers are trusting the Ocean Limited to get them to families for Christmas. It guts me to think there are widows among them, taking kids to see grandparents who lost sons in this war.

I take my sweet time. The cars rock hypnotically, a rhythm broken periodically as the Ocean butts through snowdrifts. If this were summer there would be dawn in the east, but winter night still reigns in this the Wolf Hour.

I pass the conductor lightly snoring in a booth reserved for his ilk. That's why our grub is way late. Some people have it soft.

"Heyya, Lieutenant," greets the dining car cook, a hulking, bald black fellow from Halifax's North End. "How goes the battle?"

"Tiggerty-boo and in the green," I lie smoothly. My thawing earlobes tingle, not unpleasantly.

"We were gonna come back with your eats 'n drinks, but there be an early few for breakfast." True enough, several servicemen sit at tables, looking the worse for wear. Behind Cook, sizzling eggs and bacon are music to my ears. Mailmen generally get boiled eggs, toast and a few overcooked sausages for morning repast. Cook genially hands over our mess tin and thermos. "Careful. That tea is hot enough to melt the Iron Cross off Der Fuhrer's chest."

"Thanks ever so much," I say, meaning it. These guys work wonders in their tiny galley. "The conductor is grabbing Z's, that's why he's late."

"Ha!" guffaws the cook. "More than one bottle o' Christmas rum made the rounds last night."

Rum. A sudden panic hits me. Salty is alone in the RPO with that weird special delivery to Poseidon, whoever the hell he is. Damnation, I bet my last dollar he's into it like catnip. Why didn't I see this coming? I mumble a hasty goodbye to Cook and rush aft with far more alacrity than I went forward.

I burst into the frigid RPO. Salty's chair is empty. The peculiar stone bottle rocks gently on our cluttered clerical desk. Uncorked, so it is. Half full, it loudly sloshes.

"Johnny," rasps Salty, who I discover prone on several empty mail sacks. He never uses my Christian name, testament to his seriousness. "Johnny, I'm poisoned."

"You frigging idiot! That rotgut could be wood alcohol out of a rusty still. Lucky if you don't go blind." Even though Salty is heavily bearded, I can tell he is green about the gills. He holds his bloated tummy most tenderly.

"Sorry, John. I'm a raging boozehound, what sailor isn't? By God, it tasted like cod liver oil spit outta a flame thrower."

Lovely. What to do? "Look. Salty. Let me run through the cars, see if there is a doctor or nurse on board."

"No. No, I ain't that bad." Yet, he scrunches his face like he just swallowed a spoonful of rancid butter. "Just give me twenty minutes. You get a start on Truro."

Truro. Middling farm town with more cows than people, but a ton of mail goes east toward Cape Breton and overseas to Newfoundland. Thousands of Canadians garrison Newfoundland, service folk in wait of Season's Greetings. That tips my judgment. As a former sober-sided officer, I'm all about responsibility.

"I'll help with Halifax. Double promise. Super promise. On my mother's grave."

"Okay, partner. Take thirty, grab a nap. Then a bite. You'll be right as rain." I throw a few surplus sacks over him for meager warmth.

I dive into work meant for four, popping boiled eggs in my mouth and slurping strong, flavorful tea as opportunity affords. Postal work is mentally taxing, so with all my focus on this bag and that bin I nearly forget my wingman. But all seems well, for fleeting glances tell me he's in deep hibernation, his mouth open wide enough to catch flies. Good, for there are few ills a solid nap won't fix.

The Ocean Limited is really rocking now, and when she sprints across a trestle the staccato clatter is that of a rapid-fire machine gun. It's like she can smell the Atlantic, and is hell bent for home. For just one night, I wish she would slow up.

I'm still at it as the train decelerates for Truro. I up the pace from feverish to manic. How many darned soldiers do we have in Newfoundland? A division? A lord liftin' corps? The local mail cart pulls alongside, and I fling overstuffed bags to the spindly thin local mailman who catches them with increasingly annoyed grunts. Understandably, he tosses back three hefty sacks that hit me like Grand Slam bombs. Guess I deserve that.

Each sack is twenty minutes work, on top of the Halifax-bound mail that has been collecting all night long. My heart sinks to my belly button. This is an impossible situation, but the prissy bureaucrats will deliver a dressing-down and write me up, a tart reprimand for my personnel file. It's enough to rot socks.

I cast a hopeful glance at Salty, and very suddenly rotten socks are the last thing in my mind. In fact, I stop breathing.

Salty's stomach has ballooned twice its normal size and quivers like jelly. I ... I think his beard has melted... all his visible hair has sloughed off. His eyes have rounded to the size of teacup saucers, and have grown farther apart. In absolute horror, I note that both thumbs have retracted into spongy flesh, and all eight fingers are lengthening before my eyes. Translucent, filmy webbing grows between the digits.

The flaccid mass rears up, as if in a panic. Stifling a cry, I stagger to the hind end of the car and plant my back to the door. I consider bailing, but the Ocean Limited is accelerating like crazy. One does not jump from a train like robbers in a Hollywood cowboy serial. Maybe John Wayne can do it, I can't.

My eyes flick to the stone bottle. The drink. The drink did this. It's the only coherent thought my gibbering mind can manage.

The creature heaves again, and this time an entire cabinet falls across the RPO, blocking my view of it. However, I can still hear the creature flailing and heaving. Creature? It's Salty, but he's switching into a slimy monster and I have no notion what to do. Shell shock is but a joke compared to this.

However, once in a former life, I was a Flight Lieutenant. Once, I landed a burning bomber on treacherous mudflats in Lincolnshire, saving my crew and earning a Distinguished Flying Cross. I remember that and fight absolute panic. My flight instructor once said, "Panic, and you're dead." So, I knuckle down raw fear, get control of my breathing, and wait.

By and by the thrashing stops. Then, several fleshy cables curl about the fallen hardwood cabinet and, with Herculean strength, put it back in upright position. Before me is a two-hundred-pound octopus.

I think to bail out, then. I'm only human. But I catch a glimmer in the alien eyes of the octopus. They are knowing, aware, intelligent. They study me, then dart about the RPO, taking in the junk heap that is normally an ordered workplace. It strikes me that whatever this fish is, Salty is still inside. Better put, his mind is.

I calm down somewhat. As my heart slows, I can hear a phlegmy rattle. Salty is breathing, but not easily. He still has human lungs, but for how long? Will he suffocate before — what?

Occasionally, I can connect the dots, see through a brick wall better than most. "Salty, if you can still hear me, listen pal. Rockingham. Ten minutes outside Halifax, we stop there, hard by the Bedford Basin. Saltwater, three tracks away. If … if you need that, if you can hold on, I can drag you over to the shoreline." He can't answer, he has no mouth, but I think he tries to nod his wobbly, bulbous head.

Then, for some inane reason, I blurt, "Don't worry about the mail."

The octopus starts. Its eyes flit over the mess of spilled bins, unopened sacks, and a small pyramid of letter bundles yet to be sorted. It tentatively flexes long, ropey arms.

One arm snakes out so fast it cracks like a bullwhip. With very fine suckers on the end, it seizes an oversized manila envelope. Moon-sized eyes zero in on the address, and, on the instant, the piece is flicked into a slot. With that, all eight arms start a purposeful writhing, and simultaneously eight letters find a cubbyhole. Faster and faster the arms move, as if each one is controlled by a separate brain, and each brain is twenty times faster than a human's. The arms whirl so fast that they blur and hum like a hive of agitated bees, but never do they tangle or knot. They fan the cold air, now decidedly tainted with brine. Inside the whirligig arms, the central mass of the octopus spins like a mesmerizing top.

I'll help with Halifax. Double promise. Super promise. On my mother's grave.

If only his mother could see him now.

In fifteen minutes it's all done. A quarter hour that would have taken two trained men several hours. Not a bloody paper clip is out of place.

Magic. Pure, God-awful sorcery.

But Salty is wheezing real bad. His octopus skin has a deathly, ashen gray pallor. He's … dying.

Toooooot. Unless I miss my guess, the Ocean Limited just chugged through a busy crossing on the outskirts of Bedford. I glance out the windows and see a pallid, cheerless dawn. "Salty, hang on buddy, we'll be slowing for Rockingham in just a couple of minutes."

Thinking fast, I wrench open a back-door sticky with frost and, risking frostbite, scoop up handfuls of dry snow. I sprinkle the snow over Salty. It doesn't melt, and I guess the miserable on-the-fritz heater is good luck now. Moisture and intense cold, they might make the difference. On the third trip, I glimpse between denuded maple trees a line of rusty cargo ships anchored in a line. Convoy ships on the Bedford Basin, readying to exit Halifax Harbor and transit to England. We're nearly there.

"C'mon Salty, we only have five minutes once stopped." It's icky, clammy business, but I drape a few of Salty's new arms over my shoulder and, with this improvised harness, start to shift him an inch at a time toward the rear door. My plan is to exchange mail in two seconds flat, oust Salty out the back, drag him over the snow to the Basin and get him in the freezing ocean.

From the Ocean Limited to the ocean. I giggle; that's how far my nerves are gone.

Salty's a dead weight, and I bless years of grueling RCAF morning calisthenics, the toughest drill on God's green earth. I have him on the rear platform just as the train brakes for Rockingham station, which is hard by the Basin. Drawing ragged breaths, I rush to the front door just as the train shudders to a full stop. I fling out the Rockingham sacks, making all kinds of "no time, we're well behind" comments. This is totally believable, and the guy below double times the process. Finished, I dash back toward the hind door which, as I said, is the last door on the train because some snafu nixed our caboose.

Only, Salty is not on the darned platform where I left him. He is about ten feet away, comfortably resting on the titanic shoulders of a nine-foot-tall Goliath. A more faint-hearted man would pass out dead on the spot, but after the last few hours I am immune to trauma.

The giant wears a gray mottled sealskin coat. Leggings and boots are tailored of a grainy, tough material, sharkskin perhaps. His gruff Jehovah-like beard is iceberg white, and his skin is colored a hard Royal Navy blue. Eyes are pure radiant silver, and they chill my spine, for they are otherworldly, far from human. To top it off, he wears a crown seemingly adorned with golden sea urchin spikes.

"Sa-S-Salty," I stammer, because to say I am totally gobsmacked is an understatement.

The giant — is this Poseidon? — holds out an impatient blue hand. I'm at a loss, but then it hits me.

I run back inside and return with the half empty stone bottle, the source of all this craziness.

"Special Delivery. From Artemis," I mumble.

Poseidon snatches it with ill grace. Without as much as a howdy-do, he about faces and strides for the Basin. He's at the frozen shore within a dozen paces. He eerily sinks into the bone-chilling water with scarcely a ripple. From my poor vantage point I think I see Salty slip off the giant's shoulders and tentatively bob on the surface. Then, in an energetic froth, he squirms off into the depths.

At least ... at least he doesn't have to worry about busted ankles anymore. That strangely cheers me.

The Ocean Limited jerks, starts rolling. Halifax station is not fifteen minutes off. Time enough for me to concoct a cover story.

"He just walked off the train in Rockingham. Made off with another ocean-going type of guy. I think he up and quit, sir. Gone AWOL." The supervisor curses a blue streak, but does not seem at all surprised.

"He likely joined up with the Merchant Marine, went back to sea."

"Went back to sea." I nod in fervent agreement. "Truer words never spoken."

——— « O » ———

Dwain Campbell

Dwain Campbell is originally from Sussex, New Brunswick. After his university years in Halifax, he journeyed east to begin a teaching career in Newfoundland. Thirty-six year later, he is semi-retired in St. John's and studies folklore in his spare time. Contemporary fantasy is his genre of choice, and Atlantic Canada is a rich source of inspiration. He is author of *Tales from the Frozen Ocean*, and has contributed stories to *Canadian Tales of the Fantastic*, *Tesseracts 17*, and *Fall into Fantasy 2018*. Neil Gaiman is his hero of the moment, though he will reluctantly admit to a lifelong fascination with Stephen King.

The Cake Run

Nick Svolos

Reddeth plucked a hunk of burning coal out of the firebox with a pair of tongs, lit his cheroot, and tossed it back. Fethro, the engineer, kept an eye on the engine's gauges, his hands busy making adjustments, and still managed to glower his disapproval at Reddeth as the train powered into the downgrade.

The orc twitched his massive shoulders. "Beats stickin' my head in there."

The dwarf sneered, "Ain't you got somewhere else to be, greenskin?"

"Yeah. But your boss is payin' me to be here." Reddeth levered his bulk up the ladder out of the engine and found a refreshingly dwarf-free spot on the tender to wait out the long, dull ride. Thick smoke and steam billowed past him, but he didn't mind.

"Freekin' dorfs," he muttered. This wasn't his sort of job, but insolvency had provided Reddeth with a powerful incentive to lower his standards. Low enough to babysit the weekly coal shipment from Mount Fumidor to Karith Dundol. Reddeth grimaced as the dwarfish names crossed his mind, making it itch. He wished there was a war going on. A way to make enough money to buy passage out of this Bog-forsaken country for someplace decent, with ceilings at a proper height. He'd had his fill of walking around in a stoop all the time.

Still, sitting up here in the sun, the wind whipping by and threatening to pluck away his cigar, he had to admit, this was easy money. It wasn't like someone would actually rob a shipment of coal. The only enemies he had to worry about were boredom and the train's crew. Dwarves weren't much for the company of orcs, and the feeling was mutual. Too much bad blood. The bearded little runts loved to dwell on grievances, and his people had a talent for their manufacture.

To Reddeth, these guys all looked the same from the neck up, just grumpy masses of hair with noses and eyes sticking out. Half the time, he couldn't even see that, just the bottom of a tankard. Their women weren't much better.

About an hour later, nature called, so he took a walk down to the end of the train. From his position on the caboose's roof, he found himself gazing at the sky behind them to pass the time.

Three dark pinpricks hung suspended in the pale blue of the sky. At first he thought he was just looking at a few hawks. Only, they weren't in a gyre. *Hawks don't hover out here, do they? Naw, must be somethin' else.* Reddeth mulled this over and noticed another detail.

They were getting closer.

He squatted down and knocked on the roof. "Hey, Grayson, wake up down there. Ya see this?"

The brakeman called back, "What, you're askin' if I seen you pissing off my roof? You did a fine job. Hardly any splash back at all. Congratulations."

"No, you idiot. Look at the sky."

The three objects were close enough now that Reddeth could pick out a few details. Large wings, sharp little spikes sticking out from where the bones joined. Their bodies, muscular and reddish-gray, sported patches of thick black fur on their shoulders and atop their horned heads.

Nope, Reddeth thought, *those ain't hawks.*

Grayson let out a dwarfish curse, loud and perverse, and shouted into his speaking tube, "Pick it up, Fethro, we got incomin'!"

Reddeth barely had time to brace himself before the engineer leaned on the throttle, pushing the train into headlong flight across the valley floor.

A burst of escaping smoke from the engine enveloped the orc, and he lost sight of their pursuers until it cleared. They were still coming, closing the distance to the racing train despite its increased speed.

Reddeth unlimbered his axe from the scabbard strapped to his back and spat out the long-dead cigar stub he'd been chewing on. "'Bout time I got some zoggin' entertainment."

The lead creature seemed to have a death wish. As the trio got close enough, it tucked in its wings and dove at the train's guardian, giving Reddeth a clear target for his axe. Too good to resist. Reddeth swung his weapon in a wide arc, aiming for the fool's head, only to cleave air as the thing extended its wings, caught the draft, and let the wind pull it back out of reach. The orc recovered his balance in time to hear the other two creatures land on the coal car behind him. Their faces split into cruel grins as they tucked in their wings and advanced on him with taloned fists.

"Nice trick." Reddeth adjusted his stance to account for the multiple attackers. "Smart. That means you got brains. Can't wait to get a look at 'em."

The thing on his left spoke in a voice dark, low and vile. It made Reddeth want to wash his ears. "This is not your fight, orc."

"Oh, so you'll just let me be on my way, then? That it?"

"No. My master wants you to know that you're dying for nothing."

"It's as good a reason as any." Reddeth charged at the talkative one, drawing his axe up for a quick slash. The creature deftly hopped out of range, laughing.

The laugh's on you, bub, Reddeth thought as he planted one boot on the lip of the caboose's roof and hurled himself backward. He pulled the axe in, hard, and caught the third guy in the midsection with the hilt. Foul-smelling air burst from the creature's lungs and he collapsed into a heap on the steel roof. Before the blasphemous thing could recover its senses, Reddeth solved that problem for him with a quick stroke. The creature's head rolled off the side of the car while thick, black ichor spurted from its neck.

Mr. Talkative howled with rage and hurled itself at the orc, while its fellow tried to circle around to Reddeth's flank. Talons lashed out at his face, and Reddeth ducked. Not quite fast enough. One of the claws dug an agonizing, burning furrow across the top of his bald scalp. Letting the pain spur him on, the orc jerked the axe head up, removing the offending arm at the elbow. The creature screamed and took to the air, clutching its stump.

"Guess I'll have to start callin' him Mr. Screamy." Reddeth smiled at the last attacker, who seemed to be having second thoughts. "How 'bout you, pal? Whatcha want on your tombstone? I'm thinkin': Mr. Didn't-know-when-he-was-beat."

The final attacker extended his wings and fluttered off the train. "We'll be back."

Reddeth called after him, "Well, if that's what you want, Mr. We'll-be-back. But, I gotta warn you, it's too jokey. People'll think you went out tryin' to get one last laugh. Comes off a little needy."

He turned to the corpse on the car's roof. Whatever it was, it was built for power, not beauty. If it still had its head, it would be about a match for Reddeth in terms of height and musculature. In addition to the clawed hands and wings, it had hooves, and sharp ones at that. Judging by the musculature of its legs, the creature could probably drive one through a guy's chest if it had a mind to. Reddeth rolled it over onto its back for further inspection.

Grayson poked his head up from the brake car. "Is it over, then?"

"Yeah. Thanks for all your help."

"Hey, they don't pay me to fight." He climbed the rest of the way up. "Great Digger, what the hell is that thing?"

"I was hopin' you'd know." The orc leaned in for a closer look, risked a sniff, and regretted it straight away. "Oi, that's foul! Like rottin' garbage and bad sex." He gulped a few deep breaths of fresh air. "Whatever it is, I don't think we've seen the last of 'em. Better get yer buddy on that talkin' tube of yours and figger out a plan before round two starts." Reddeth gave the creature one last look before kicking it over the side.

"Here." Grayson handed Reddeth a bit of burlap.

"What's this for?"

"You're bleedin'." Grayson pointed to the top of his head.

Reddeth grinned. "You're not goin' soft on me, are ya?"

"Hardly. Don't want that green glop drippin' on th' controls." He climbed back down into the brake car.

Now that his attention had been called to it, the wound on his scalp re-announced its presence. Reddeth winced as his hand went to the gouge. His body bore the scars of many such injuries, but this one felt different. It burned, but not like fire. That would be clean and wholesome compared to this. It felt more like malice, if such a thing could be given physical form. Maybe it was some kind of venom, but it felt alive. Whatever it was, his orcish physiology seemed to be immune to it — it was all but impossible to take out an orc with anything other than steel or booze — and that just made the toxin angry. He could feel it in the wound, seething with impotent rage as his seeping blood forced it from his body.

Reddeth affixed the makeshift bandage and joined him. Grayson already had Fethro on the horn, describing the incident.

The engineer didn't sound happy about it. "Well, I don't know what you expect me to do. I can make this thing go fast or slow. Take your pick."

"Let's go with fast. How long 'till we're outta this valley?" Reddeth asked.

"Top speed, maybe three hours."

"That's how long we got, then. Time for you guys to level. What're you carryin'?"

Grayson's head shot up. "What? Coal. That's it."

"Bullshmuck, dorf. Whatever them things were, they weren't after your coal. Coal don't need guardin', and dorfs don't part with a copper unless there's a damned good reason for it. Out with it. What're they after?"

The dwarves went mute. Reddeth let them simmer for a moment before grabbing Grayson by the collar. "Have it your way. Grayson an' me'll be up there in a second, Fethro, and then I'll ask you one more time. Only, I won't be so amicable about it."

"Wait!" Grayson cried. "Alright, alright—"

Fethro interrupted him. "Grayson, you shut yer yap!"

Reddeth pressed his nose against the brakeman's. "If you want to keep your yap, you better use it."

Words spilled out of Grayson like ale from a freshly-tapped keg. Smelled a bit like that, too. "It's something the miners found. Some kind of artifact. Don't know what it is or what it does, just that it's worth a lotta gold."

"Keep goin'."

"That's it! That's all I know."

"Grayson, you're tryin' my patience. Those guys didn't seem the type to share our mutual admiration for the profit motive. What's this thing do?"

The dwarf shook his head in dismay. "I really don't know."

"Alright, let's try this a different way. Who's takin' delivery?"

Grayson looked lost and worried about his prospects for a long life. Reddeth calibrated how hard he could hit the little guy without disconnecting something he'd need to answer questions.

Fethro saved him the trouble, his voice coming over the speaker. "The Order of Gereth. They're supposed to have an escort waitin' at the platform."

"Gereth? Who's he?"

"It's not a 'he,' greenskin. It's a secret priesthood. They protect the realm from dark magic. Demons. Whatever our cargo is, it's important to them."

Reddeth ran a hand over his face. So that's what the red guys were. Demons. "Dammit, I ain't gettin' paid enough for this."

"That's your lookout, greenskin. If it's any comfort, we're not gettin' paid much more than you."

Like hell, Reddeth thought. The greedy runts were probably getting a big, fat bonus for this. "Alright, here's what we're gonna do. Where's the artifact?"

Grayson jerked a thumb toward the head of the train. "Buried at the bottom of car seven."

"Right. Fethro, stop the train. We're gonna dig it out."

"What? Why?"

"So we can throw it overboard. That thing back there said somethin' about a master, and whatever it takes to boss around a buncha demons is way outside the bounds of what we signed on for. Time to cut our losses."

"No! We can't do that!" the engineer cried over the speaking tube.

"Oh?" Reddeth's eyebrows rose. "Fethro, I'm beginnin' to think you're still holdin' out on me. Right. There's lotsa ways to get answers outta dorfs. I'll show you the one I think is funniest." He climbed the ladder out of the compartment and started making his way forward.

Grayson followed. "Reddeth, you can't kill 'im."

"Yeah, yeah, I know. He's the only one what can drive this thing. He don't need legs for that, though."

As his boot came down on the top layer of coal on car seven, a shock ran up Reddeth's leg. He jerked his foot away with a yelp. It wasn't quite like touching one of the dwarven lightning gizmos, although it moved the same way through his muscles. It felt like liquid darkness. Like ravenous hatred manifesting itself as a physical force.

"Bog, what the hell?"

Grayson caught up with the orc, set a hand on the coal, and jerked it back. He muttered some ancient and elaborate dwarfish curse. "Well, that's new. Can't be good."

"You think? 'Course it ain't good." Reddeth thought for a moment. Make that a couple of moments. Orcs didn't spend a lot of time thinking and the lack of experience made it take longer. "Grab a shovel and start diggin' that thing out."

"We're not throwin' it over." Grayson's eyes took on a stubborn cast. In all the world, no race of people could match the hairy runts in the time-honored field of obstinance, and the brakeman looked like he might have graduated at the top of his class. Reddeth decided it was best to just move on to Plan B.

"I just wanna get a look at it. Maybe there's some way we can use it."

Grayson shrugged and went back aft to find a shovel. Reddeth hot-footed it down the length of car seven, leaped onto six and continued forward. When he reached the tender, he poked his head up, just for a second, and dropped into a crouch. A loud report barked from the cabin and a blast of whirling bits of metal whizzed over his head.

Reddeth jumped into the cabin, swept the long-barreled blunderbuss from Fethro's reloading hands and pinned the engineer up against the overheating engine surface, leaving him to kick the air in futility.

"Let me down, you green-skinned fool!" Fethro shouted.

"Not until you tell me everything you know about that thing. Let me know when you start burnin' and I'll press harder."

The dwarf's hair began to cook, and his nerve broke. "Dammit, orc. Lemme down, for Gereth's sake."

Reddeth set him down, keeping his fist on the dwarf's collar so he could give him another taste of boiler heat if his mood turned less cooperative. "So that's it. You're one of those priests, ain't you?"

Fethro shook his head. "No. I'm just an initiate." He pulled an amulet out of his shirt, a bronze circle of flame. "It's my task to make sure the artifact stays out of demon hands."

"You're doin' a fine job of it. What's the artifact? What's it do? Why do they want it?"

Grayson hopped down into the engine, a burlap sack in hand. "Found it." He dumped the contents on the deck. It was smaller than Reddeth expected, a square box about the size of his fist. The cube's surfaces bore intricate, bronze-inlayed carvings, arcane symbols that seemed to squirm as he looked at them. It made his eyes hurt. He had an urge to stomp on it, destroy it.

Reddeth got the feeling that the urge came not from him, but from the box itself. He looked away. The urge faded, although it still seemed like a good idea.

"You can feel it now, can't you? The evil?" Fethro asked.

"Yeah, but you haven't told me why we shouldn't just smash it. Whatever it is, I'm pretty sure letting it keep existing ain't gonna end well."

Fethro glared at him with contempt. "What is it with you greenskins? Anything you don't understand, you wanna smash."

"Most of the time it seems to work."

"Well, not this time." Fethro drew a deep breath. "Six thousand years ago, my order battled what you might call a demon lord. It was too strong to banish, so they trapped it in that box. Buried it deep where they thought nobody would ever find it." He scowled. "Just our luck, the mining guild decided to start diggin' right on top of it twenty years back. So, we've been watchin', waitin' for them to find it so we could get it back and find a better place to hide it. Maybe now we can banish it once and for all."

"So, if we smash it, we let the thing inside loose."

"Exactly. Glad to see somethin' finally made it through that thick skull." He kneeled down to examine the box. "These runes are what's keepin' it in. Looks like they got a little dinged up when the miners found it." He pointed at a couple of spots, but Reddeth's stomach turned when he tried to look. "Now it's leakin' nether. That's why we got demons on our asses. It's callin' to 'em."

"So the master that demon guy was talkin' about...?"

"Is in here." Fethro gave the box a nudge with his boot. "If they get ahold of it, they'll let him loose. Then we got a much bigger problem on our hands. That's why we can't chuck it over the side, orc."

Reddeth muttered a few choice words on the matter of dwarves, gods and demons, their lineages and reproductive habits. "Alright, so whaddya propose we do?"

Both dwarves shrugged. Fethro added, "Security's your job, ain't it?"

Reddeth glared at the runty little piece of schmuck. Fine. He mastered his revulsion, picked up the demon prison cube and shoved it into a toolbox bolted to the bulkhead. "Lemme see a map."

With Grayson standing an uneasy watch topside, Reddeth and Fethro spread the map out on the deck. The engineer pointed at a spot on the parchment with a thick, soot-smudged index finger.

"We'll hit the grade coming up outta the valley in about two hours," he said.

"That's where they'll hit us."

"How do ya know that?"

"It's how I'd do it." Reddeth shrugged. "Wait 'till you're movin' at a crawl and then give ya what for."

"Spoken like you got a bit of experience." Fethro glowered at the orc.

"All in good-natured fun."

"What you people think of as fun, other folk call atrocities."

"Some folk ain't got no sense of humor." Reddeth gave the dwarf a hard look. "You wanna discuss the finer points of comedy, or you wanna figger a way outta this mess?"

Fethro did something few dwarves ever did. He let it go. "Fine. What you got in mind?"

"How fast can this thing run if it ain't hauling all them cars back there?"

The light came on in the dwarf's smudged eyes. He grinned. "A damned sight faster, I'll tell ya that."

"Good. We'll grab some provisions outta the caboose and cut everything loose but what we need for fuel."

Fethro nodded his approval. "Top off the tender with the coal in car one."

"Works for me." Reddeth stood and clapped the engineer on the back. "Looks like we got us a cunnin' plan. Let's get to it."

By the time the train worked its way through the foot-hills on the far side of the valley, and the rails bent upward into the mountain pass, they had the tender topped off and plenty of rations from the crew car. The rest of the train coasted along on the valley floor behind them. As it passed from view, Reddeth could just make out a troop of demons descending upon it, tearing it apart as they searched for their prize.

"Damn, there's a lotta them things," he muttered.

"Yeah, but they don't seem to be all that bright," Grayson commented as he joined the orc on the top of the tender. He laughed. "Look at 'em! Diggin' through that coal for somethin' that ain't there."

"They'll figger it out soon enough." Reddeth fiddled with his axe handle. "Then they'll be comin' for us."

Grayson gulped, looked up the mountainside at the rails ahead. "Maybe they can't fly this fast."

"Yeah, and maybe your king'll offer me his daughter's hand for gettin' that demon box to 'im safely." He shook his head. "If I was you, I'd keep that boomstick close."

The locomotive chugged its way up the pass, eating up miles with unfettered speed as the long, tense afternoon wore on. The demon horde, finished with the coal train, now hung in the sky behind them. Reddeth and Grayson maintained their vigil as the pursuing demons gained ground with each passing minute.

A shout rose from the engine compartment, "Reddeth, get up here!" The orc swung down to find the engineer leaning out a window on the side of the machine.

"What now?" he asked. The initiate didn't answer, just pointed forward. Reddeth gripped a stanchion and leaned out to get a view unobstructed by smoke and escaping steam. A series of low, guttural and particularly creative curses sprang from his lips.

A troop of demons stood waiting on the tracks before them. Reddeth tried counting them, but gave up when he ran out of numbers and decided to just chalk it up as "a bunch". That would have been bad enough, but they had brought along a friend. A big one. From what he could see at this distance, the jumbo-sized demon was regarding them with a grimace the orc guessed to be the demonic equivalent of a smirk.

"Fethro, how much faster can you make this thing go?"

"Not much. If I put too much more coal to 'er, the boiler's sure to blow."

"I don't think it'll matter in a couple of minutes. Give 'er all she'll take. We're gonna ram this thing down their zoggin' throats." He called back to the fuel car, "Grayson, git your arse in here. We're gonna have guests."

The brakeman made his way back to the engine, joining Reddeth in piling shovelfuls of coal into the firebox. The engineer monitored the gauges and finally called a halt to their efforts. "That's it, lads. Any more and she'll blow."

Fethro threw the throttle all the way open, well past the spot marked with red paint. The engine leaped forward.

Grayson lurched backward and cried in mortal terror as the change in velocity bounced him off a stack of rations and over the edge of the engine. Only a quick grab saved him from a gruesome fate, as his thick hand found a grip on the rear wall. Reddeth gave him a hand back into the compartment.

"Sweet beard o' the All-Mother," Grayson exclaimed, "that was close."

Reddeth chuckled and clapped him on the back. "Shoulda seen the look on your face. Now that's comedy!" The dwarf shot him an angry look, but his rejoinder got lost in the jolting confusion as the engine struck the wall of demons in its headlong flight. Boxes of provisions slid across the crowded cabin as the engine lurched up onto its right side. Not all of the demons got out of their way. A tangle of broken red and black corpses flashed by on the tracks behind them. The engine righted itself, slamming back down onto the rails. Reddeth pulled his axe from its scabbard.

The remaining demons came at them from every angle. Numbers were on their side, and their attacks were relentless. The engineering compartment, however, proved to be a decent redoubt for the train's crew. Fethro and Grayson maintained a steady stream of blunderbuss fire through the windows. Reddeth's axe whirled, cleaving claws, snarling faces and whatever other pieces of crimson demon-flesh happened to get in its way. Soon, stinking black ichor and demon pieces coated the floor.

And still, they came.

A set of talons reached into the compartment and raked Reddeth across the back. He howled in pain and rage, and took the enemy's arm with a downward strike. A pair of attackers took advantage of the sudden gap in the train's defenses and swept in through a window. Fethro went down under them. Reddeth shouted something unintelligible, grabbed the horn of one of the demons, and yanked its owner away from the engineer, giving the crimson fiend an axe-head to the belly as a consolation prize. Grayson's boomstick sang out, smearing the other one's head across the instrument panel. Fethro squirmed out from under the remains, covered in black goo and his own blood. He tossed his weapon to Grayson, who caught it while tossing his own back to the driver for a reload.

Another demon dropped down into the compartment. Reddeth kicked it in the gut and it fell back out through the doorway, catching itself upon leathery wings before it hit the ground.

"Enough!" a voice above bellowed. Two thundering steps boomed, denting the roof, and a massive claw reached down, tearing the aft bulkhead and a good section of the overhead away. Sheet metal squealed in protest and tumbled off, crashing somewhere out of view.

"Aw, we're zogged now," Reddeth muttered.

The claw's owner swung heavily down onto the exposed rearmost portion of the cabin. The engine shuddered at the force of its landing, the front pony wheels rising momentarily into the air before landing again on the rails, steel shrieking on steel.

Grayson yelled some obscure dwarfish battle cry and fired his blunderbuss. Black spots appeared on the hulking demon's breast, ichor spilling out onto the deck.

The demon smiled.

Reddeth snarled and hurled himself at the monstrosity, axe arcing to bury itself in the thing's grotesque face. The demon swatted him with a massive backhand, like he was an annoying bug. The orc fell back into a pile of spilled coal and his axe flew from his hands, glanced off a stanchion and spun away into the gloom.

"You mortals have fought well." The smile never left the demon's face. Its voice was corruption in verbal form, deep and rich, and it rumbled like thunder across a lake of fire. "Give me what I seek and I will reward you with a swift death."

Reddeth's hands scrambled for a weapon. A tool. Anything to continue the fight. He found something, hard and rectangular, buried in the detritus.

The toolbox.

He fumbled for the latch, got the thing open, and fumbled some more until he found what he was looking for. Grabbing it, a shock of darkness jolted up his arm. Images of despair, torment and debauchery — all woven together like a profane tapestry — appeared in his head. He ignored the disturbing sensation and rose.

"This what you're lookin' for?" He held up the arcane box, and the demon's eyes lit up, baleful and glowing in the twilight.

"Yes." Its voice sounded almost reverent. It reached in with a leathery claw the size of a bull's head. "Give me my master."

"Reddeth," Fethro croaked, "you can't."

"No zoggin' dorf's gonna tell me what I can or can't do," Reddeth growled. He took a sidelong step. "I'll make ya a deal," he called to the demon. Another step. "This thing here's your master, right?"

"No games, orc. My patience is at an end."

"Right. But I gotta know somethin'. I'm the curious type." Reddeth opened the firebox door and shoved the box in front of it. "What happens if I do this?"

The big demon laughed. The sound echoed with malice and contempt through the cramped engineer compartment. "Go ahead, little green fool. My master will be freed and you will know such torments that death would seem a welcome friend."

"Yeah, and you get your boss back. No more bein' in charge for you, eh? Sure you won't miss it?"

The demon's head jerked back in surprise. The light in his eyes changed. The light spoke of realization. Opportunity. Greed.

"Ah, you get it now, don'cha? You want this 'cause your boss wants you to want it. Kinda makes you wonder if he has your best interests at heart, doesn't it?"

"What are you playing at, orc?"

"I ain't playin'." He swept his free hand in a wide arc, taking in the lesser demons flocking behind them. "You're the biggest, so you're in charge. That's how it works with orcs, anyway. I figger it's about the same for you guys. I could give you this thing, and you can go back to makin' sandwiches for it, or whatever it makes you do. You get to be this thing's top toady again. Or, maybe you'd be interested in making your promotion permanent." Rage and hatred flowed from the box and through Reddeth's arm.

The demon was listening, his focus intense. The orc took that as a good sign, ignored the demon box's fury, and continued. "These Gereth guys could lock it away. Maybe even boot it outta this world for good. What do you guys call it, Fethro?"

"Banishment," Fethro gritted through his pain.

"Yeah, that's it. A one-way trip back to the nether. That leaves room for a new boss, don't it?" Reddeth shrugged. "Could be your chance at the big time."

The giant demon was silent, pondering the possibilities. Steel wheels clattering on the tracks, the steamy chugging of the engine and the rhythmic beating of leathery wings from the following horde were the only sounds.

"Very well," the demon said at last, with a grin reeking of malevolence. "We have an accord." He roared a command to his demonic army and took to the skies. The troop greeted their new master and followed.

Grayson broke the stunned silence. "I can't believe that worked." He crawled across the detritus and began tending to Fethro's wounds.

Reddeth returned the demon box to its spot in the toolbox. "Never underestimate the lust for power, fellas."

"Sure, but didn't you just give a horde of demons carte blanche to run around the country causin' trouble? Seems like that's gonna be a problem."

"Probably. I can help you guys sort that out later, I suppose." He dug a fresh cheroot out of a pouch on his belt and lit it from the firebox. He took a deep pull, held it for a while before letting it out. He watched the smoke rise, mingling with the engine's billowing exhaust.

"Of course, that'll cost extra."

------ « o » ------

Nick Svolos

Nick Svolos dropped out of high school in his senior year, joined the Navy and spent the next several years sailing around the western Pacific on the USS Enterprise.

After discharge, he roamed around a bit and finally landed in software development. After his most recent job ended in a layoff, he decided to take a timeout and indulge the voices in his head by writing a novel. Now, he ekes out a living as a freelance web developer and spends the rest of his time writing about the stuff he loves, namely, mysteries involving superheroes and orcs.

He lives in Crescent City, CA, with his lovely wife Charlotte, their youngest son, Tommy, and a couple of layabout cats, Sprocket and Daphne. Everyone in the house is an avid gamer, and their home often resounds to the sound of tumbling dice. The cats prefer games involving small birds and lizards, but they're more than happy to take a whack at a d20 if they get a chance.

His website is www.NickSvolos.com, and he maintains a Facebook page at www.facebook.com/NickSvolos. He's also been known to tell jokes on Twitter as @NickSvolos.

Steampunks needed for a post-apocalyptic world

Do you have interest in steam power? Do you want to help salvage humanity in a post-apocalyptic world? Well then, Russia, Sweden, Great Britain and the United States might have a job for you.

In case of a nuclear attack, or other catastrophic event, all these nations have a hidden strategic reserve of steam engines. Though Great Britain and the United States still won't admit to their steam reserves, all experts agree that, like Sweden and the former Soviet Union, they too have mothballed an array of steam engines in the event that the fossil fuel powered electric grid is destroyed. This need for steam power would be further magnified as the devastation wrecked by detonating nuclear warheads would render electrical and electronic systems of diesel motors useless, requiring that all supplies be transported by steam locomotives.

In recent years, Sweden and Russia have declassified information about their strategic steam power reserve. And despite their insistence on keeping their steam reserves secret, both Britain and the US have had trouble keeping theirs' under a lid.

The British Government insists that a Royal strategic steam reserve is a myth. Yet, periodically Royal British Army Engineer battalions are required to take training on how to operate large steam boilers that would be used to power trains and electric power plants, as well as be used to provide steam heat in the winter.

The government of the United States neither admits nor denies such a reserve, but the author of this article, a licensed mechanical engineer, can attest that at times the US government will contact stationary mechanical engineers to gather information on alternative ways to fuel their steam boilers in the event of a national emergency.

So steampunks, be certain, your steam vapor skills are not only valuable today, but in the event of a catastrophe, they will be downright precious.

Pluck Versus the Giant Rat of Sumatra

David Worsick

I trust you shall find this story inspiring, but heed the future it foretells. But let us first have some of the best port from Portugal and superb chocolate from the Netherlands to complete our meal. I do believe these chairs are suitably stuffed for your comfort.

Now, as an employee of the prestigious Willet and Woodendit Engineering firm, I had been commissioned to inspect the newly completed coastal railroad of New Guinea. Therefore, along with our equipment, I had brought the latest design dreamed of by our engineers: an armored locomotive.

As you know, lush New Guinea is by no means a flat, lagoonal island, but rather a rugged set of magnificent, wooded peaks and impressive, lush valleys. To link this large island together, we needed an engine of no small effort. Therefore, our engineers started with the largest locomotive which that American genius, Ephraima Shay, could offer. With her consent, they dismantled it, replaced the boiler and firebox with one meant for a small warship, and created a class E, six-cylinder, eight truck behemoth. Its first test was pulling an iron-clad turreted cutter through a canal in Devon. It was a smashing success, despite the fact that the cutter was a smashing failure as it broke the canal lock.

Now, if you have never gazed upon a Shay, I do confess that it is an odd platypus of a steam engine. All of the massive cylinders are on the right-hand side of the locomotive and every one of them is vertically aligned, pumping in the direction of Mother Earth and Father Sky. They propel a massive crank that directs power to all of the trucks under the lopsided locomotive, allowing the partial slip needed for excessive gradients.

And we had excessive gradients, I do say, and a commander excessively eager to earn the grade of Knighthood through service to the Queen. Ah, we were pawns of that ambition, but at least this iron rook could shield us. In front of the engine was, not a New World cowcatcher, but an ironclad's ram. On top of that intimidating wedge of steel and iron was an armored cupola for a sharpshooter with a double-barreled grenade launcher. To take out fallen trees and wayward water buffalos, we said.

Well, to be honest, we were there to discourage the belligerent and altogether uncooperative Sultan of Indonesia from waging war on the outskirts of Asian Christian civilization. We had also hoped to convince newly-independent Australia to purchase our freshly prototyped designs. As the Queen had commanded our directors, it would be unseemly for the Empire to help repel the steel-clad river monitors of the wrathful Fenians in the defense of young Canada of the North, but then fail to aid young Australia of the South. Rather poor impression that would have cast.

So we tested every bit of the track and found it most adequate, and then retested it. I became friendly with the commander because of our shared love of chess, though he really should have stopped relying on the Tarrasch maneuver in his openings.

Of course, the train used the latest composite armor, hard steel facing our enemies, tough wrought iron backing it like fans of a football club, all clinging to a cast iron frame like fans around a football star. Over the wheels of the locomotive and the trucks of the cars we hung sheets of soft steel as protective aprons. The Shay cab itself bore no weapon more threatening than the engineer's revolver and the stoker's rod. Yet behind the tender full of coal, we pulled an armored car with a well-shielded, sixty pounder breech loader, using steam-driven recoil absorbers and employing the new rubber-sealed breeches of Monsieur de Bange. Beside this stood a turreted, four-barrel, steam-loaded automatic Nordenfeldt, firing one-inch slugs and looking more like the drying racks for carp than a weapon of mass projectiles.

Then came a Yankee-style caboose with Gatling mechanical guns, a small boiler and long hoses to the other cars, followed by another artillery car, two box cars and three garrison carriages with thin iron plating over oak, slits for riflemen and hooks for hammocks above the seats. Finally came the requisite combined galley, first aid station and officer's lounge. I do admit that we, contrary to policy but very common among our fellow regiments, allowed the non-commissioned and the civilians to enjoin us in that lounge. Behind that was the two gauge and surveying cars, with their engineers and smithies. At the end of all that was a sand-bagged flat car with a Krupp field gun and two belt-fed, gear-regulated Gatling's. And the best crew we could have prayed for. One was a skillful train engineer who was a Black American son of a former slave. He made me proud to be descended from abolitionists. The rivet tightener and valve adjuster was a lively German technician, very knowledgeable. A third of our crew were Empire, mostly British but also whites, blacks and browns from the colonies, and the rest were local natives, the Fuzzy Hairs that have never disappointed us. I insisted that they have two of the garrison cars. None of this colonial arrogance, you know.

Yet, those superb subordinates and our tough bulldog of a train might not be enough. Rumors whispered about the Sultan's obsession with steam-powered monsters, engineered to travel over any terrain. First the rumors said he started with a Gatling-clad "Gerbil" resembling an ill-tempered switching engine, then a malicious "Mouse" the size of a one-two-one locomotive, then an even bigger horror, the "Hamster" with two field pieces. They said he next reared up the rapid-fire "Rabbit" from Hades, and finally ratcheted together a massively armed giant which he called the "Rat". The more nervous of our neighbors feared he threatened to build a giant amphibious Beaver to terrify the Empire. Yes, a giant beaver would have shattered our imperial composure. How these monsters were armed and armored, we knew not for sure. We did know that massively-sized pontoons had been built to carry an enormous cargo between his islands. And he most surely wanted our large island as one of his, glowering over our friends down under. Therefore, we prepared ourselves for the worst.

However, the worst was in no hurry to arrive. And so we waited, tested the rails, cleaned our weapons and waited some more. Thank the Heavens for the shipment of fortified wine, distilled grain and IPA. And one day a man who would drink none of that came to visit us.

The regional Imam was a friendly, if somewhat fastidious, fellow who occasionally rode down to greet and talk with us to practice his English. We assured him that our weaponry was for defense only, and as nobody had yet designed sea-worthy rail tracks, he knew we were telling the truth. But this one time he did not smile.

"Good day, honorable Imam," I said. "How has your week been? Would you like some tea?"

He replied, "My week has been recently upsetting."

He paused formidably and then continued.

"I have received orders from the Sultan of Sumatra to mobilize a militia from the local believers. I have refused to do so, as I know we do not need defense from our neighbors. But I now fear that you do."

I responded, after much thought, "We worry about that too. We have heard rumors of a giant war machine called the Rat. And one of our near-submersible scout boats had spotted a giant raft of pontoons approaching a fifth of a fortnight ago."

"So, the rumors are true. Can you try to oppose such a device?"

"We are part of the British Empire. We can try to oppose anything. Whether we succeed is the proper question."

"I admire your bravery. I will gather the good people around me and try my best for peace. Be aware, though, that this Sultan is well known for beheading scholars who criticize his actions. None of our lives are safe."

"Thank you. But I am puzzled as to why you would risk the censor of your neighbors by helping save those who do not believe as you believe. May I ask you this?"

He responded immediately. "I will censor no questions about my behavior, so you were correct to ask. What our world demands we do and what our souls need us to do are often at war with each other. I have chosen souls over world. And you? You could be safely and comfortably away from this humid heat with all your friends and family, but here you labor to build the defenses of strangers. And now I ask why."

I thought for a bit more and said, "I have determined, with all my years and my study of the Sciences, that we live in a world where a man, no, a human, can gain increasing power. Power is like fire. If you control it, you can do wondrous things. If you cannot control it, it will do horrendous things. I believe that my life should strive to do wondrous things in order to stop the horrendous things. Well, to be truthful, I do moderately impressive things, all the time wondering about horrendous things."

The Imam laughed. "Well spoken, sir."

"Thank you. Would you like some tea?"

"Yes, just a small cup, thank you."

I always kept tea handy in those new double-glass and vacuum canteens, with porcelain cups and a local sweetener nearby. He finished his tea, saluted with a bow and left.

I saluted back according to my service as a sergeant. "Then fare well, scholar. We troops will stay watchful."

I knew that many of the army and the New Guinea inhabitants strongly disapproved of me dealing with such non-Christians. I dared not mention that I, myself, was not a believer, not in any religion. But, curse it, I still know how to tell apart people who deserve the paradise they won't get, from people who deserve the damnation they won't get. Never mind, though. What happens upon death is the one mystery every mortal will always solve. I'll find out then. For now, I believe that I can read a man's true nature. And I read him as truthful.

Then, one early afternoon two days later, I was in the lavatory when one of the native troops knocked on the door and cried out, "Good God, sir, it's enormous!"

"What's enormous?" I asked, buckling my belt.

"The machine on the beach!"

This was not a time to be out of uniform. I hurried dressing and washed my hands, latched my helmet on and climbed atop the nearest box car while the commander jumped to the ground to peer around the curve. And so it was, barely visible beyond a ridge that, by fortune, hid us.

The technician shouted, *"Dee grossair Ratteh fun Zoomatra!"*

As usual, he was correct. This grossest rat was about two miles away from us, crawling along the beach that lay serenely next to our elevated track. The massive metal rodent looked like the bastard crossbreed of an enormous millipede and a scandalous battleship. It had, not a circular turret like its wayward father would have, but a rotating box, square in front and rounded in back, with abstract Oriental designs painted upon it. This held what looked like two long and intimidating breech-loading cannons. Monsieur de Bange must be getting filthy rich from his invention.

Immediately behind this double-threat were two large black smokestacks, richly decorated in chrome arabesque. Well behind those was another turret with a smaller naval gun. Between these rotating threats were two pedestal-mounted field guns with bullet shields. These guns could brilliantly be tilted upward to threaten airships. If only we had airships to be threatened.

The entire monstrosity rode on eight giant studded steel wheels on each side, each a dozen feet in diameter. With my binoculars, I could see Gatling's studded throughout its front and sides. The two main cannons must have had calibers of at least eight inches. The barrels looked like they were forty calibers in length, longer than any piece I'd seen before. With modern cordite charges, each cannon would have been able to fire two hundred pounds of shell and explosives with each shot.

This was far more power than our armor was designed to resist. They'd easily outrange us and we would not withstand one hit. And if they hit the railroad, we would be immobile while that monstrous metal rodent could ford the bay and attack us from any angle.

Then doors opened on the side of the beast and out came a mechanical elevator descending with two cavalry troopers. Scouts on horseback, riding off in search of us. Then a roar charged toward our train. The big guns had fired.

Seconds later, two shells plowed deep into the railway twenty yards in front of us, shredding the tracks and shaking our cars and our troops. One of those shells had landed near the reconnoitering imperial commander, leaving only his shredded red jacket. Bloody Hades. I was now next in command. No more shall he Tarrasch his knight!

"What do we do?" said the engineer. The native major next to me was studying the behemoth with his binoculars. Then he shook his head.

Come on, sir, I thought to myself. Think! For the Empire, the pubs back home and for your sorry little life, you scoundrel. Think. Yes, of course! The sorry little Nordenfeldts! Now I knew what to do.

I told the major that his troops should detach those four-barreled weapons from their turrets and remount them on the wheeled caissons we used to move ammunition. I also had the wheels of several Gatling's unlatched from the car floors and the Krupp gun rolled off the flat car. The troopers worked quickly and efficiently. In front of us, the train crew was now cutting down jungle trees and placing them in front of our locomotive and cars. Fortunately, so fertile was this volcanic island that long weeds made the railway tracks impossible to see from the beach. Though I suppose the commander might have disagreed about that had he still been around.

Another two shells overshot our position and gouged cellars out of the sand. And not beer cellars, either. I grabbed my favorite but useless sword, a more practical Lee-Colt repeater and my tall helmet, dyed khaki with tea. We left our scarlet jackets behind. The native troops always wore dark mottled green, and we had indeed learned from them.

We heard the giant approaching with a grinding, clanking noise and saw its engine smoke rise over the bush.

It was heading for the main seaport that we had just left. The raiders could attack where the town had no defenses: from the land side. We picked an ideal spot for the ambush and cleared bushes so the heliograph relays could reach the sand-bagged and foliated train.

"Now," I instructed, "keep the Gatling's out of sight and fire them in an arc over the ridge. We want bullets to fall around the exposed field guns. Aim the Nordenfeldts at the hubs of the front wheels. Not the back wheels! The grenade shotguns will fire smokers, and the riflemen will aim for the mechanical guns. Remember, you don't have to kill the gunner, just dismantle the gun."

The riflemen would try this with their rotating box magazines, seven five-round clips per cylinder. Bulky it was, but these troopers could handle them well.

"How are we going to work the Nordenfeldts without a steam line?" one of them asked. "Do we have to do it by hand? That would really slow down our rate of fire."

"No," I said, pointing to the train crew who was laying down the agricultural hoses we employed to extract river-birthed water for the boiler. "These aren't designed for steam, but they'll last as long as our ammunition will."

"The steam hoses are primed," said the technician in his cute accent. We prepared as fast as we could, for the Rat moved as speedily as a jogging soldier. The monster fired two more shells at our train. We heard a crash and saw shattered lumber fly into the sky. A box car had become tinder and now we would be short of supplies. And time.

Then the massive rodent was almost broadside to our train and from it not a single firearm pointed at our hiding spot.

"Now fire," I shouted with the appropriate flourish of my sword.

And we let loose with the field gun and Nordenfeldts. Overhead, a sixty-pounder shell flew from the train into the hulking Rat, where it exploded with much drama and little damage. Their mechanicals returned fire blindly, but thoroughly, through the jungle growth. That many rounds improved their chances and three of our brave men fell dead.

Five of us staggered back, wounded. I swore at the lead shot that had just broken one of my blooming ribs.

Their field guns were even deadlier, ramming their explosive shells into the earth near our positions. Five more of us fell forever and eight more needed the field surgeon. I refused to call for his help myself as I wasn't in danger of dying yet.

Our English train guards arched smoke shells around the Rat, trying to confound their gunners. A sixty-pounder hit the big turret with scant effect. Now both enormous turrets were slowly turning toward our hill. Hand-cranked. Thank goodness the Rat didn't have the mechanical turret drives of the battleships. Another of our sixty pounder shells hit the big turret again. Its rate of turning slowed not a bit.

Two dozen native troopers and seven train guards were down already. The Krupp gun fired valiantly until a small shell hit its barrel, wounding the crew. One of the Rat's field guns was still fighting, throwing dirt and vegetation over us. Our large-bore mechanicals also still roared. One of them was then blown apart. Fortunately, the natives manning it had flung themselves away and were unhurt. Most of our small-bore mechanicals still rattled away at the field guns. My left hand held my handkerchief to my right side, while my right hand gestured with my saber, with less and less speed and enthusiasm, I do admit. With one more flourish I encouraged the troops on, and nearly killed the man nearest to me when my grip failed on my saber. I apologized for what I did to his shirt.

Finally, the Rat's top-side field guns had been un-crewed. But the turrets were invulnerably facing us, and their barrels were rising. The cannons stopped moving when they had us in their sights.

Then, all three front wheels sequentially fell off the Rat. It collapsed like a rejected suitor, the forward right side lurching toward the ground just as its turret fired. Their shells assaulted the base of the ridge. Carbonate sand flew everywhere and the ground under our feet shook. The ridge began a slow crawl toward the monstrous Rat. We pulled our weapons and our casualties back barely in time. Trees and earth buried part of the metal beast as its remaining right wheels failed. Then the smokestacks flew into the air and landed well behind us, almost reaching the train and felling several trees. The boilers of the beast had exploded. One last sixty pounder shot descended within the broken roof and exploded right where the machine's magazine would likely be. We covered our ears and watched the pedestal guns and Gatling's fly over the beach into the ocean. One field gun dove barrel first into the azure waters and stayed there, sticking up half submerged with its breech and bullet shields looking like the head and shoulders of a forlorn scarecrow.

A handful of turbaned men climbed out and ran away from the flames, carrying another handful with them. I shouted to cease fire. No sword flourishes this time, though. The survivors waded into the sea along with the bewildered cavalry, toward a nearby cutter we had not noticed before.

Seven of our native troopers and four of our British soldiers were lost. Seventeen other troopers and soldiers required time in the local hospital. Sixteen more needed cleaning and bandaging but nothing else, I being one of those. The round that had hit me had bounced off my ribs instead of burrowing deep, so I only needed carbonic antiseptic, bandages and a stiff glass. Not that I didn't visit the hospital, of course. Regulations are there for a purpose.

The railroad was repaired, and the mechanical failure of a giant rodent was salvaged for its metal. The Imam and his helpers buried the unfortunate ones who had fatally crewed the Rat. Amazingly, the Sultan's envoys never gave any mention of his lost toy. Rumors of the construction of a giant Beaver soon died out. A quarter year later, celebrated as I was in the daily news and my ribs fully healed, I returned home, but not before giving a crate of the best tea to the Imam for his help.

Now, in my drawing room overlooking the Thames, sipping our port by the glow of an autumn's fire, I suppose you would think me happy about my adventure. True, the British Empire is secure, and I have my accolades and rewards. But I am not relaxed. Just because that first steel monstrosity had done little damage, it does not mean an even more brilliant engineer cannot dream up something far more threatening and deadly. This is not the path I want for our beloved technology, but I know many do. And now my associate, that cheerful German technician from our train, has written me to say his niece, Ottoma Diesel, has invented a new and more compact type of engine that runs on petroleum products. She said it will eventually replace steam and coal. Maybe it will, but I hope sincerely that this invention will never find its way to the battlefield.

——— « O » ———

David Worsick

David Worsick descended from the Canadian son of English folk and inherited his father's books on steam trains and British heroes. He now attempts to ascend the list of Calgarian writers.

The Conductor

Maurice Forrester

Mary was walking along the railroad tracks and thinking about trains. She liked to think about trains. She had come west from New York City on an orphan train a few years after the war and a year before the trains came to life. She didn't remember much from the city except for hunger, a crowded room, and quarreling children. She and some of the other children had been pulled from an orphanage, bundled onto a train, and sent west for a new life away from the dirty, crowded city. On the train west, she was given food and a seat all of her own. Many of the children were scared and some cried, but for the first time in her life Mary was happy.

She had been adopted by the Miller family and immediately put to work. From morning until night, there were chores to do. There was cooking, cleaning, laundry, and mending. Outside, there was a garden to plant, weed, and harvest. There were eggs to collect and chickens to be slaughtered. She cared for the younger children, was bullied by the older, and she waited on the guests that came to the Miller home.

One of her early memories was hearing Mr. Miller and his friends talk about the trains. They argued about why the trains had come to life and what should be done about it. They talked about a silver hammer driving a golden spike to complete the railroad that ran across the country, and Mary treasured that image in her mind. She pictured trains waking up from a long slumber, stretching out, and running as fast as they could along the tracks.

Mr. Miller and the other men had a less happy vision of the trains. They talked about trains not stopping when and where they should. They talked of helping the railroad men bring the trains back under control by starving them of the coal and water that they needed, and by blocking the tracks on which they ran. But the trains were not ready to be controlled again. They refused to run at all, or they ran dangerously fast. And then there were some people, Mr. Miller called them traitors, who helped the trains.

Finally, an uneasy truce emerged. The trains began to run more on schedule than not. The railroad men helped to keep them operating with coal, water, and occasional repairs to the rails. There was no communicating with the trains, but this was the arrangement that seemed to work. People didn't ride in the same numbers as before and freight cars were less numerous, but the trains were still the fastest way to get from one place to another — as long as they stopped. They stopped often enough in the little town of Greenville that the Millers and their friends stopped talking about trains, but Mary never stopped thinking about them.

Now, ten years after she had arrived on the train, Mary was growing from a girl into a young woman. She felt awkward, and she was unsure how to move or stand in this new body. Her unruly dark hair that had been an inconvenience when she was younger now seemed like a curse. Mrs. Miller let her know regularly that she wasn't very pretty and was a poor prospect for a wife.

Sometimes Mary wondered what might be out there for her in the wider world. She thought about leaving the Millers and maybe the town of Greenville entirely. She tried once and got as far as the railroad station, but she had no money and the railroad men wouldn't let her board the train. After that, she saved what little she could, hiding it under a floorboard in her attic room, but she earned so little that it seemed impossible she would ever have enough money to leave.

Mrs. Miller noticed Mary watching the trains and dreaming. The older woman never failed to remind Mary of how much she owed them. "Dead in the streets or worse," Mrs. Miller said. "That would have been your life had we not adopted you."

The adoption and the reminder that she would never be fully part of the family was a constant in her life. There were others who came to Greenville on the orphan train, but they had very different experiences. They were members of a family, part of the community. They had gone to school and played along the river. They were confirmed into the church. They found employment or they worked alongside their new family. The older ones were married by now. Mary was never part of that group. She had chores.

On that particular spring day, she was sucking on a peppermint and returning to the Miller home with sugar, flour, and coffee. Mrs. Miller didn't always trust her to go to the grocer, but Mary had been particularly good the past week. The railroad track wasn't the shortest route back home, but it was her favorite. In the distance, she could see the smoke of a locomotive. She heard the pop of the rails as it got closer, and she wondered if it would stop in Greenville. You could never be sure.

Mary stepped from one crosstie to the next with her basket of groceries in her hand. When she returned to the house, Mrs. Miller would scold her for taking too long and put her to work cleaning. Mr. Miller would stand in the doorway, watching her work.

And Mary realized she didn't want to go back.

The train could hit her, and she would be out of the Miller home and the town of Greenville for good. She could dodge at the last minute, dumping the groceries that Mrs. Miller had paid for, and let the train roll by, but then Mrs. Miller would be even angrier. The train might see her and stop, but what did trains care about one girl on the railroad track?

Her feet kept moving forward toward the oncoming train.

Mary heard the shrieking of the brakes. The train was slowing but there wouldn't be time for it to stop before reaching her. How fast would it be going? How much would it hurt if she didn't jump? She continued to walk forward determined to see how close she could get.

The train stopped. She was seconds away from jumping out of the way or being hit, but the train came to a stop in a cloud of hissing steam.

A door opened on the locomotive and a stooped, gray-haired man stepped down. He wore a dirty uniform, and a conductor's cap was perched on his head. He reminded Mary of the crew on the orphan train that brought her west. He motioned for her to come forward, but she hesitated.

"Why did you stop?"

"Didn't," the conductor said. "The train stopped. Get on board." He closed the door to the locomotive and waited.

Mary turned toward town. The Miller home wasn't very far away, and she thought she could see Mrs. Miller on the front porch watching for her to return with the groceries. She imagined the woman muttering complaints about her adopted child. There would have to be a punishment for being late. No sweets, no trip to the grocer, no time off on Sunday. Extra chores.

Finally, Mary stepped off the tracks and looked down the length of the train. There was the locomotive followed by the coal tender and then a string of passenger cars. A few heads popped out of the windows to see why the train had stopped. A man and woman jumped out of one of the cars and ran toward town. The man was burdened by two suitcases but paused long enough to holler, "Don't get on. She might never stop."

The conductor checked his pocket watch and looked at Mary. A man leaning out of the window shouted at her. "Come on, lady. This train ain't moving until you get on."

"Why me?" she asked the conductor.

He shrugged. "Who can say. The trains will do what the trains will do. We only ride along."

Mary turned back to the Miller house. The figure on the front porch was looking her way now. She was sure of it. She could picture Mrs. Miller, hands on her hips, glaring at the train and her missing groceries.

Mary set down the basket and stepped forward. She was no thief, and Mrs. Miller could still collect her things. Maybe she'd even find the coins under the floorboard in Mary's room. "Where are we going?"

Again the conductor shrugged. "Wherever the train takes us."

—— «» ——

They entered the first passenger car. The conductor had to help Mary up. "Had a step stool," he said. "But it got left behind when the train started moving a little quicker than I expected."

There was a jolt as the train began to move and Mary grabbed hold of a seat back to steady herself. As the train picked up speed, it settled into a gentle, soothing sway.

The old man took her through the train. "There's a boy up front who shovels coal," he said. "No need for an engineer or a brakeman anymore. The train decides where to go and when to get there."

The passengers were a mix of people. Many knew where they wanted to go, although some of them had missed their destinations when the train rolled through Lafayette and Bradford without stopping. Others were riding because they had nowhere to go.

"Why am I here?" Mary said.

"Where do you want to be?" the conductor asked.

Mary wasn't sure she knew the answer and said nothing.

He took her to the very last car. "The caboose is where the crew sleeps. That'll be your spot."

"I'm not part of the crew."

"Are you a passenger? Did you pay your fare?"

"No. I don't know what I am. I was just walking home."

"Really?"

Mary stopped to think about that. Was it her home? Or was it the Miller home? Her name became Mary Miller when she was adopted, but in her dreams she was still Mary Black. "It was where I lived. I had groceries."

"And now you have no groceries and are on a train. Maybe you were walking home."

———— «» ————

The conductor said she was part of the crew, but he didn't assign her any work. When Mary asked, all he said was, "You'll learn what to do. Pay attention to the train."

While she waited to learn, Mary found things to do to keep herself occupied. The passenger cars weren't very clean, so she began by collecting trash and sweeping. That was something she knew how to do well enough and somehow, without Mrs. Miller bossing and Mr. Miller watching, what was once a chore now became a pleasure. She took pride in how much nicer the passenger cars looked under her care.

At the next stop, Mary welcomed new passengers and said goodbye to those who disembarked. When the train was moving again, Mary took time to listen as the passengers told her their stories. Some were headed to a new home, some were going to or coming from visiting family, some were traveling for business reasons, and some never gave a reason for being on the train but they still had a story to tell.

When the train stopped, the conductor would send Mary to a store to replenish their supplies. Mary worried that the train would leave without her, but it never did. There was always time for her to bring food back to the train and take some of it to the locomotive.

The boy who worked there was black with coal dust and sweat. From behind that dark mask were two bright eyes and a shy smile. "Toby," he said by way of introduction.

He appeared to be about Mary's age, but it was hard to tell under all that grime. He was short but with broad shoulders and strong arms. He moved like a well-oiled machine as he shoveled fuel into the boiler. The locomotive was hotter than baking bread in the summer. The engine rumbled and hissed and clanked. There was room enough for two if they didn't mind being close, and Mary didn't. She studied the many levers and dials while Toby gulped down water. "How'd you get this job?" she asked.

Toby bit off a hunk of bread before speaking. "The train stopped. The old fireman said he needed a helper and it looked better than sharecropping. He left the train and now it's just me up here."

Mary wanted to stay in the locomotive, but she knew the passengers would need looking after. When she returned to the cars, the train again began to move.

———— ‹›› ————

There was a man on the train who kept looking at Mary. He was tall with heavy boots that made him look taller still. He dressed well and might even be considered handsome were it not for the sour expression on his face. His gaze reminded her of the way Mr. Miller had begun to look at her.

The almost handsome man approached her while she was mopping the floor of a gently rocking passenger car. "You must be pretty important," he said.

"I'm nobody special," Mary said. "I just clean the train."

"The train stopped for you. Not at a train stop, not because you were waiting. It just stopped."

The passenger car shook, and Mary was thrown off balance. She dropped her mop and fell into an empty seat. The man fell backward to the floor. The bucket of dirty water tipped over, washing across his slacks, and he cursed.

"I'm so sorry," Mary said instinctivel.0y.

The man rose to his feet. "Just an accident. Some of the rails on this line need to be repaired. With a little luck, we'll get it fixed soon."

"You're with the railroad?"

"Henry Moore, railroad agent, at your service. But let me change out of these wet clothes before we continue our conversation."

Mary found the conductor in the front car leaning out the door. It frightened Mary who imagined the old man falling out, but he assured her he was always safe on the train. "Just wondering if she'll stop," he said after pulling himself back in. "Got a passenger who wants off at the next town. He's a nag. Wouldn't mind getting rid of him but I wouldn't lose any sleep over him missing his station either."

"I was wondering about a different man," Mary said. "The tall one who always looks unhappy. He's with the railroad."

The conductor nodded. "He's been riding for a while. Don't know what he's up to. Toby said he came up to the locomotive at one stop and started nosing around."

"I don't think he likes me very much," Mary said. "When the train shook back there, he fell down and got soaked with water from my mop bucket."

The conductor shook his head. "I didn't feel her shake. She's riding nice and steady."

———— «»————

Mary was cleaning one of the sleeping compartments. An angry businessman had been the last occupant, and he had to stay on the train two stations past his destination because the train decided not to stop. The man expressed his displeasure by deliberately missing the spittoon and littering the floor with empty Century tobacco packets.

From the corridor outside, Mary heard Henry Moore. "I was a bit worried when we missed two stops," he said.

"The train will do what she will do," the conductor replied.

"Oh, I think you have a little more influence over the train than you realize. A train likes its conductor, or the conductor doesn't last long."

Mary wondered if she should be hearing this conversation, but she felt trapped. If she left the sleeping compartment now, she would call attention to herself. If she stayed, she might hear more than she was supposed to. There had been a few times when Mrs. Miller thought Mary had been eavesdropping and she ended up with a whipping. On the other hand, there were a few times when she'd overheard something useful. She stayed in the small compartment and kept quiet.

"We'll have a number of passengers waiting to get on at the next stop," Moore said. "The town has always been good for us and it's very important we stick to the schedule. If they don't ride, we don't get paid."

"I can't tell you what the train will do," the conductor said.

"No, but you can tell the train what you want it to do."

"Nobody's figured out how to talk to the trains."

"It knows what you want. If you want it to stop — I mean, really want it to — it will stop as scheduled."

"I let the train take care of the stopping and starting. I stick to my job."

Mary heard something heavy thud against the wall of the sleeping compartment and she jumped. The conductor cried out in pain, and Moore hissed something too low for Mary to make out. She reached for the door to help the conductor when Moore's voice returned to normal. "It's up to you. If you don't want that to happen to her, you'll make sure we stop."

Mary paused, listening to Moore's heavy boots as he left the car. Were they talking about her, she wondered? She opened the door and saw the conductor slumped against the wall. "Are you hurt?" she asked.

He shook his head and Mary saw that his eyes were wet before he turned away.

———— «» ————

The train did decide to stop at the next town. Passengers got off; passengers got on. The railroad man stayed on board.

The next day, the train left the main line and headed into a switchyard. "Why are we stopping here?" one of the passengers asked.

Mary shrugged. "The train will do what it will do. I expect we won't be here long."

They came to a stop. Passengers and crew stared out the windows. There were lines and lines of branching tracks. Water towers stood ready to fill the boilers. Mountains of coal waited to be shoveled into the hoppers that fed the engines. Freight cars, passenger cars, locomotives, and cabooses were all scattered about the yard. Men were making repairs to a few of the cars and a locomotive was being prepared to leave. Some older men sat on benches sharing a bottle and watching the trains.

Their own locomotive stopped under a water tower. Toby had warned Mary and the conductor that they would need to fill the boiler soon, but the train knew where to go.

"This is where I get off," the conductor said after the locomotive was made ready.

"I wouldn't mind a chance to walk around myself," Mary said.

"I don't mean that. I'm done riding the train."

"Here? But why? Where will you go? What will you do?"

"I'm old and tired," he said. "More than that, I'm weak. It's time for me to move on."

"No!" Mary said. "I'll come with you. You stopped for me. I can help you."

"It wasn't me that stopped," the conductor said. "From here, I go alone. Your place is with the train." He passed her his conductor's cap and pocket watch.

"I'm just a girl! I can clean the cars, but I don't know how to be a conductor."

"Be good to the train and the train will be good to you."

Mary moved to step out of the car to join him, but the train started to roll out and she was jostled backward. The conductor waved goodbye as the train picked up speed and left the yard. She shoved the watch into a pocket but couldn't quite bring herself to put the cap on her head.

«»

The train stopped next on a siding in a lonely prairie. A small herd of cattle turned to study them. When they saw no threat, they resumed grazing. Mary checked the pocket watch and realized that Toby must be ready for some fresh water. She hurried to fill a jug and grabbed an apple. The railroad agent was already in the locomotive when Mary arrived.

"The train likes both of you," Henry Moore said. "Otherwise it wouldn't have stopped to pick you up or stop for Toby here to get a drink and some food."

"I'm nobody special," Mary said. "The train liked the conductor, but he had to leave. Maybe the train likes me today but won't like me tomorrow."

Toby took the apple and nodded. "You can't tell with a train."

"Trains aren't like people," Moore said. "I've studied them. They're slow to make a decision but stick with it once it's done. The train decided it was time for a new conductor and it chose you."

"So what?" It was hot here by the boiler and crowded with the three of them in the cab. Mary didn't know how the coal boy could stand it for hours at a time, but he did it and kept the train rolling.

"You have to see we can't continue like this," Moore said. "The trains need to be controlled. The railroad companies are hurting and if they fail, who will keep the trains running?"

"We will," Toby said around a mouthful of apple, the fruit now black as coal.

"You two? Who's going to lay new track, repair the engines, bring in the water and the coal to keep them all running? It's fine for you to shovel coal and mop floors, but it takes a company to keep the trains running."

"You still make your money when people ride the trains," Mary said.

"Not like we should. Look at what the trains are doing to the schedules. Sometimes they come on time, other times they're early or late. Sometimes they don't stop at all. How can we have a railroad that operates like that?"

"Why are you asking me?" Mary said. "What can I do about it?"

"The train likes you. You can help us take back control of the train. This train and then others until we have all of them back under control. There are repairs that need to be done but how do we lay rails when we don't know if a train might decide to come barreling down the track?"

"The rails look fine to me," said Toby.

"And that's why you won't keep the trains running," Moore said. "You don't know what to look for."

"I know you hurt the conductor," Mary said. "I don't think I want to help you." Mary had tried to tell Mrs. Miller that once. It had not gone well for her. She didn't have much hope this would be better, but she was going to try.

Moore took a step forward. So did the coal boy.

"She said she's not helping you," Toby said and dropped what was left of his apple.

The railroad agent pulled a double-barreled derringer from a pocket and waved it from Toby to Mary to Toby again. "Back," he said. "This isn't a negotiation. All I'm telling you to do is talk to the train about how important it is to stop. Everything else stays the same. You ride the train. Maybe you even get a salary from the railroad. The train's happy. You're happy. The railroad makes money."

Mary kept an eye on the gun. "The train will just find another conductor. One who doesn't ask it to do things it doesn't want to do."

"If it does, we'll do the same thing with the next conductor. It just means you won't be on the train. Look, we've learned a few things since the trains started running on their own. They like people. They need people. Without people, they've got no reason to live. So we need people who can tell the trains to do what we want them to do. You could be one of those people. You could really go places."

Mary looked at the gun and looked at Toby. She thought she saw the boy shake his head ever so slightly. "I can't do it," she said. "The train has to do what it wants to do."

Moore cocked the hammer of his pistol. "I can shovel coal as well as this boy. We're going to do this. It's your choice who's shoveling coal for you."

"Wait," Mary said. "I'll help you. Just put the gun away."

Moore didn't put it away, but he did ease up on the hammer. "Do it," he said.

Mary reached a hand out to steady herself. She grasped the no-longer-needed throttle and felt a little tremor in her hand. This is it, she thought. We're either all going to stand up to the railroad company or we're all going to end up doing what they want.

Something told Mary to grip the controls more tightly. The fingers of her left hand tightened. The water jug hung heavy in her right. She looked at Toby and saw the coal boy shift to widen his stance. The engine roared and the train lurched forward. Taken by surprise, Moore struggled to stay on his feet.

Toby pulled back on his coal shovel and it clanged against the boiler. Moore brought the gun back up as he fought to regain his balance.

Coal dust arced from the shovel as Toby swung it up at Moore's head. In the narrow space, there wasn't room for the boy to bring the full force of his muscles into play. The shovel connected, Moore's finger tightened, and the gun exploded. Mary's ears rang from the noise.

The train was accelerating faster than Mary had ever felt it move before. She realized it must have decoupled from the passenger cars and wondered what the passengers were thinking. She had no time to dwell on that thought. Moore had fallen but so had Toby. The boy was clutching at his side with one hand, and the railroad man was again raising his gun. Mary stepped forward, swinging the jug down on Moore's hand as hard as she could. She had lost the conductor and she was not going to lose Toby as well. The ceramic jug smashed into the railroad man's fingers and he screamed in pain.

When the gun fell loose, she grabbed it. It was heavier than she expected and hot in her hand. She was shaking and wasn't sure she actually knew how to fire the gun, but she pointed it at Moore all the same.

"Are you hurt?" she said over her shoulder to Toby.

"Winged me. I'll be all right." The coal boy stood up and took the pistol from Mary. Blood was seeping through the coal dust on his left side.

The train slowed and Moore looked up at the two of them. "You ever fire a gun before, boy? You don't want to pull that trigger," he said. "You'll get hurt worse than me."

"Maybe," Toby said. "Might be worth it."

Mary reached out and put her hand on Toby's back to let him know she was there. "We'll see what the train thinks about it," she said.

The locomotive slowed to a stop and the cab door opened. Moore pulled himself up to his feet. Blood was trickling down his face from where the shovel hit, and one finger stuck out at an unnatural angle. "You'll regret this," he said.

"The train wants you to leave," Mary said.

Moore backed out of the door, keeping an eye on Toby and the gun. The door closed and the locomotive began to ease back to recouple with the rest of the cars. Toby moaned and pulled off his shirt. Blood flowed down his side. "Think I cracked a rib," he said.

Mary took the gun from Toby and set it down carefully. "I'll get you cleaned up," she said. "Then I'll go check with the passengers. There's a few on board that would be happy to help."

Toby nodded. "And don't forget your cap. Conductor."

——— « 0 » ———

Maurice Forrester

Maurice Forrester is a software developer living in central New York. Recent publications include stories in *Middle Planet*, *Daily Science Fiction*, *The First Line*, and *Unrealpolitik* (JayHenge Publishing). Long interest in both 19th century American history and in train songs helped to inform this piece.

Mr. Turner on the Great Western Railway

Michael Johnstone

Nor shall your presence, howsoe'er it mar
The loveliness of Nature, prove a bar
To the Mind's gaining that prophetic sense
Of future change…
— William Wordsworth, "Steamboats,
 Viaducts, and Railways" (1835)

Joseph Mallord William Turner stood upon the grassy hill looking west toward Maidenhead. His gaze followed the line of the nearby railway tracks in anticipation of the cloud of steam announcing the approaching locomotive. The early September afternoon was gloomy, intimating rain perhaps that evening. Behind him, the Thames flowed dourly south. As a breeze whispered by, he pulled his coat tighter about him and adjusted his scarf to cover his neck more securely, yet still he shivered a touch.

Then he spied the gray-white steam puffing heartily into the air and billowing back as the locomotive sped toward him. Taking his sketchbook and a pencil from his coat pocket, he found a blank page and began drawing. First, the shapes of the steam. Next, the dark railway tracks almost converging in the distance as the front of the oncoming train appeared. He scrawled a few words — slate gray, black, iron, shadow, yellowing fields. Swiftly, he moved to a new page and outlined the front of the locomotive, with a horizontal rectangle topped by a half oval, which was topped by a thrusting vertical cylinder fluted open at its crown.

"Dear God, it is monstrous," grumbled a gentleman close by Turner.

"Don't be so spiteful, Mr. Fleetwood. I declare it to be a marvel," said the gentleman's wife, seated next to him in their phaeton. A snort from their horse suggested he also disagreed with her. They had arrived some ten minutes gone.

"What do you say, sir?" Mr. Fleetwood queried.

Turner, having begun another page of sketches, kept peering to the west, grunting lowly while he concentrated upon the wheels of the locomotive. Three of them a side, the large driving wheel between the smaller leading and trailing wheels. They propelled the train forward, urged by the pistons churning the driving wheel.

"He appears not to have heard you," the wife said.

"You may be right, Mrs. Fleetwood."

At last, the train rumbled and whistled and clattered past them. Turner halted his sketching to enjoy the quaking of the ground and surge of wind that would have carried off his hat had he not clapped a hand upon it just in time. As the passenger cars hurtled by, all seemed to slow down for a mere breath, and Turner saw a man seated by a window nod and tip his hat to him. A gentleman, with a dark and well-trimmed mustache, wine red jacket, white gloves, indigo cravat, and black top hat. Yet most striking were the gentleman's eyes, which glimmered despite the somber day, appearing also to contain tiny flickering blue and green lights. In the next breath, the train hurtled on again, crossing the bridge over the Thames and continuing east toward London.

"Mr. Fleetwood," the woman said once the train passed beyond the bridge, "I suspect he may be the painter, Mr. Turner. There is talk he is currently lodging at the Bear Hotel in town."

"Yes, yes. Good spot, Mrs. Fleetwood," the gentleman mumbled. He cleared his throat and said, "If you are indeed Mr. Turner, sir, I am honored to make your acquaintance and to welcome you to Maidenhead. Have you come to paint one of these devils of Hell?"

Turner raised his hand holding the pencil, gesturing for silence. He looked east now and watched as the back of the train eventually disappeared beyond sight, dissipating puffs of steam wafting above the railway tracks the last vestige of its recent presence. How, he wondered, would he ever devise a means of rendering such speed on the canvas? A conundrum, to be certain.

Returning to his sketchbook, he hurriedly drew the strange man at the window. When he had finished, he closed his sketchbook, put it and his pencil back in his coat pocket, and turned to face Mr. and Mrs. Fleetwood.

"My sincere apologies, sir and madam," he said cordially, proceeding a few steps toward them. "I was making some notations about the light of the afternoon and its effects upon the train. I am indeed Mr. Turner, and I am pleased to make your acquaintance as well. Do you come often to view the trains?"

"This is our second visit this month," Mrs. Fleetwood said brightly. "We were already out in the phaeton, and I proposed to Mr. Fleetwood that we would be in time to see the afternoon schedule on its way to London. My husband, as I am sure you overheard, does not find the new locomotives to his liking."

Mr. Fleetwood *humphed* and sat up straighter in the phaeton. "These railways are cutting up the country. They're rubbing out some of the most picturesque spots. Good heavens, what is the use of traveling that rapidly? You cannot even see where you are going. I have said to Mrs. Fleetwood more than once, what happens if there is an accident? Those beasts can wreak untold havoc."

"Fine questions, Mr. Fleetwood. I shall ponder them during my supper this evening, I am sure, while I review my notes. Are you staying in Maidenhead as well?"

"We are visiting with my brother a little south of the town," Mrs. Fleetwood said. "Can we offer you a lift back?"

Turner bowed slightly and tipped his hat. "Your offer is very kind, Mrs. Fleetwood, but I must respectfully decline. I prefer to walk back to the hotel. I know the way, and it is only a mile or so. Good day to you, sir. Good day to you, madam."

⸺ «》 ⸺

Two days later, Turner boarded the train as it lingered in Maidenhead station before resuming its journey to London. The gloomy skies had persisted, and the rain at last was heavy and unremitting. He grunted as he took the steps into the passenger carriage, ruing his advancing years and the stiffness of his joints. While the train had arrived in the station, he saw the queer man with the glinting eyes, who once again nodded and tipped his hat to him. Well, he must engage the stranger in conversation, as the gentleman seemed to know who he was.

First, he set down his luggage and located his seat at the back of the carriage. Though the rain fell, he pulled down his window, for the air in the carriage was a tad stale. Once the train left the station, he would proceed up the car to greet the stranger.

A stumbling commotion nearby startled Turner, and soon a young man scrambled into the seat across from him. He started slightly at the disturbance, crossing his arms upon his chest and assuming a displeased expression.

The young man smiled broadly. "Terribly sorry for the intrusion, sir." Thrusting forward a hand, he said, "Thomas Darbyshire. Are you traveling to London?"

Although the lad's spirit was infectious, Turner shook his hand briskly and said curtly, "Good day, Mr. Darbyshire. Mr. Booth, and yes, I return to London." The alias would afford Turner anonymity. It had served him well these past many years when absconding to Chelsea and the comforts of a certain esteemed woman's home and company.

"I must confess, this will be my maiden voyage on the Great Western Railway," Darbyshire said. "I am to see my uncle about a position in accounts in his company. Truly a fantastic feat of engineering, the whole system, wouldn't you say? Brunel is a true genius."

A train enthusiast, then. Turner concurred with respect to Isambard Kingdom Brunel, whose bridge he had been sketching two days previous, waiting for the train to materialize.

"As you say." Turner nodded. Just then, the train lurched into motion. "Are you also an admirer of Daniel Gooch's locomotive?"

"The Firefly? Indeed, I am. I see, Mr. Booth, that you are familiar with your engineers. Did you know that we may attain an average speed of fifty miles per hour? One cause is the width of the tracks. The gauge it is called. Brunel decided upon a gauge of just over seven feet, for greater stability. Bloody brilliant, if you ask me. But some claim that Gooch's use of the 2-2-2 wheel arrangement, with the large driving wheels in the middle, is the principal cause. How fast might a train go in the future, Mr. Booth? It is only 1843. Perhaps in twenty years' time, Maidenhead to London will require mere minutes. Progress astounds me!"

"And it should, lad." Turner grinned as he stood. "A shame you are going into accounts," he said, winking. "I beg your pardon, but I thought I should take a walk through the carriage."

"I shall await your return, sir."

《》

Turner paused a few rows of seats behind the strange gentleman before approaching him. Slipping his sketchbook out of his coat pocket, he reviewed his drawings and notes from the other day. Even for him, the forms and lines struck him as rushed and slap-dash. The train was more like an apparition than a solid, menacing, thundering machine of steel. Ah, and he had forgotten about the hare, scampering ahead of the train. Well, that may be a key to expressing the train's speed.

In an attack of curiosity, Turner moved to a set of empty seats on his left. Opening the window, he stretched up and put his head out of the train.

The fierce wind flung his hat back into the carriage, and cold rain lashed at his face with such severity that he could see only by blinking swiftly. His heart raced and he began to shiver as he felt through his hands the rumbling power of the train. Suddenly, the Maidenhead bridge came into view, and just as promptly they had crossed it, the Thames below frothing and gray.

Turner pushed himself back into the carriage and dried his face and head with his scarf. Exhilaration and distress warred within him. Such fabulous force, yet he had hardly been able to make sense of the landscape as it streaked past him. He despaired that a painting could ever reproduce this discord of emotions and impressions.

After retrieving his hat and settling his coat, he proceeded to where the stranger sat. At first, the man seemed not to notice Turner, his gaze directed ahead and his eyes shifting from left to right as if he were reading something. Like two days past, Turner swore he glimpsed a dot of pulsing blue light in the stranger's left eye and green in the right.

"Good afternoon, sir," Turner said gruffly yet, he hoped, genially.

Turner was prepared to dismiss the gentleman as ill-mannered when at last he adjusted his eyes and looked up at the old painter.

"My dear Mr. Turner, well met!" The gentleman's accent was London, but a shade off, as if practiced. "It pleases me immensely at last to have you before me. You are shorter than I anticipated, but no matter, there is so much I desire to speak with you about. Have you decided yet what you will do for the painting?"

"The painting?"

"Forgive me, Mr. Turner! I dash ahead of myself. I have not even invited you to sit with me, nor offered my name. Please do me the great honor of joining me. I am Hermes."

The gentleman was decidedly eccentric. His name was German, which at least accounted for the peculiarity of his accent. Yet Turner's curiosity was undeniably piqued by Mr. Hermes appearing to be familiar with him. Turner lowered himself into the seat opposite the gentleman and said, "You travel to and from London frequently, Mr. Hermes."

"I am ensuring that I experience fully this part of the Great Western Railway at this particular time, before I must transpose back to when I came from. All of it owing to you, sir."

Mr. Hermes spoke animatedly, gesticulating with his hands and shifting about in his seat. His eyes mesmerized Turner, for they were too shiny, and those blue and green dots of light pulsed more rapidly as he spoke. Had the man said *when* he came from? Surely not.

"You know of my work," Turner said. "May I persuade you to visit my gallery in London? You might happen upon a piece that interests you, I wager."

"I would wish for nothing else, but I do not have the time, I am afraid. Besides, there is just one piece of yours which could ever interest me, and its purchase is now beyond the means of all but the astronomically wealthy. That painting is why I have transposed here, however."

"My apologies, sir, but I do not take your meaning."

For what felt like several minutes, the gentleman did not respond. Though he looked at Turner, his attention appeared involved with his own thoughts, and the lights in his eyes ceased pulsing. Turner stifled a gasp.

Suddenly, Mr. Hermes smiled, clapped his hands together, and moved nearly to the edge of his seat. He smoothed out his waistcoat and trousers, and straightened his top hat, as if arranging himself for an important occasion. Turner could not account for such perplexing behavior.

"There can be no chronohistorical harm in what I am about to do, Mr. Turner, rest assured. I am indeed most fortunate! Before we begin, I hope you will not consider the question too impertinent if I ask once more about your painting."

Not only did the gentleman speak nonsense, but he pressed the bounds of propriety. Turner desired to indulge such singularity no longer.

"To which painting do you refer, sir?"

"Why, the one you have been making sketches and notes for these last several days! It is why you stayed in Maidenhead and why you stood upon the hill the other day. I have an awfully keen interest in your painting, Mr. Turner. It is ... well, it is a most extraordinary Temporal Inflection."

"Sir, you presume too much, and you speak rather queerly, indeed." Turner was vexed and baffled. "A painting is not simply decided upon like one selects a waistcoat or a cravat. A painting is discovered."

"Of course, of course," Mr. Hermes said, eager and conciliatory. "Could you at least tell me how you conceive of addressing the matter of the train's speed?"

His temper swelling, Turner prepared to wish Mr. Hermes a good day and return to his own seat at the back of the carriage. Yet the man was oddly enthralling, a puzzle unlike any he had met, missing a piece or two that would allow him to fit the whole together.

"I do not know." The timidity in his response surprised him.

"I believe I can assist you."

Mr. Hermes leaned forward, opened his mouth, then exhaled a white vapor that swirled about Turner's head. Turner coughed once, yet the vapor soon disappeared as it swept up through his nostrils and down his throat.

———— ⟨⟩ ————

The carriage dissolved and reformed into a gleaming, pristine, pleasantly warm car. Abruptly, Turner perceived that the entire car was like a single, large window. He was surrounded by a sky the blue of a robin's egg. When he looked down, he saw beneath his feet a dark greenish line perhaps a hand's breadth wide, interrupted occasionally by red squares. He surmised the car was moving only by the fact of the red squares blurring into and out of view. The sensation was of floating.

Turner leaped out of his seat, which had shaped itself to his body for exemplary comfort. He nearly collapsed to his knees from a surge of dizziness, preventing his fall by grasping onto the top of his seat. Whether he glanced up or left or right, nothing appeared material. If not for the solidity of the seat in his hands and the floor upon which he wavered, he feared he could reach through the walls of the car. He would be reaching into the sky.

"A miracle, isn't it?" Mr. Hermes's voice sounded in Turner's mind. "It goes from Bath to London now in a shade under ten minutes, traveling at approximately twenty kilometers per minute. The speed is achieved by a combination of a highly sophisticated antimatter propulsion system and briefly slipping through quantum space-time. You feel as if you are floating because there are no wheels and there is no track. We discarded such constraints very long ago. It has charmed me to think that a man such as Isambard Kingdom Brunel would approve."

"Where am I? Where are you?" Turner said aloud.

"You are on the train to London, Mr. Turner. I am quite literally in your head, though not for much longer. I desired a great deal to show you the world your painting helped to create."

"Who are you, Mr. Hermes? I demand an honest answer."

"My name truly is Hermes. I selected it myself. I am an android, or what you might consider an automaton, although I am no mere senseless machine. You can think of me as a historian, specializing in the representation of trains in the visual arts. My particular focus is non-virtual mediums from the nineteenth to the twenty-third centuries. Hence my passionate interest in your painting *Rain, Steam and Speed – The Great Western Railway*. As I said, an extraordinary Temporal Inflection."

"I do not understand one jot of what you are prattling on about, Mr. Hermes. Not one jot. And I do not care for it. What in the devil is *Rain, Steam and* ... and the rest of that drivel you mentioned? Release me from this immediately."

"I promise that I will do so soon, Mr. Turner. I beg your indulgence a little longer. I have dreamed of this encounter a great deal. It is the climax of my scholarship. You see, your painting renders a turning point that, upon hindsight, has led to the train you are experiencing now. Over the centuries, it has become a chronohistorical threshold, so that we can say, 'Yes, this future was seeded *then*. We began imagining this future *then*.' And I must remark, the hare was a brilliant touch. It justifiably drew praise at the Royal Academy exhibition in 1844."

Turner resumed his seat, fatigued and bewildered. The only rational explanation was that he lay in the grip of a powerful hallucination. A train made of glass with no wheels or tracks. Bath to London in ten minutes. A voice in his head jabbering about bizarre, impossible things.

"This is not real," Turner whispered.

"It is, and it is not. The nanites you breathed in have allowed me to manipulate certain centers of your brain and play for you a quantum-sensory video I prepared. You have my word that I will emend your memories precisely so you suffer no recollection of this. Otherwise, the chronohistorical damage would be … incalculable."

———— «» ————

With a snort and a cough, Joseph Mallord William Turner jerked awake.

Mr. Hermes still sat across from him, smiling as if he looked upon an amusing child.

"I must have nodded off." Turner straightened himself in his seat. "Terribly sorry, Mr. Hermes. Rather rude of me, to be sure. I blame my advanced years."

"It is of no matter, sir. We had a most enchanting conversation about painting and locomotives. We are nearing London now, and I must transpose soon after we arrive. Thank you, Mr. Turner, for the honor and pleasure of your company. I will cherish the memory of our meeting for all my days."

"You are kind to an old man. Do take my card. If you are ever inclined to visit my studio, you will be welcome."

Turner stood, produced a small silver case from the inside pocket of his coat, opened it, and held his card toward Mr. Hermes. The gentleman took it almost reverently, his attention fixed wholly upon the card and the hand presenting it.

"A good day to you, sir," Turner said, replacing the silver case in its pocket.

"And to you, sir," Mr. Hermes replied in a hushed tone, gazing still upon the card.

Stepping into the aisle, Turner proceeded to the back of the carriage, where he found young Mr. Darbyshire reading a book of poetry. As he sat, he observed that it was a volume of Wordsworth.

"You are an admirer of Mr. Wordsworth, I see. A proper English poet. Very keen eye for landscape. He has a fine sonnet on railways, I recall."

Thomas Darbyshire glanced up from the book. "Welcome back, Mr. Booth. The Wordsworth is at my father's insistence, though I am becoming sensible of his virtues. Has your journey been pleasant?"

"Quite, yes," Turner said, looking out the window to his left.

Through the rain, he could discern the edges of London in the distance ahead. As he looked upon the rapidly approaching city, he felt as if the final piece of the puzzle slid into place. In that moment, he apprehended he was between the past and the future, and the train hurrying east to the great, boisterous, clamoring city was carrying him from one to the other.

The problem of speed was not, in fact, a problem at all. On the contrary, it was the very essence of the painting.

As the train hastened across the land and over bridges, it smudged out the past and propelled him to the future. Both were shadowy and obscure. There was loss along with the inexorable forward motion of progress.

Turner smiled mischievously, as if appreciating a particularly witty quip.

He would put the hare in the painting, scurrying ahead of a black, nearly formless train upon the bridge.

Was the poor creature doomed? Did it herald a grand new age?

Let everyone make it out as they wished.

« O »

Michael Johnstone

Michael Johnstone has short stories published in *On Spec*, *Tesseracts Twenty: Compostela* (EDGE; ed. James Alan Gardner and Spider Robinson), and *Andromeda Spaceways Magazine*. He teaches speculative fiction as well as nineteenth-century literature at the University of Toronto.

Website: www.michael-johnstone.com

Twitter: @mikejwrites.

The Boy on the Train

Neil Enock

The screech of steel on steel echoing through the tunnel was the first sign. After years of silence, the tracks had only recently started to complain as the train rounded the curve into the area under the Zone. Then the lights flickered, and the train seemed to shudder. She closed her eyes, took a deep breath and forced herself to relax into her seat. When she opened them, she gasped involuntarily.

The wispy apparition of a young man had again appeared in the aisle in front of her, walking along the train car, clearly searching for something or someone. She stood up and ignored the curious stares of the other passengers as she waved and tried to get his attention. He did not respond, so she gave up, stood still and let her inner scientist study him. He appeared to be in his mid-twenties, with dark hair and twinkly brown eyes. He wore a colony ship uniform, but the regulation boots were different. Suddenly, he vanished!

Abruptly left staring at her reflection in the window, she turned away, only to face a train car full of people staring at her. Clearly, they had not seen the boy. Self-conscious, she half smiled, half grimaced and quickly sat down, landing squarely in the lap of a sleepy old mine worker.

"Mmmm." He roused. "Hello?"

"I'm so sorry!" She tried to get off and almost fell. Smiling, he steadied her then slid aside to make room for her on the seat.

"Are you all right?" he asked, genuinely concerned, then jokingly added, "You look like you've seen a ghost!"

Her cheeks flushed as she blurted, "Actually … I think I may have."

To her amazement, the old miner's smile widened. "Ah, well, you're one of the lucky few then. That'd be Curly's ghost. Few are those that can see him, and lucky are those that do." As she looked at him in bewildered amazement, he winked. "Parents never told you that one, did they?"

"No," she admitted. "Can you tell me more?"

"*Second Chance Mines,*" the PA announced as the train slowed.

"This is my stop," the miner said, his voice apologetic as he stood. "But you should talk to old Curly, the station master at First Landing. He'll be happy to tell you the story."

"I will, thank you!" she said as he headed to the door.

"Oh, don't thank me, and don't let the old bugger scare you," the miner cautioned. "He'll likely be a bit touchy about it."

"Why?" she called after him as the doors slid open.

"Nobody's seen the ghost in years!" He winked at her as he stepped off the train.

———— «» ————

Sarah smiled, pleased that none of her inner turmoil showed. The elevator glass reflected a calm and composed woman. She had ignored the stares the rest of the train ride to the spaceport, but she had felt every one of them. She knew that she'd seen the ghost boy, but couldn't understand why nobody else did.

Her glasses darkened as the elevator broke the surface and began its crawl up the tower base. Morning sunlight glared across the unfinished spaceport, glinting off the structures that protruded from the ground. Her view slipped away as the elevator entered the bottom of the control tower.

The doors slid open to the astro lab. She heaved a deep sigh and strode into the lion's den.

"Good morning, Sarah." Her mother smiled, looking up from her console. Her father glanced at his watch.

"Hi Mom, hi Dad," she chirped as she headed over to her own desk. It was strewn with an assortment of sample containers.

"You finished collecting those samples last week. Why are you still coming in late?" her father asked pointedly.

"Don't bother her, dear," her mother interjected. "Maybe she met a nice boy and is *finally* thinking about settling down!"

"Mom!"

"We live in hope my dear," her mother said unapologetically. "We all have to do our part to grow the colony."

"*Hrumpfff,*" her father said. "I'm sure she hasn't miraculously discovered '*Mr. Right.*'" He made air quotes around the words.

"As it happens," Sarah said, "I did see a very handsome someone today. Someone that I would love to meet."

"Where's he work?" her father asked.

"I don't know, Dad!" She was beginning to regret saying anything.

"What does he look like?"

"Mom!"

"Where did you meet him?"

"On the train."

"Is that why you're late again?" He kept the questions coming. "What do you know about him?"

"He has nice eyes," she offered.

"That's what you know?" her mom asked.

"I haven't got him to notice me yet."

"Why not? Is he blind?"

"Dad!"

"What? You're an attractive young woman. What's wrong with him?" His eyes narrowed. "Is he married?"

"What?" She shook her head in disbelief.

"Is this really why you're coming in late?"

"Yes, Mom! Well, no. It's … not like that!" She was exasperated. "I'm just sick of you guys trying to pair me off."

Her dad seemed like he was going to back off, but suddenly asked, "So, is there a guy, or not?"

"Well…" She looked at them carefully. "Sort of." She hesitated. "I think he's a ghost."

"What!" her mom screeched.

"An old miner on the train said he might be Curly's ghost. Do you know who that is?"

"It's just an old tale told to scare kids out of the tunnels under the Zone," said her dad.

Her mother stayed silent.

"You shouldn't go around talking about it." Her dad seemed quite concerned.

"Why not?"

He clammed up and turned back to his console, but her mother had more to say. "We lost thousands of souls that day."

"And our connection to Earth." Her dad spun around to face her again. "Curly's ghost is a cruel reminder of the Crisis. A bad joke."

Her mother interjected. "Not according to Curly."

Her dad scowled and turned back to his work. The conversation was over.

"Well then, I'll just go ask Curly," Sarah blurted out.

"You will do no such thing," her dad insisted.

"Why not?"

"Curly was on the train when it happened. He's … damaged."

"What do you mean?"

"Bad radiation scarring," her mom explained.

"And his brain is messed up," her dad added.

"George!" her mom chastised.

"Well, it is. He cooked up that whole ghost story, and he keeps trying to funnel colony resources to mount a search for it. You just stay away from him! He's dangerous."

Her mother shook her head, warning Sarah to let it go.

"Fine," Sarah said, and started sorting the samples she'd previously collected, labeling them according to their Patreon concentration.

——— «» ———

Curly, the station master, lived deep in the train tunnels under First Landing. At the back of a poorly lit side tunnel, an old stripped-down train car sat beside a knocked-together platform. The awning and rocking chair on the platform made it look like it might be a residence, so she climbed up the steps and knocked.

"Hello?" a grizzly voice growled from inside.

"Hi," she responded. "Are you Curly?"

A shuffling noise, footsteps and then the door opened. He stayed in the shadows.

"Yes."

"They said maybe you could help me."

"Let me guess?" he said. "You're doing a term paper on why colony ships establish railways as the primary transportation grid, and you want some quotes and pictures?"

"Well, actually—" she started, but he launched into a speech he had obviously given many times before.

"Interstellar colonization requires that almost everything be brought from home, and since the ships hold thousands, there's a lot of people and things to move about when we get there, er, here. By designing components of the ship to be converted into train cars after arrival, well let's just say that it is by far the most economical use of weight, space and materials possible. Can you imagine if we had to bring individual vehicles for everyone like they use at home? The ships would have to be twice the size."

He paused, so she jumped in. "Thank you, that's great to know, but not why I'm here."

"Why did they send you to me then?" he said suspiciously. "Hey, you're not here to try and take my house again, are you?"

"I — no. What?"

"Ever since they've been working on the line to New Hope they send people around every once in a while, to try and put my house back into train service."

"No. Definitely not," she said.

"Well then?"

She didn't know how to start.

"Why'd they send you to me?" he asked again.

"He said you might know what's going on."

Curly leaned into the light. A radiation burned face is not a pretty sight, but Sarah didn't flinch.

"Who said?"

"A miner I met on the train."

He slowly withdrew, turning back into the shadows.

"I keep seeing a boy on the train," she blurted out. "But — he's not really there."

Curly spun around and glared at her. "Who put you up to this?"

"Nobody!" she said. "Nobody else can see him. I don't know what to do."

"Get out," he said quietly.

She didn't move.

"I said GET OUT!"

She turned and ran.

——— «» ———

"How are you honey?" her mom asked when they sat down for dinner that evening.

"Not too good," she admitted. "I went to see Curly this afternoon, and he yelled me out of the place."

"What?" Her dad was instantly angry. "I wasn't kidding. You can't go see that crazy fool! I never thought you would actually go there. You stay away from him! Nobody talks to Curly … and Curly talks to nobody. Ever."

The door chimed for access.

"System?" her mother asked.

"Curly Adams, station master, to see Miss Sarah."

Her mom and dad just looked at each other, shocked.

"Admit him," Sarah instructed. "I'll be right there."

——— «» ———

Sarah brought Curly into the living room and invited him to sit.

"I'm very sorry … Sarah, is it?" he apologized. "I'm sorry for my behavior earlier. See, nobody has mentioned seeing him on the train for…"

"At least ten years," her dad finished as he joined them. "Curly."

"George." He looked at Sarah again. "I apologize for startling your daughter, but I thought I was being pranked again."

Her dad started to say something but Curly held up his hand. "Then I realized nobody remembers that stuff. There's no way it could be a prank."

"The ghost hasn't been seen for so long," her mother said gently as she came in and sat down beside Sarah.

"Well Marion, the old car is back in service again," Curly said, as if that explained it. "They need every car now that the train is running all the way to New Hope."

"Who is he, Curly?" Sarah asked.

"A ghost," he said sadly. "From the Crisis."

"I don't see what good it does bringing this all up again," her dad said.

"But she's the one that saw him!" Curly said, a bit defensively.

Her mom looked worried, so Sarah added, "I don't see him all the time."

Curly was shocked. "You've seen him more than once?"

"Uh, a few times, yes."

"That's incredible."

"Curly." Her mom used that firm voice that meant she was going to get what she wanted. "It's really good to see you again, but I think it's time for you to go."

Curly looked down, acquiesced, and stood up to leave.

"Thank you," he said to her parents. "Sarah, I'm very sorry I startled you today, but I'd appreciate it if you would let me know if anything further develops."

—— «» ——

Sarah sat on one of the chairs on the platform, lost in thought about what she should do differently if she saw *him* again today.

"Miss Templeton?" Curly was standing right in front of her.

"Curly," she said evenly. "What can I do for you?"

"Nothing, but maybe I can help you," he said. "The boy on the train, he doesn't know you're there, does he?"

Now how did he know that? "No," she admitted. "I've even tried jumping up and waving my arms, and nothing."

Curly sat down beside her. Reaching into a small equipment bag slung over his shoulder, he pulled out an odd-looking wrist-rack device. "This should help him to see you. Just strap it on your wrist and touch this button to turn it on."

"What does it do?" she asked.

He hesitated, so she cocked her head, pursed her lips and awaited his answer.

"It's a Matreon particle emitter."

"What good will that do?" she asked. "Matreon particles are everywhere. That's why we colonized this planet."

"Well you know your history," Curly said. "This emitter concentrates the particles and focuses them into Matreonic Waves."

"And you just *happen* to have a Matreon emitter in your bag?" she asked wryly.

Curly laughed. "You don't beat around the bush, do you?"

"I'm a scientist. It's not in my nature."

"Well … good. Then you will understand that this is a prototype and that I need you to test it to see if my theory is sound. I need to determine if it will attract his attention…" Seeing she was waiting for more, he added, "…to you."

Sarah looked quizzically at Curly.

"Years ago," he continued, "I started tracking the 'ghost' from the Crisis and I've been refining my theory ever since. Now that he has reappeared, I can take the next step."

"That sounds reasonable," Sarah said as she strapped the device to her arm. "Now I just have to find him."

"Car 47," Curly said. "He'll always be in Car 47."

She nodded, and Curly stood to leave.

"And Sarah?"

"Yes?"

"Not everybody can see him."

"Don't I know it," she said wryly.

—— «» ——

Sarah hopped the next train, but Car 47 was not attached. A couple of trains later she found the car. A few trips and a couple hours later she was ready to give up. Then she heard a familiar squeal of steel on steel as they entered the Zone. The lights flickered, and seconds later the boy appeared and began his walk along the car. When he was in front of her, she tapped the button.

The ghost stopped, backed up a step, and began waving his arms frantically. Behind her a passenger screamed. She ignored the scream and waved back. Sarah moved closer to the boy and they locked eyes. His face was a mix of shock and relief as tears welled and rolled down his cheeks. Then he vanished.

The car was abuzz. *"What the hell was that?"* *"It's that damn ghost story come to life."* *"Did you see that?"*

Sarah sat down and sighed. He was real, very real. She wiped her face and discovered her own tears.

———— «〉» ————

"You're sure he could see you?" Curly said.

"Absolutely," she replied.

Curly looked deep in thought, as if he were wrestling with something.

"Okay," he said, and took a deep breath. "Shall we try phase two?"

"What's that?"

"Getting an image of him," he said. "I need proof. The council has doubted me for twenty-five years and I need to prove he actually exists."

"Okay," she said. "How do I take a picture of him?"

Curly smiled and grabbed his equipment bag. He handed her a standard looking digital capture device. "I've added a Matreon emitter."

"That's it?"

"Yes," he said, as he adjusted the emitter and handed it to her.

"Tomorrow morning then," she said. "Will you be there?"

"No. I need to work on a few things."

"What could be more important than this?"

He looked at her and smiled happily. "Phase three."

———— «〉» ————

The next day Sarah boarded the mid-morning train intent on capturing an image of the boy on the train. She entered Car 47, oblivious to the other passengers and to her parents who had surreptitiously taken a seat at the back of the car.

Her parents' whispered discussion about why they should and shouldn't be spying on their daughter was interrupted when Sarah jumped up and quickly moved to the center of the train car. They watched, open mouthed, as Sarah tapped the device on her arm, then as the boy appeared and came directly over to her. She snapped his picture, and they smiled at each other. She extended her hand to see if they could touch and he copied her. Before their fingers met, the lights flickered, and he was gone.

Sarah sighed, then turned to see her parents standing at the back of the train car.

"We saw him." Her mom wiped a tear from her eye. "Sarah, we saw him!"

———— «〉» ————

"Who is he?" her dad asked Curly as they crowded into his cluttered home.

A fuzzy image, displayed on Curly's monitor, was being systematically enhanced, and it quickly came into focus.

"It's … my twin brother Raymond," Curly said, his voice cracking. "He's looking a bit older than when I last saw him." Curly choked back a sob. "We were sixteen at the time of the Second Landing Crisis. The second wave colony lightship was about to land at the spaceport, and our family was on the train going to meet it. I was one car back, chasing Raymond through the cars. Suddenly, there was a flash of light, and the train slammed to a halt. The front half of the train, the tunnel, tracks, everything in front of Car 47 vanished as if it had never existed. The car I was in and everything behind it was fine. Car 47, the car in the middle, the one that Raymond and the rest of my family had been in, was still there, but … empty. Everyone was gone."

Sarah knew what she'd been taught about the Second Landing Crisis. The ship's light drive had exploded. Everything and everyone near the ship, whether on the surface or underground, had disappeared. Starling City, Second Chance Mines, the spaceport — all gone. Vanished as if they'd never existed. All communication equipment had been lost and no lightships had arrived since. The surface for hundreds of kilometers was still desolated, and that had been twenty-five years ago.

"How come he looks so young?" Sarah asked.

Curly shrugged. "Perhaps he's trapped in some sort of anomaly. Nobody really knows what happened when the explosion occurred."

"Maybe that's why he looks like he's standing in a bubble." Her dad pointed to the background of the picture. The fuzzy background did look like the reflection of a bubble.

"How were we able to see Raymond today?" her mom asked.

"Patreon particles. From the ship's exploded light drive," Curly said. "For the last ten years I've been collecting them on the surface and augmenting them with the planet's natural Matreon particles. That's what's in the emitter Sarah has."

"But that makes a Faster-Than-Light drive!" her dad said. "You put an FTL drive on my daughter's arm?"

"Dad, it would need a lot more to be an FTL drive," she said.

"Sarah's right," Curly said. "The emitter simply exposes the particles to each other, and the resultant excitation makes things visible to Raymond. We'll need a much bigger event to bring him back."

"Bring him back?" her dad asked incredulously.

"Phase three." Curly smiled happily at Sarah. "Bring my brother home."

———— «» ————

Sarah's parents had always been stubborn, 'go with the flow' types, so they amazed her when they agreed to support Curly in his efforts to bring back his brother. They petitioned the council for assistance, citing Curly's years of data collection, the recent photo of Raymond, and Sarah's experience of finding the boy on the train.

The council shocked them when all but two of the councilors voted to let them attempt proper communication with Raymond and cleared the way for them to use the train under the Zone for up to one hour at a time, as necessary.

The two naysayers on the council rode along on the first few trips where Curly and Sarah used whiteboards to schedule times with Raymond for communications. As soon as they saw the boy on the train was real and communicating back, the council vote became unanimous.

———— «» ————

"Why did they have to announce what we're doing?" Curly grumbled as they pushed their way through the crowd to the train a few weeks later.

"It's in the constitution," Sarah reminded him. "Unanimous votes have to be publicized."

"Bah! They'll look good if they help bring someone from the Crisis back," Curly said. "That's all they care about."

Sarah shrugged. "Either way, they're letting you do it."

"Us," he said. "This couldn't have happened without you — and your parents."

She smiled as they boarded the train. It wasn't long until Raymond was reading the whiteboard that explained their thoughts on the anomaly he was trapped in. He shook his head, and put his hands one over the other, as if there was an invisible ball between them, and rotated the ball 180 degrees.

"What's he trying to say?" Curly asked.

"I don't know," Sarah said. "Something is turned around?"

Raymond began writing a complex formula on his own whiteboard. He vanished before he could complete it.

Back at the lab, they studied a video of the exchange.

"It's impossible to tell what he thinks is turned around," her dad said. "This is the first time you showed him our thoughts on the anomaly?"

"Yes," Sarah said. "We wanted to give him context for what we are doing."

"Speaking of what we are doing," Curly said, changing the subject, "we haven't discussed how we are going to get enough Patreon particles to make this work."

Sarah smiled. Her mother got up and opened the frosted glass door of the cabinet that housed Sarah's samples. "Sarah's Interstellar Comm Array experiment had her collecting samples with high Patreon concentrations for months," she told Curly. "Based on your calculations, we should have far more than we need."

Curly looked at Sarah, then at the samples, then back again. "When did you start to see Raymond?"

"When I started to come in later in the mornings," she said. "I needed to collect the samples in daylight."

"That's why you could see him when no one else could." Curly slapped his forehead. "You were saturated with Patreon particles!" He looked down at the plans laid out in front of him. "This really is going to work!"

"This confirms your 'phase three' theory?" asked Sarah.

Curly nodded. "Now we just have to build it."

――― «◊» ―――

Over the next two months Curly, Sarah and her parents worked tirelessly to develop and build the phase three device.

Time passed quickly and before long the day that the council had decided to call Re-Union Day had arrived.

"It looks like everyone in the colony is here," Sarah said as they made their way through the throngs gathered outside the First Landing Station.

"It stands to be a rather significant day," her dad said.

"Let us hope so," her mother added.

"Bloody crowds," Curly muttered. But he was smiling.

Accompanied by the encouraging cheers of the crowd they eventually pushed their way through to the train, which had been reserved especially for the entire day. Selected Council officials, a medical team and the colony news crew were already on board. The news crew had set up remote cameras in Car 47, ready to livestream the event to the entire colony.

"What a circus!" Curly said as the door closed behind him.

"Let's get to work," Sarah said as she rolled forward the emitter array. It consisted of three circular metal hoops with pods for the Patreon packs, Matreon exciters and a separate EM ring for focusing the energy.

"Five minutes," her mother called out.

"All ready," her father said as he checked the console.

"Power on!" Curly instructed.

The indicators glowed and the emitters began to hum as they came up to temperature. The needles on the dials jumped up, wavered and then settled down to normal.

"Okay."

Sarah caught Curly's eye and gave him an encouraging smile. Her mother gave the signal, and the train started moving. "Here we go," she said.

They rode in silence as they approached the Zone. Sarah tensed as she heard the squeal of steel on steel. It was time. "Ready…"

The lights flickered. "Patreon injection … now!" Curly hit the switch.

Space within the emitter array seemed to distort, shimmer, and settle into a flat field as Raymond appeared on the other side. There was no time for contemplation. Careful to avoid touching the field, Sarah extended a handwritten note toward and then into the shimmering field. Raymond reached forward as it emerged on his side ... and took it from her!

"It works!" Sarah cried, surprise and delight in her voice.

Smiling, Raymond pushed the note that he had prepared into the portal. But, as the edges of his note touched the field, it disintegrated and vanished!

"What happened?" Curly said.

"I don't know—" Sarah began hopelessly.

Sparks flew from the emitters, and the train shuddered, just enough to throw Sarah off balance. Instinctively she reached out to steady herself, but her hand went straight into the field. Her mother screamed as Raymond lunged forward, grabbed Sarah's hand before she could pull it back and — pulled her through the portal.

The lights flickered and they were both gone.

———— ‹›› ————

"What have you done?" Sarah yelled as Raymond caught her and steadied her from falling.

"I couldn't let you pull back," he apologized. "That would have cost you an arm, or more."

"But where..." she trailed off as she looked around. The moving train car they were in looked nothing like Car 47. It had the shape of the train car, but it had been outfitted like a lab, and they were standing inside a sphere of glowing emitters right in the middle of it all.

"Where are we?" he finished for her. "Can I let go?"

She realized she was still hanging on to him and nodded. "We were supposed to bring you back."

"Please don't move!" he cautioned, letting her go. Moments later the lights on the emitters clicked off and the train car began to slow.

"It's safe now," he said. "Come and see."

He moved to a control panel and clicked a couple of buttons. She took in the racks of equipment as the train car began moving again, this time in the opposite direction. From behind her, a shaft of sunlight lit up the interior as the window shutters retracted.

She spun and looked out over the most beautiful sight she had ever seen. Crystal lakes dotted lush greenery. People strolled along paths that connected lakeside villas. The paths led to a sprawling, modern city off in the distance. It seemed like they must be in a crater, as the city rose up from the lush floor and climbed up the walls to where tall stone spires seemed woven between the tallest buildings. Off in the distance, one spire was much too symmetrical to be stone. She gasped as she recognized the forward cone of a colony lightship!

"Welcome to First Landing," he said.

"What?"

He pointed out the window. "This ... is First Landing." He watched her intently.

Her mind reeled.

"But. I live in First Landing."

"Yes, you do," Raymond said. "I'm Ray."

"Sarah," she said. "Pleased to meet you ... in person. You're Curly's twin brother."

"Hmm," he said. The train slowly came to a halt. A sensor dinged and the train door automatically opened. "Come with me."

They left the train and instead of a train station, they emerged into a series of labs. As they walked by each lab, people stopped what they were doing and stared at them, at her. He ignored them all, leading her to a glassed-in café, then out the door onto a patio where they could look back at the facility.

He pointed along the crater wall. A long thin building attached to the lab circled the crater wall for about a fifth of its circumference.

"The train line?" Sarah asked.

"Yes," he said. "Let me try and explain. Maybe we should sit?"

"This can't be First Landing."

"Well," he started carefully, "many years ago, the second lightship to arrive had a drive failure on landing and exploded directly over First Landing, which created the crater we are in now."

"The Crisis, yes … but First Landing is fine," Sarah protested. "And the ship was to land at the new spaceport, not First Landing."

"True. But it ended up here, where it exploded. First Landing was vaporized … or so we thought."

"But—"

"Maybe its best I get through this all, then you can ask questions after?"

"All right," she said.

"Everything was gone right up to the train tunnel and part of the train. The tunnel and remaining train were found in the crater wall here. As it was being rebuilt, people started seeing what they called 'ghosts' of their missing relatives in one train car. Everyone dismissed it, except one person, who realized that you were seeing us as well."

"You?" Sarah said.

"No," he said. "But I'll get to that. For years it was assumed to be a ghost story, but after a while, the appearances became regular, almost scheduled. We think it was just luck that the train times coincided. Eventually it was thought that you were all trapped in an anomaly and an effort was mounted to coordinate an attempt to bring you back.

"Just as things were getting started on that effort, part of the crater wall collapsed, taking out a portion of the tunnel as well. It took about twenty-five years to rally the effort and expense of trying to rebuild the line. Eventually this facility was built and the track restored. But, although we could see you, people from your side couldn't see us any longer. Until you came along." He smiled.

"I was exposed to Patreon particles that came from the exploded light drive," she said. "Curly said that's why you could see me."

"That makes perfect sense," he said. "That's the missing piece!"

He smiled happily, but then looked at her apprehensively.

"There's more?" she asked.

"Yes." He smiled again. "My name is Ray. Raymond is my grandfather."

"Impossible!" Sarah scoffed. "Curly is only forty-one years old."

"How long since the Explosion?" he asked her.

"Twenty-five years, of course," she said.

"Sixty years. By our measure," he explained. "We noticed the effect even before the crater collapsed. The timing difference was measurable. It may even be why the crater wall collapsed. That's why the train was separated from the mainline and put in a controlled environment. It's why we have the dilation bubble set up in the train car."

"And that's why we couldn't see anything behind you in our Car 47," she said. "Because of the dilation bubble."

"And why we couldn't build a portal from this side," he said. "Until now."

"What do you mean?" she asked.

"Your exposure to the Patreon radiation and the fact that we, um, safely moved you through the portal. We'll need a bit more time, but we have everything we need to build a portal that will work both ways now."

"I can go home!" she said, happy tears spilling down her cheeks.

"Or," he smiled, brushing her tears away, "you can *come* home. And you can bring everyone home with you."

—— « O » ——

Neil Enock

Neil Enock has been called a modern day renaissance man. He is an author, actor, director, artist, singer, songwriter, screenwriter, filmmaker, inventor, and media presenter. He created and hosts "Train Talk TV" on iTunes, which has over a million viewers/listeners, and just completed his first televison pilot, *SomeWhen* – which Neil both wrote and produced. In addition to his many talents, Neil has a vast knowledge of trains (real, toy and imaginary) and a passion for storytelling.

The Siren and the Switch

Christine Hanolsy

The Train is in your blood, my mother would have said, if she had lived. She'd said it of my father often enough. She would curl up on their bunk in our cramped residence-coupé and stare out into the Undertow night after night until we pulled into the next Station. Envara to Andalus Minor via Kazimir — that was our route, the only route I have ever traveled. Even through the Undertow it takes three months to traverse the Spur end to end. I celebrated my twelfth birthday halfway between Andalus and Kazimir and my thirteenth on-station at Envara. My mother braided ribbons into my heavy black hair.

Some people, I know, live their entire lives groundside, or on the concourses and resupply hubs between planets. Stationary lives, we say, smiling at our own pun to cover up disdain. My mother was born on Remera Segunda, just one stop beyond Envara on the Orion-Cygnus line. She never loved the Train, but she had loved my father. Me, I can't imagine staying in one place, can't fathom waking up day after day with the same landscape on my doorstep. On Remera Segunda, my mother said, one could walk for weeks and never leave the grain fields nor come out from the shadow of the mountain.

The Train is in your blood, she would have said, and my father would have agreed. Home is the space in between

Stations, the motion of the Train, the ever-changing landscape of the Undertow. I was a born Engineer, like him.

Sometimes, when I was small, my father would take me with him to the control car. I would sit on his knee and watch the dials and blinking lights.

"Steady, girl," he would caution when I reached for the levers. "Trust the Train. He knows the way." And so I learned to sit, to watch and listen, to feel the hum and sway of the engine and hear the faint hiss of the mags against the force-rails. Groundside trains are different, I've heard. They clack and clatter, squeal and groan from city to city, shackled by gravity and friction and other limitations of subsonic speed. Union Galactic Trains are nearly silent, unless you know what to listen for.

And outside, between Stations, there is the Undertow.

They say the Undertow is like an ocean, though I have never seen the sea, only this infinite expanse above or below or overlaying the space between the stars, separated from our own reality by a barrier both impermeable and fragile. It shifts and seethes; it swallows. It is non-traversable by ship or shuttle or any other means that requires set coordinates, bearings and lines of position. One might as well fix one's nav-system on a stick floating on the waves. Countless ships had been lost before the force-rails were invented. And now Trains crisscross the Undertow from Station to Station on routes opened and fixed generations ago by the Switchman's Corps. We used to be explorers, we humans.

———— «◊» ————

I checked my timepiece. Even without it, I could tell by the pulse of the force-rails through the floor that my Train was waking up from his on-station nap. I say his, as my father did, though a Train is not alive. Trains don't even have artificial intelligence. They're just machines, vehicles. This particular Train was the property of Union Galactic, even though I called him mine.

Affection and a familiar impatience settled in my belly and I bounced on my toes a little, waiting for the doors to slide open. Next stop: the resupply hub at EA-51, and then four more weeks along the Spur to Andalus Minor itself —

the End of the Line, colloquially. There was nothing beyond, nothing we could reach, not without a Switch to open a new path and an Engineer to guide the Train. Nowadays, Union Galactic was not interested in expanding into the Arm. Nowadays, we stuck to the schedule.

At least Andalus Minor had plenty to recommend it, including the best teahouse I had found along the Spur, where I'd met a girl with violet eyes and long, elegant fingers. I wondered if she was still there, if she would remember me after so much time or if she'd found a more permanent liaison. A hazard of the traveling life, I suppose. Not everyone was as lucky as my father.

My job was a simple one, a sinecure, really; I stood on the platform as passenger after passenger presented wrist or claw or pinion for the scan, each Citizen's data uploaded to the Station's network to be passed along to Central. The job didn't pay much, but it didn't need to; Union Galactic's insurance policy was one of the best. They had offered to re-home me, after my father died, to house me with the crèche children on Envara, or to send me to my mother's family on Remera Segunda. They had promised a steady income and a one-time pass to anywhere the Trains ran. I had refused everything but a monthly stipend in exchange for my parents' coupé and the run of the Train. This Train, my Train, was already too much in my blood. Union Galactic let me stay; a relic, if a young one, of an earlier time when Conductors were necessary personnel, and Engineers, too.

You'd have thought the passengers would interest me as much as the places we visited, but people were ephemeral — no matter how exotic, they passed in and out of the Train unremarked and unremembered. I noticed the girl now only because of how she glared at me when I reached for her arm. The boarding process was so routine that most people barely gave me a second glance, but this girl stiffened and looked me right in the eye.

"Apologies, Dama," I said, taking her for one of the Sky-Touched. But no, she wore no gloves, nor the enveloping robes of the Order. She was just a girl, and a nervous one. I'd seen those nerves before, gotten used to reassuring first-time riders. It's perfectly safe, now. Even the Sirens are few and far between, these days.

The couple in the line behind her stirred impatiently, the woman opening her fan with a loud snap. The girl started and thrust her wrist toward me.

"Sorry," she muttered.

I ran my scanner over the invisible chip lodged under her skin until it beeped softly.

"Welcome aboard." I sketched a half-bow. My mother had taught me to be polite.

Her gaze did not soften, but she favored me with a stiff nod. "Could you tell me, please, which way is my room?" she asked. Definitely a first-timer, then. Her consonants were soft, muffled, like the whisper of the mag-wheels.

I checked the scanner again. Stena au'Tenebrae, it read. Private coupé, second class. "Your coupé," I stressed the word, and gestured. "One flight down, fifteen cars to the fore." First class was closest to the locomotives on either end, third class in the middle where the sway was most noticeable and gravity had a tendency to play tricks. "Mind your step in the vestibules."

She nodded again and brushed by me. Her scent lingered, ozone and something else, something sweet. I watched her glide down the corridor, her fingers trailing along the brass handrail, until the fan snapped again and I turned back to the line.

⸺ «◊» ⸺

I might have forgotten her had it not been for the fragrance. It seemed there were traces of it wherever I went. In the corridors, in the dining car, on the observation deck. It was insidious, like a Siren's song; it drew me into unfamiliar waters. I had always been content to let people drift by, unmarked and quickly forgotten.

Now I found myself watching for the girl. I didn't dare loiter outside her coupé, but I looked for her at breakfast, at supper, in the lounges. I imagined what I might say when I caught up to her, what she might answer. The observation deck was always crowded, but there were other places I could have shown her, where the passengers did not go and where one could drown in the beauty of the Undertow. Only, I rarely even caught glimpses of her, and when I did she was never looking at me, no matter how much I wished she might. I thought of her hand on the rail. Had her fingers drawn sparks? I did not think so, but I imagined they could, at times.

Her data record was oddly sparse. I shouldn't have looked — it was against UG policy — but I was curious.

Citizen ID: N70056886-49AC.

Date of birth: 2901-352 Standard.

Birthplace: Alpha Crucis

Nothing else. No travel history, no employment data, no medical records or family chronicle. Even the holo that accompanied her file was unconvincingly bland: a flat, blurry image of a somewhat younger girl, perhaps thirteen years Standard, with pale skin and hair. There was no mention of her perfume.

A week after leaving Kazimir I finally came upon her in one of the observation lounges on the upper deck. She sat cross-legged in an armchair, cradling a cup of kaf in both hands and watching the Undertow. Our surroundings pulsed blue and green, like pictures I had seen of the oceans on Envara.

The girl looked up at me, her eyes heavy-lidded and bruised with weariness. At least she didn't look anxious anymore. Whatever fear had held her, she had left it on-station.

"Careful," I said, gesturing at the cup. "They brew it strong here. Stuff'll keep you up for days."

"Good." She spoke softly. I resisted the urge to lean in close to hear her better. "I would rather sleep a little less."

"Ah." I took the chair next to hers, as if it was the most ordinary thing to do. Me, little more than a Train-thralled mendicant, and her a mystery. "Is it vertigo? It does take some people like that, Train travel. We have a medic—"

"No, no, it is only bad dreams. The kaf helps. I'm called Stena." She held out her hand and I braced myself for the shock of electricity. There was none, of course, just her palm warm against mine. When she turned the full force of her smile on me, I forgot the medic and the Undertow and almost my own name.

I released her hand, curled my fingers around the lingering sensation of heat. "I'm Adeet. I'm the Train's resident vagabond," I explained with a grin that had charmed other girls often enough but could not possibly match hers for intensity.

That surprised her, I could see. "You live here? On the Train? How novel."

I shrugged. "I like to travel. Besides, I like to think he'd be lonely without me. The Train," I clarified. "He's like family."

Stena was silent a long moment, and my cheeks grew hot. It had just slipped out, that last bit; I didn't usually invite strangers into that piece of my heart.

"Look." I tapped the window. Outside, a nebulous, undulating shape kept pace with the Train, fell back, reappeared. Another shot ahead, crossed the tracks, and dropped back alongside its fellow. "Sirens. They're not usually so daring, these days."

They would be singing, I knew, hoping to lure the Train to a standstill. They hated us, the Sirens did, for intruding into their demesne. For the violence of our passing, of punching through. I couldn't hear them — had never heard them, despite my years of crossing the Undertow — but my father had described their song to me.

"It's not a song, exactly," he had said, one hand flat against the window. "It's like … if you took a melody, wrapped it in the scent of jasmine, and tied it around your heart. It pulls on a body." He had cleared his throat then and sent me back to the coupé to "keep your mother company." My father was too gruff to be a poet, but that night he had come close.

"They say the Sirens' song is irresistible," I told her. I had leaned close enough that her breath stirred the fine hairs on my cheek, sent a pleasant shiver down my spine. "The longer one spends near them, the harder it is to ignore."

"I'm sorry," Stena said. A shadow crossed her face. She set the cup down on the window ledge as she stood. "I ought to try to sleep after all, I think." And then she was gone.

Her cup, I saw, was nearly half-full.

------ «» ------

I thought I'd missed my chance, but the next night she was there, in the same chair by the same window, with the same circles under her eyes. I took it for a good sign and sat down with her again, pulling my chair just a little closer. We talked for hours, or rather I did. She wanted stories of the places I'd been, anecdotes about the passengers. She wanted to know about my parents and what it was like, growing up on the Train. She had grown up on Envara, herself, in a crèche until Union Galactic sponsored her admission to the Academy. To study astronavigation, she said.

"Wow. They don't do that for just anybody. You must be pretty smart." I shoved her gently. It was a risk, teasing her.

She just shrugged. "They never said." And shoved me back, surprising a laugh out of me.

We found each other the next day. And the next night, and the next. After a while, I didn't even have to look for her. We pretended it was coincidence when she ended up behind me at the buffet or browsing the same shelves in the library car. It was an unspoken arrangement, that we would take meals together. She walked with me on my rounds to check on the passengers. She wanted to see the locomotive, but I said no; I was breaking enough rules already. The expression on her face was nearly enough for me to break that one, too.

"I was hoping to meet the Engineer."

I blinked in surprise. "This Train doesn't have one. The line is automated. You didn't know?"

She cocked her head, then, and I saw that her eyes were nearly the color of the rails. "The Union directory listed a name."

"Your information is old. The last Engineer died five years ago." Went off the rails; that's what they call it when an Engineer gives in to the Undertow and steps into the abyss. They were automating the route, they had said; they didn't need an Engineer anymore. They had wanted him to retire. "My father," I clarified, and left it at that.

"I'm sorry," she said. "That's so sad." She put her hand on my cheek, then, and kissed me.

Later, I introduced her to the other staff: Jera, the day cook; Lorn, the head of security; Anfis, the medic. Stena made polite conversation, a proper passenger standing a proper hands-breadth apart, until she could draw me away someplace private — and I knew all the private places on this Train where we could make another sort of conversation, less polite, more honest.

Not her coupé, though, nor mine. It wouldn't do, she said, and I respected that. Respected her privacy the way she respected mine. Besides, who would settle for a narrow bunk and tiny porthole when one might have a pile of blankets in the forward cupola and all of the Undertow limning a woman's skin in blue and gold?

——— «» ———

At Resupply we took on a new passenger. Staas Endreche was a Union rep and an old friend, practically a brother. It was Staas who had taught me the dials and displays, after my father died.

"Wasn't expecting to see you till Andalus," I said, unfolding myself from his bear hug.

This close to the Station, the Train was still running slow. Most of our departures took place in the morning hours, Train-time, but tonight the passengers would go to bed watching the stars flash by their windows, and they'd wake up to the swirling colors of the Undertow. It was a few more hours yet before we would punch through at the prescribed coordinates.

He shrugged. "Union got word of contraband on the Line and sent a few of us to look into it. A Switch, somewhere this side of Envara. UG's checking all the hubs."

Train lore said Sirens could smell a Switch; that they'd chew through metal to reach one, to stop a Train from punching new holes in the Undertow. It's why UG had retired them; it's why we only travel the established routes. We used to be explorers, we humans.

I glanced outside. Some immeasurable distance away, a Siren rode the crest of a copper-green wave of light, then vanished into the depths. "Wow. You find anything?"

"Not yet." His gaze followed mine. "But we will. There are only so many routes, ya'know?"

We made small talk for a while, light, comfortable conversation. I liked that I never had to try too hard with

Staas. If I didn't feel like talking, he was perfectly happy to rattle on about whatever came into his head. He had a big, easy laugh, and he liked to tease me in a way that never hurt.

"Too bad you didn't overnight at Resupply," he said, in the middle of a story about some new restaurant he'd discovered there. "Moira was asking after you. You remember Moira?" His eyes narrowed. "You don't remember Moira. She's gonna be pissed."

"Well. You know me. A bunk on every Station." It was an old joke. Only, somehow it wasn't funny anymore.

"And none of 'em your own, yeah, Addy?" Staas grinned and made a rude gesture. I rolled my eyes.

Which is when I caught sight of Stena over Staas's shoulder. Her naturally pale face had gone bone-white, and I swore under my breath. She was already hurrying out of the car before I could explain that Moira wasn't, that I wasn't—

Staas turned. His eyes followed the sway of Stena's hips, and I balled my hands into fists. I had never been jealous before, not on account of a lover.

Steady, girl, I chided myself.

"Friend of yours?" Staas asked, his voice as bland as protein paste.

I loosened my hands and reached for my cup as I sat back down. "She's interested in the Train."

"The Train, eh?" If you didn't know him, you'd think Staas was just making conversation. But I heard a thread of something else in his voice. "Union doesn't condone liaisons with paying passengers, you know that, Addy. They'll bounce you faster'n a penny floater in zero-g."

"Don't worry," I said. "It's nothing." I could still feel the electricity in her touch, the pleasant shock of her lips on mine. Her fingers, I had discovered, did indeed draw sparks, or near enough. "It's nothing."

Staas looked at me for a heartbeat, two, before his shoulders relaxed. "Yeah, you love this bucket of bolts too much to fuck it up. Me, I can't wait to get to Andalus. I've been traveling too long."

"No such thing." I grinned, on a more stable platform now. "I've been traveling as long as you have, and I'm not bored yet."

The conversation turned to more comfortable topics: mutual acquaintances, upgrades in nav-tech, the latest news from Central. All the while I kept sniffing the air for ozone until Staas asked if I was feeling all right.

"Allergies," I mumbled, and made a show of blowing my nose. "I should maybe get home, take some meds. Catch you tomorrow?" I made my escape amid promises of breakfast and a beer over lunch.

When I knocked on Stena's door, she didn't answer.

———— «» ————

The pattern of my days changed abruptly. I kept company with Staas instead of Stena, eating tasteless food and trying not to show that I was only half-listening to his stories. Stena herself was nowhere to be found, and I heard from Jera that she had started taking meals in her coupé. When I finally gathered the nerve to try her door again, I was honestly startled at the sight of her face in the viewpanel. But she only shook her head.

"I'm sorry," she said. "I can't." And the viewpanel went dark.

In the evenings, I sat in the Engineer's chair and watched the Undertow. Outside the force-rails glowed faintly, two silver lines converging some immeasurable distance away. They did not need to glow — it was a concession to the Engineer, when the Train had one. How else could a person tell up from down in this formless place? It was easy to lose oneself in the Undertow.

Just like, somewhere between Kazimir and the hub, I had lost myself in Stena.

Staas finally caught on that something was different, but I couldn't exactly tell him. He was right; I'd be bounced for sure if UG found out. Station time was our own, but on the Train we were employees first. Even me.

A week Standard after Resupply, a week of silences and solitary cups of kaf, I smelled electricity again. I knew she was there before I even stepped into the cab. She was perched on the Engineer's chair — my chair, I thought jealously — gazing out at the rails. My face made a dark smudge in the window past her shoulder.

"This car is off limits to passengers," I said, with perhaps more acidity than was warranted. Still, it was true and I was heart-sore and a little angry.

She spoke not to me, but to my reflection. "I'm sorry," she said.

She was made of apologies, it seemed.

Outside the window, I caught a flash of jaws, a shimmer of blue: the biggest Siren I had ever seen, racing the Train.

"For what? For this?" I gestured at my chair. "Or for pulling a disappearing act? It was stupid, what Staas said. What I said. But you didn't even let me explain. You just—"

"I should never have boarded this Train." Her words were so soft, I only fully understood them by reading her reflection's lips.

"If you hadn't," I said, "I would never have met you."

"Exactly," she said. One word, one resounding note, and it pulled at my heart like nothing I'd ever felt before. I let it draw me into the cab, to the chair.

"Don't say that," I said, and leaned over the back of the chair to nuzzle her cheek. "Stena—"

Her hand was resting on the brake lever.

I froze. "What are you doing?"

"She's trying to kill us," came a voice from the doorway. Staas, and he was holding a gun. "She's the Switch."

She's the Switch.

Stena's apologies fell into place, started to make sense. Already I had spotted a third Siren, and a fourth appeared just at the edge of my range of vision.

"Get out," Stena said, and her voice was firm now, unwavering. "Both of you, get out or I'll stop the Train right here and we'll all be lost." Something slid up and past the window: a pale underbelly, a flickering tail. The Sirens would be waiting, if we stopped. I imagined I heard a faint melody, felt a gentle tug.

"Stena, please." This Train was my home. My family. This locomotive was my heartbeat, my breath — or had been, until I met her. "You don't want to do this. It's just the Sirens. Stay with me; fight them off."

"Do you know what they do to Switches? To people like me?" She was speaking to me, but looking at Staas. He had something in his other hand. A collar, I realized. I put a hand to my own throat.

"Switches are unpredictable, Addy. Dangerous." The Train rocked. The enormous blue Siren flashed by again. "See? There's a reason we keep them apart. Controlled. Move, Addy. Get behind me. Let me take her, and I won't mention any of this to Central. They might even let you stay on the Train."

"I needed an Engineer. I found you. Any other Train…" She trailed off, met my eyes in the window. "It's not the Sirens. I never wanted to hurt you, or him." She lay her free hand on the control panel, patted it gently. "I'm sorry."

I didn't know if she was apologizing to me or my Train.

The Sirens' songs were irresistible, I had told her. Odysseus in the ancient epics had his sailors stop up their ears with wax so they wouldn't go mad and jump into the sea, but Odysseus wanted to hear it for himself. My father had never denied the pull of the Sirens' song. It was part of the traveling life, part of the Train. Whether or not he had finally succumbed, as UG said, I still don't know. Maybe he had, or maybe he had just missed my mother that much. A melody wrapped in perfume and tied to your heart.

Four steps took me from the Engineer's chair to the door of the cab. I kept myself between Staas and Stena the whole time.

I looked at Staas a long, long moment. Staas, my near-brother, my friend.

"Go. If you hurry," I told him, "you can power up the tail. Take the Train back to Resupply. You've got thirty seconds to get to the next car and decouple." And I slapped the panel, shutting the door between us. Staas looked at me wide-eyed, then turned and bolted down the corridor.

I watched him go, counting under my breath.

Five.

Five steps back to the control panel.

Ten.

I was ten years old when I met Staas.

Fifteen.

I was fifteen when my father went off the rails.

Twenty.

I was twenty years old when Stena kissed me.

Twenty-five.

My Train had twenty-five passenger cars. The first one behind the locomotive had been my father's, until it was mine.

Thirty.

Stena pulled the brake.

The Train shuddered and jolted; worse, he screamed. Trains weren't meant to stop in the Undertow. Trains drowned here. I felt his aversion in the pit of my belly, a nauseating twist that had nothing to do with gravity and everything to do with the utter wrongness of what was happening.

I lost my grip on the chair back, lost my footing, too, and slid into the opposite wall. I sat there, dazed, as the engine fell silent and the floorboards grew still under my palms.

The light of the force-rails wavered and diffused into sparks as I watched. Blinking, I scanned the depths for something to latch my gaze onto, some sort of anchor or buoy, but there was none. Just the slow rolling waves of pale light that told me we were still in the Undertow. In the Undertow and stilled.

Lost, I thought. There were no rails. There was no path out of the Undertow. Panic bubbled up, and I shoved it back down, covered it with something not unlike wonder.

"You really are. You're a Switch."

"And you're an Engineer," she said. Her teeth were bared; it was not a smile. "Or you could be. Your Train will die if you can't get him moving again. Or the Sirens will take us." Outside, an enormous shape slid by the window, followed by another. The Train lurched. Something scraped against the hull.

"I can't see the rails." The air in the cab felt close, stale. My words scratched against my throat.

"An Engineer doesn't need rails. Don't you know anything?"

I bristled. "I know that you can't get back on the rails once you've gone off."

"You don't need them," she insisted. "You just need to get him moving again. I'll do the rest." She stroked the control panel again. The hair on my arms stood up as the cab filled with the scent of ozone.

Trains are not living ships; they do not breathe, think, move independently. Still, they are more than machines, or I have always thought so. A stalled Train is little more than a corpse. And my Train, right now, was dying.

"Move," I said, and she did, sliding out of the chair to stand at my elbow as I took her place. The instrument panel glowed faintly; various displays blinked and flashed. This wasn't my job; I wasn't an Engineer, had never trained for this. But I had watched my father often enough, spent enough time in the cab with him and without him. I knew what to do. I released the brake and started adjusting dials.

Had Staas reached the tail before the Sirens caught up to the severed body of the Train? I couldn't be sure. I could only hope. The rear camera feed showed only static.

The engine began to spin up, a hum that started at the crown of my head and vibrated through my bones until it steadied and faded into the background. I checked each dial twice before I realized I was missing the thrum of the mag-wheels against the rails.

"Where are we going?" A question I had never needed to ask before. Envara to Andalus Minor via Kazimir. My pulse quickened.

"Wherever we want," she said, and smiled. Her fingers crackled with static, and the Undertow flashed in response.

———— «›» ————

The Train is in our blood, or the traveling is. Our Train is seven cars long now, including the residence-coupé that Staas had left us — a kindness, that. We take passengers, sometimes, and goods. If the authorities ever seize us, if Union Galactic manages to track us down, we'll be grounded. Worse, they'll collar Stena again, make sure I quietly disappear. Went off the rails, they'll say, like her father, and it would be true. I won't let that happen.

"Steady," I tell my daughter as we prepare to punch through. "Trust the Train." And I cover her tiny fingers with mine so we can release the brake together. The Train is in her blood, too.

———— « O » ————

Christine Hanolsy

Christine Hanolsy is a (primarily) science fiction and fantasy writer who simply cannot resist a love story. She serves on the editorial staff of the online writing community YeahWrite, where her main portfolio includes microprose, flash fiction, and poetry. She completed her first novel—*The Copper Dragon*, a post-technological pseudo-steampunk sci-fi adventure—in 2018, and is currently writing its sequel. Christine lives in the Pacific Northwest with her wife and their two sons. She blogs at christinehanolsy.com and can be found on Facebook (facebook.com/hanolsy) and Twitter (@hanolsy).

One Way Journey

Peter Hargraves

The end of another work week, the boss in his face every five minutes, angry as hell most of the time. It couldn't end soon enough. However, the thought of the walk to the diner in the blizzard had filled him with dread. But here he was now, almost.

Cold, so cold. The wind was biting, the snow in his face. He stumbled on. With a numbed hand shielding his eyes, he spied the narrow diner. It stood with curtains drawn, showing only chinks of light hinting at the life inside. He stepped forward, opened the door at the end and blinked in the sudden brightness. The occupants looked at him in friendly silence. He nodded at a couple of people he knew. There was nowhere to sit so he ordered a coffee over the heads of those at the counter.

The diner lurched slightly. He grabbed the edge of the counter between two people, just in case. Gradually people got up and made their way to the exit. He sat down on a vacated stool and drank his coffee while the diner swayed gently to and fro. The crush of people had left the curved-roofed car overly warm. He took his coat off and slung it over his shoulder before following the others to the exit.

Here came a moment of fear. He stepped onto the vibrating steel plates, afraid — as always — that there might be nothing but the snowy ground outside. Then he relaxed as he saw the narrow corridor of the sleeping car beyond. True, large patches of nothing partly obscured the walls and the floor, like a painting that hadn't been finished. But these quirks were always there at the beginning. He grabbed a handhold for support, before it vanished for a moment, leaving him lurching. Gradually everything flickered into life, leaving everything solid; the sleeping car stood complete unto itself. Dreaming car. Through the windows, the night went by: a parade of streetlights, the lights of the occasional farmhouse that were there for a moment and then were gone.

A steward led him to a cabin. Hanging up his coat inside he walked on, through several more sleeping cars, through a car where earlier arrivals played board games, past the bar car, to one where a folk circle had assembled. A young woman about his age in a plaid skirt and knitted wool tights sat cross-legged on the beige carpet and played guitar and sang. He took one of the few seats left and listened.

When she finished, to applause and calls of "Bravo!", her face lit up. She moved her arms around herself just slightly, unseen unless you watched carefully. Protective, shy.

He got up and asked her what it was she had just played.

"Oh, I know that singer," he exclaimed, after her answer. "Just never that song before."

"Do you play?"

When he nodded, she handed him the instrument. He was self-conscious of his voice and he fluffed some of the finger-picking, but got some polite applause at the end of his song. Taking back the guitar, she whispered in his ear, "Your voice is full of emotion."

"Dreadful technically, though."

"Divinely emotional. Like the song might last an eternity." She laughed. "I mean that in a good way."

The circle progressed several more times around, guitars interspersed with banjos and ukuleles, until it was very late. They shared her guitar. Out of the corner of his eye he caught her looking at him a few times. At some point after many people drifted off to bed, he found her on the seat beside him. He placed a hand on her knee. A hand appeared on top of his in affirmation and she leaned into him.

"I'm tired," she said. He helped her up. She didn't let go of his hand as they headed together, by unspoken agreement, for the sleeping cars.

The sleeping cars started to sway and they placed their hands on the walls once in a while to steady themselves. A young man, as small-boned as a woman, with coiffed hair dyed purple, yellow pants, and a bright floral shirt, blocked the aisle as he fiddled with the latch to a cabin. He turned and the three of them smiled at each other and gave nods of recognition. When the young man had disappeared into his cabin, they continued on down the corridors, through two more sleeping cars until she indicated that they were at her cabin. Once she had unlatched the door and they were inside, she leaned the guitar against the wall.

"You've met him before?" she said, a slight tension showing on her face.

"Yes. I've shared a table with him in the dining car. And I always see him around. Looks as if he rides the train all the time, as if he's reluctant to leave."

"You like him?"

"Yes."

The tension on her face melted away and her eyes lit up. She reached forward and kissed him on the lips. They kissed and cuddled on the bed like high school sweethearts. She pulled him close, the tiredness she'd complained of earlier seemingly gone. Anyone who saw them wouldn't have believed this might well be just a one-night stand. He feared for a moment she might not be real, might disappear like parts of the sleeping car had at the beginning. When the knitted tights and plaid skirt came off, he found her thighs were considerably more substantial than those of a fashion model's. His pants and shirt fell to the floor; he fumbled with the buttons to her blouse, and then the clasp of her bra. Then they were intertwined, he with his hands all over her torso. She writhed and moaned, climaxed with an out-of-control shriek. She laughed at her own loud passion and he laughed with her. They slept well, he without dreaming, as if the evening had been enough in itself. He woke up once on the narrow bed as she jerked to and fro, moaning, trying to escape a nightmare. He held her until she calmed.

———— «◊» ————

It was late morning when they woke. The tracks were better laid here and the train didn't sway or lurch. She pulled up the blind to a cold sunny day with snow-covered trees. Snow drifts lay sculpted on the roads, visible whenever the train broke from the forest. He walked down to the diner. He supposed he should call it the dining car now, since a locomotive pulled it at considerable speed behind the rest of the train. It turned out they'd missed breakfast, but there was space at the first lunch sitting. He took two lunch tickets from the waiter, loaded up with muffins and coffee to tide them over, and headed back to the cabin.

The train came to a halt at a major station as they were finishing lunch. He said, "I usually get off here and catch the next train back home."

"So do I."

A question hung in the air unasked. Go back, as always, or keep going. Given that a romance might be budding … that might last forever, or fizzle in just a few days… He looked at her over their empty plates.

As if she had read his thoughts she said, "Someone once told me that further ahead you go through spectacular mountains. Snow-capped ones, often with cotton ball clouds low enough that the train goes through them and disappears into the fog."

They got their coats, stepped down from the train and took a walk along the platform. The return train wasn't due for an hour. The sun warmed them and no wind blew.

They walked past car after car until they reached the locomotive. In preparation for the next leg of the journey, the fireman shoveled coal into the open firebox that revealed the orange-yellow glow within. A little steam issued from the cylinders. Smoke wafted from the chimney.

"Can you live here all the time?" he asked. "On the train, I mean."

Her head jerked up just slightly, as if the question had been hanging there, perhaps just below normal awareness, now surfaced like a buried memory.

"I mean," he said, "what about money and stores to buy clothes in, and stuff like that." Some distance off, he saw, out of the corner of his eye, the young man they had run into the previous night walking away from them, still in his bright clothes. She looked around to see what had grabbed his attention and, without saying a word, ran after the man — the man who, as far as he knew, rode the rails all the time, reluctant to leave. A reluctance he was now discovering in himself.

The train whistle sounded, shrill and loud. She reached the other man and he turned to her. A lively conversation took place. With a second shriek of the whistle, the loco chuffed and its wheels did a half rotation, sliding on the rails.

The wheels came around again, this time gaining some adhesion; the train inched forward. She was a bit too far away for him to see the look on her face as she ran back toward him, but she leaped up, fists punching the air above her head, for a moment, an eternity. The coal tender traveled past him, and he climbed aboard the first car. She climbed onto a car farther back, leaning out, hanging on by one hand, the other waving free, her face visible now, radiant as a sunburst.

Back in her cabin they lay on the bunk in each other's arms. Her thigh disappeared into nothingness as did his calf. He stroked her side, having to stop each time he reached her vanished thigh, until finally she became whole again.

"Do you think all this ... is real?" she said finally.

A long pause. "Maybe it doesn't matter."

—— « o » ——

Peter Hargraves

Peter Hargraves has a Ph.D. in Physics and has spent most of his working life in the high tech sector of Ottawa, Canada. Somewhere along the line he decided he preferred writing to Physics and turned to corporate writing and (in his spare time) to fiction.

Facebook; https://www.facebook.com/peter.hargraves.35

The Horn of Winter

Jason Lane

It was in the wind moaning over the steppes. It was in the howls of the wolves echoing through the woods. Singing through the Siberian night. Clear. Pure.

The Horn.

Anya heard it. Felt it. A tremble through her. A song, calling to her. Calling to her as she was forced out of the cabin with her father, her mother, her sisters and brother, and into the fresh fallen snow.

The scream of the train's whistle wrenched her from her dreams. She sat up sharply, blinking. The world closed around her and took the shape of the cramped rail car. Peasants swaddled in heavy clothes filled the seats, a number clustered around the stove in the corner.

Captain Berlitz looked at her from the seat opposite. Broad, with a drooping mustache and bristling salt and pepper beard, he wore a heavy winter overcoat with a wolf fur collar.

"Something the matter?"

She shook her head. "Nothing."

He maintained his stare. She looked away. It was so beastly hot in the train. All the bodies crammed together. The smell of them was near overpowering. And dark. So dark with the winter night outside, the wind howling. The train swaying and beating the tracks with a *shakka shakka* sound.

She reached up and touched the locket around her neck. She popped it open and looked at the people within. A man with a swooping mustache in a fine red military coat and a blue sash. A woman, stiff and proud but with eyes of deepest compassion and pain. Children gathered before them. Girls and a boy, all smiling up at the camera.

"Put it away," Captain Berlitz said. He was glancing about the car. Some of the peasants had raised their heads.

She scowled at them, but snapped it shut with a sound like a steel trap and tucked it under her heavy coat. A few looked over, but at the sight of Berlitz in his military jacket they wisely turned away.

"You should not bring that out," Berlitz said.

"Why not? I don't care if they see. They should see what they did."

"Anya…"

"Don't call me that."

She looked out the window. She had seen the other name on his lips. She huddled into her thick woolen coat, the fabric itching and rough. She remembered the softness of silk and the smoothness of a carriage ride, bells tinkling along the sled.

"Why should I help them?" she said again.

"They are our people."

"Are they? I wonder who forgot that."

Berlitz's dark eyes glinted. She turned away from him. He had his opinions. She had hers.

She watched the barren landscape swoop by as the train rattled on. A light winter buried the deep forests and fields. Weeks they'd ridden the trains. Weeks of hiding, ducking from soldiers, fleeing the west, always heading east. East, into the lands the Cossacks claimed inch by bloody inch in years gone by.

Russia.

Her Russia.

She leaned her forehead against the cool glass, watching it all pass by. She dozed, soothed by the swaying of the train, its whistle screaming in her dreams.

A different scream woke her.

Anya sat up. Ice crawled down her spine as the shriek pierced through the air. The other passengers were awake, milling in confusion. Berlitz grabbed her.

"Down!" he shouted and pulled her beneath the seat. The scream roared over the train. Bullets pierced the ceiling, stitching through the aisle and seats, sending splinters flying. A man fell by her hand, his eyes staring and glassy. And blood, red blood, spilled across the floor.

Anya stared, fascinated. The scream grew fainter. Fell away. She scrambled away from the body and rose to the window, peered out into the white of the day. A shape like a bird swung about through the sky. Soaring back toward the train. It began to dive, screaming like a banshee.

She winced, covering her ears, shutting tight her eyes. The winter wind gave a great howl. A sheet of white washed over the window. The scream of the plane fell away, coughing in the dark.

Faded.

Somewhere, she heard a muffled *whoomph*.

Anya cracked open her eyes, peering through the storm. A figure flickered just at the edge of sight, standing on a snowy mound. A man in black, a soldier's coat whipping about him.

She blinked. He was gone.

The train moved on, winter bleeding into the car through the bullet holes. People sobbed and shuffled about. Later, they passed by the tail of a plane stamped with the Iron Cross, sticking out of the snow like an arm raised in stiff salute.

≪≫

They rolled into the station hours later. Anya stepped off with Berlitz and stood aside as soldiers carried out the bodies, stacking them like cordwood on the station platform. Anya turned away from the men in red, pulling her hood lower.

Berlitz's heavy hand landed on her shoulder. "Come, Anya. We must go."

She nodded stiffly and turned. Her face was as white as the snow as they walked down the street of the former peasant village.

"We will meet guides," he said. "They will take us on."

"They know the way?"

"It is the old country," Berlitz said.

It was all the old country, she thought. Yet new buildings rose about them. Heavy, brutal things of cement and brick. Far more were the old, wooden ones that slumped beneath snow and their years, blending into the background of the encroaching forest and the drifts of white piled against their sides.

They reminded her of the monk. The one with those powerful, intense eyes. The one who gazed into the face of her brother and calmed him and stopped his weeping wounds. She grew a little warm at the memory of him, speaking in a soft, deep voice to her and her sisters. She remembered him passing by them one at a time, smiling, speaking. She remembered him pausing when he reached her and placing his hand on her shoulder, staring deep into her eyes.

"You," he had said.

Later he had spoken in murmured conference with her father.

But that had been before. Another life. Another name.

Berlitz brought Anya to one of the slumping buildings and pushed open the door. A samovar simmered in the corner and icons were gathered on the wall. Two men were within. One, his feet propped up on a stool, was big as a bull. His head was slumped forward, a heavy fur hat resting on the back of his chair. Not far away, a second man, thin as a rail, was meticulously writing on a bunch of papers, his hair slick and black, tongue sticking out the corner of his mouth.

The thin man looked up as they entered. His eyes flicked to Berlitz.

"Berlitz?" he said.

"Rogozhin," Berlitz said, then to the large man, "Boris."

Boris grunted. Stirred and raised his head.

Rogozhin rose, his legs creaking faintly. He stalked forward and peered at them. "So, this is her, is it? The one who will blow the Horn and save our Mother Russia?"

"Yes," Berlitz said. His heavy hand rested protectively on her shoulder. "You'll take us on?"

Rogozhin peered closer, ignoring the tall soldier for the moment. "I saw a portrait of you. A very long time ago now.

In the papers before the Revolution. And such comics! Is it true what they said about the monk?"

Anya shied away from the man. His intent eyes and thin-boned face reminded her too strongly of another man from a life before. He grinned.

"Rogozhin!" Berlitz barked.

Rogozhin jerked upright. He waved his hands errantly. "Yes. Yes. All prepared. Not uncommon for men to make the trip along the mountain. Bourgeois used to do it all the time. I sometimes took generals along it before the war. But these days you need papers. Used to be just a few bribes but these new men are all about papers. Fine with me!" Rogozhin chuckled and swept a hand back toward the desk. "Cheaper than it, I say! Always new men too. Very keen. Hard to get a good word in."

Berlitz moved over to the papers and looked them over. Left alone, Anya's eyes trailed over to the samovar, the fireplace, the chairs and desk. Anywhere not at the leering Rogozhin.

"Yes! All ready. Boris!" Rogozhin barked, kicking the bigger man. "Get up! We go now."

Boris rumbled, yawned and rose unsteadily. He crouched down and picked up a pair of massive boots, jamming his feet into them one at a time. He stood slowly and grabbed the fur hat, pulling it over his ears. "Yes," he said, fetching a rifle.

"Not many go there now," she heard Rogozhin continue. "Wolves very aggressive. Soldiers have been warning people away. We think they are too hungry."

"Do you?" Berlitz said.

"Oh yes," Rogozhin said, delighted. "But we will make it. I know all the short cuts to the mountain. So long as you know what you are looking for."

"We do."

"We should not bring the girl," Boris rumbled.

"We must," Berlitz said.

"Then we best go soon," Rogozhin said. "There may be shooting. I hear one of the German's planes shot up your train. They do not usually fly out so far. Very far from the front. Do you think they know?"

"They may," Berlitz said. "I expect there will be trouble."

"Good," Rogozhin piped, patting his pistol. "I could use some new boots."

«»

The winds of winter sliced across the barren steppes. A Cossack village, ruined, tumbled upon itself, clawed out of the snow like bones of timber, nail and spar. They walked through it, single file. Heavy furs against the cold, rifles slung over backs.

Anya alone carried none. She trudged, the rough cloth of her coat scratching her skin. Exhaustion plagued her after the long march from the village and through the snows.

"Only a little further, Anya," Berlitz said. "Only a little further."

"I'm coming," she gasped. "I'm coming."

She lifted her face and, in the distance, saw the peak. It rose out of the landscape, bald and terrible. The nearer to the mountain they drew, the harsher the wind cut and the snows stirred.

They went on. Captain Berlitz led the way, his drooping mustache and beard speckled with ice. Boris followed, the heavy man's trudge breaking a path through the choking snow, his stolid face red from the biting wind. Behind them came Rogozhin, thin as a rail, but of the hardy peasant stock.

"My father took me hunting this way," Boris puffed as he forged ahead. "He was big man. Knew every trail. He hunted with rifle. Good rifle. Still used old flintlock in those days. I remember sound when it fired." He made a popping sound with his mouth that made Anya wince. "It was good rifle."

They rested in what had been an old tavern. Rogozhin grumbled as he searched the basement for a drop of vodka or beer. Boris collapsed on a chair, and Berlitz kindled a fire in the hearth. A glow began, filling the room, light flickering on corners and edges of dust covered barrels and old cracked steins. Anya bundled down in a chair near the hearth, flinching as Berlitz broke a table into kindling and fed the fire.

The warmth pushed away the cold, but the darkness of the abandoned place lingered just beyond, crouched in corners like the *domovoy* her nanny had once spoken of, describing the little house spirits that the peasants still had faith in. An altar stood in the corner, the once fine gold paint faded and smudged.

"Driven out," Rogozhin said, stomping upstairs. "Long gone I'd say. The Reds came through."

"Could have been the Whites," Berlitz said.

"Doesn't matter. Soldiers! That's all I know. Only soldiers take all the liquor and burn everything else." He spat into a corner and slumped into a seat. "Left the icons. Probably the Reds. We'll stay here tonight. Take the mountain tomorrow."

"Is it far?" Berlitz asked.

Rogozhin laughed, a sharp, biting sound that Anya hated. "Noooo. Not far. Just near the foot of the mountain. People about don't like it, though. Probably why no one else took up residence. No one ever goes near the mountain. They fear a curse. Peasant stories talk of the cold and a winter that never leaves. That it gathers in the valley even during summer. Hah! High time we got rid of all that."

"My grandmama talked of the valley," Boris said. "She said we must never go. That it is too cold and always cold. Not a place for men. But wolves. Many wolves."

Anya left them to their conversation. She went to the smoke-stained window and looked out into the snow. Winter hung heavily over the remains of the village. The forests grew thick on the outskirts of town.

She squinted, staring, spotting a dark figure against the tree line.

"Something's happening."

Instantly all three men were moving. Boris went to the door, rifle in hand. Rogozhin drew his own and dashed up the stairs, peeking out a hole in the wall. Berlitz joined her, peering out at the night.

"What did you see?" the old soldier asked.

"A man. I ... think."

"You think?"

"I saw him before. At the train. After the plane attacked."

His mouth tightened. "We're leaving."

"Now?"

"Now."

Boris grunted and threw his pack back on. Rogozhin came running back down the rotting stairs with a sound that sent Anya's spine rattling. Berlitz grabbed her and pulled her to the back of the old inn.

The kitchen was caked with dust, and pots and pans clattered under their feet as they moved to the back door. The way through was open, the door smashed in by some boot in years past. Through it they reentered the snow choked village. The ruins rose around them in ragged shapes. The sun was setting, stitching the sleet gray sky with a blaze of colors.

"Move. We must move!" Berlitz grunted.

There was a crack. Anya barely heard it. Then Rogozhin reeled about, clutching his chest. He fell into the snow with a thump, and in moments the snow was filling the hole his body had made.

"Run!" Berlitz shouted.

And they were running.

Anya looked back and saw other figures chasing. Men in storm gray coats and helmets that swept down to cover their ears raced from the tree line. Near a dozen of them. Berlitz turned, firing with his pistol. One of the gray men went down, feet flying from under him, looking as if he had slipped while skating on the Saint Petersburg canals. He never got up. The others came on. Grim, purposeful men like those who had taken her and her family out behind the cabin.

"The trees!" Berlitz bellowed. "The trees!"

The soldiers in gray kept coming, firing wildly now. The snow puffed with every missed round.

Over the gunshots, she heard the howls.

The wolves streamed past the trees. Ragged, mangy, starving things. The men in gray shouted in surprise. One swung about but the wolf was already on him. Teeth fastened on the man's throat. Both went down, struggling in the snow. The others fired again. One's weapon jammed in the frigid winter air, and he went down screaming under a mass of fang and claw and bristling fur.

Boris bellowed as a wolf tackled him into the snow.

"Run Anya!" Berlitz roared as more wolves raced for him. He fired, drew his saber from his belt and hacked the first one down. Blood spilled, red and so warm it steamed when it hit the snow. She heard the sobs of her sisters. Her mother and father's painful dignity as they looked down the men in red. The maids whimpering and crying. And a voice echoed through time, shouting at her the same word from that dark night.

"Run!"

Anya clamped her hands over her ears to silence the screams, the howls, and ran into the woods.

《 》

The winds roared down through the trees.

The snow had risen to her knees. Every step was a fight through snow so hard the crust broke with a crack under her feet, leaving solid pits in the white that swiftly filled. Her breath steamed in the air. Her lungs burned with effort and her face tingled to the roots of her hair with that cold. That terrible, terrible cold.

Berlitz was dead.

She shuddered and buried her face in her collar.

Father was dead.

Mother. Olga. Tatiana. Maria. Alexei. All dead. All gone.

She was alone.

And in the distance, she heard the howls.

Closer.

Closer.

She fought on. Fought forward. There wasn't anything else to do. If she stopped, she'd freeze, perhaps even before the wolves got to her. She almost laughed at the thought of the animals breaking their teeth on her blackened, frozen face. But that was too near hysterics, and instead she choked on the sound.

A root, hidden under the snow, caught her foot. With a cry, she went down. For a moment, she lay in the snow, gasping, sobbing.

The wind died to a whisper.

She raised her head.

The man stood before her. His booted feet only just touched the snow. His dark soldier's cloak was wrapped about him and a sloping helmet not in fashion for a hundred years or more sat on his head. A saber was sheathed at his side. His beard was a thick white thing, mustache sweeping in a style popular when Frenchmen marched across Europe under their emperor.

But his eyes were older. Far, far older than mere centuries. Not even the monk's eyes had held such power. The casual ease to carry death. The utter absence of any warmth. A thousand could die at this man's boots. A hundred thousand could claw at his cloak and he wouldn't even look down at them as they stiffened with frost and stilled. He could pass through fields and leave whole villages to starve without an ounce of interest. He didn't mean to. He simply did. He simple was.

Anya had faced death before. Looked down the barrels of rifles as she stood, soaked in the blood of her mother and sisters in the cold snow behind the cabin.

She saw something worse than death in those eyes.

The fur of her collar was stiff like porcupine spines around her head as she stood. Her tears froze on her cheeks, burning with the numbing pain. She looked him in those eyes.

"Where?"

He moved his head. An acknowledgement? A greeting? She wasn't sure. But he stepped aside, and, like a white curtain to the stage, the blizzard parted.

A cave lay before her, cut into the mountain's face. Stone worked with strange designs flanked it in a pair of heavy pillars. Shapes without forms she could recall spiraled across the two *bautasteiner*. They reminded her starkly of the writing in the old illuminated manuscripts. But this was rawer. More unevenly cut, like the winds had carved the stones.

He said nothing. Merely stood aside. Waiting. She glanced his way, then ventured through the cavern mouth and into the darkness.

Her footsteps echoed hollowly within, chimed off icicles hanging from the ceiling. She breathed in. Out. Her breath no longer puffed in the air.

A blue light shone ahead. She forged on until the light became a doorway, and she stepped through, and into a memory.

The walls were made of clearest ice, like she had walked into a room of crystal. Elegant filigree curled in corners and arched above. Pale light glowed from a chandelier hanging above, its every candle lit with a blue flame. It was a place she knew. The palace at Saint Petersburg.

In the middle of the room stood a throne. And on it rested a woman of striking beauty. She sat, still, her skin like marble. Her hair was white as snow, and her gown as blue as the water from the freshest spring. Her throne was worked from the trunk of a single great tree, its branches rising into the air to spread out and clasp the roof of the palatial chamber.

On her lap, in her hands, was a horn of antler.

Anya stared at the woman. Slowly, she approached, her footsteps chiming in the stillness of the chamber. She climbed the cut steps up to the throne and looked down at the Horn.

She reached out and grasped it. It was stuck. With a scowl, she yanked.

The woman shattered like glass. Anya gasped, stepping back as the woman's flesh fell to pieces on the throne. The shards dissolved, melting on the ground.

The throne was empty.

Anya held the Horn.

She ran her fingers over the ancient thing and traced designs like those on the stones outside. She felt the heft of it.

So, this was it. This was what would save her country? Yet, even as she held it, she knew there was more to it. She turned slowly, and he was there.

He stood in the middle of the room, his black soldier's cloak rustling in a wind that wasn't there. Around him, wolves made of the rotting, black ice of spring crowded around his feet. The old man stared at her. Not accusing. Not eager. He simply waited. The wolves sat on their haunches, expectant.

She stood before the throne beneath the mountain and put the Horn to her lips.

And blew.

The sound boomed through the cavernous palace. Rang off the icicles in the passage beyond like a chiming band of the Moscow Concert Hall. The wolves sat up straighter. The rotting ice of their forms grew more solid. Clearer until they shone like the finest diamonds, the bared fangs quivering with eagerness. Anya drew back her lips, gasped, her throat raw with the cold like she'd swallowed razor blades.

She blew it again.

The sound boomed past the mountain and into the valley. She saw it reach out, swirling the snow and wind. She saw more men in thick gray coats and helmets fighting through the snows stop and listen. The wind picked up, rustling their thick winter garb, biting them with the bitterest cold. They screamed, shielding themselves, hunkering down as the buffeting winds ripped through them.

Anya gasped; her mouth hot with the bloody iron taste. She blew again.

The long note rang deep. The wolves of ice lifted their muzzles and howled with it. The old man touched his sword and drew it. He turned and left the space beneath the mountain. The wolves carried past him, running with the wind that raced out before them, carrying them beyond the frozen shapes of the men in gray, flesh blackened, frost crusting them, and arms raised like statues in torment. The wolves surged past, rising into the air. The wind in the valley churned with them, ripping the snow from the trees into a column of ice.

Anya took her lips from the horn. Breathed in.

And blew once more.

The Russian Winter surged from the valley, spreading across the country. Rivers cracked as they froze. Men and women hunched in their homes and huddled near stoves. She saw them all. Saw the stormy winter clouds race in every direction. North and south and east and west. The winds howled with the voice of wolves. And above them all came the thundering roar of the Horn.

Winter swept down, deepening. To the west it blanketed the landscapes in drifts of white. Aircrafts painted with the Iron Cross sputtered and struggled. Tanks creaked as they fought to advance, their engines freezing. Trucks ground to a halt. Trains screamed, ice encrusting them, streaming away in ribbons of steam as they struggled over tracks shining with frost. Men died huddled for warmth and were buried in the snow.

The winds swept through broken buildings, attacking men in red and gray without distinction. Freezing hands and feet and faces. The ground hardened like cement in the terrible cold. She could fairly hear the earth tighten in the grip of true winter. As if on a map, she saw the dark advance from the west stall and halt across her homeland. She saw the men who ordered the deaths of her family sit back and order preparations as the winter rattled the windows of their snug, brutal buildings. She saw forges billow smoke and factories rumble to life with the toils of industry, turning white snow black with ash and smog.

The note died. Her thoughts receded from the country and back into the valley, down the passage and into the palace beneath the earth. She lowered the Horn and touched her numb, blue lips. She exhaled, and the thin puff of warmth died in the air.

Slowly she sat down on the throne at the root of the mountain. She sighed, a sound that whispered through the room of ice and stone and crystal. She set the Horn in her lap and closed her eyes, and dreamed her winter dreams of palaces and czars, and a Russia that had once been.

———— « O » ————

Jason Lane

Jason Lane is an aspiring author from Whitehorse, Yukon. He was born, raised, and educated there with brief forays to the south where the weather is milder. He has a number of self published works and has been featured in numerous anthologies.

If you enjoyed this read

Please leave a review on Amazon, Facebook, Good Reads or Instagram.

It takes less than five minutes and it really does make a difference.

If you're not sure how to leave a review on Amazon:

1. *Go to amazon.com.*

2. *Type in Fantastic Trains edited by Neil Enock and when you see it, click on it.*

3. *Scroll down to Customer Reviews. Nearby you'll see a box labeled Write a Review. Click it.*

4. *Now, if you've never written a review before on Amazon, they might ask you to create a name for yourself.*

5. *Reviews can be as simple as, "Loved the book! Can't wait for the Next!" (Please don't give the story away.)*

And that's it!

Brian Hades, publisher

About the Editor

Neil Enock is an author, actor, screenwriter, filmmaker, inventor, and media presenter. He created and hosts "Train Talk TV" on iTunes, which has over a million viewers/listeners, and just completed his first feature Science Fiction film, SomeWhen – which Neil both wrote and produced. In addition to his many talents, Neil has a vast knowledge of trains (real, toy and imaginary) and a passion for storytelling.

About the Ads

The ads on pages 54 and 138 were created by Kim Solem. Kim is a licensed mechanical engineer who is fascinated by steam power and has been operating a recycled 1887 steam locomotive engine to heat a brownstone building. "Sadly, the old boy developed a crack and is being replaced by a modern steam boiler."

Need something new to read?

If you liked Fantastic Trains, you should also consider these other EDGE-Lite titles…

The Black Chalice

by Marie Jakober

Award Winning Novel...

It's 1134. In a bleak monastery somewhere in Germany, Paul of Ardiun begins the chronicle he has been ordered by his religious superiors to write: the story of the knight Karelian Brandeis, for whom Paul once served as squire, who fell prey to the evil wiles of a seductive sorceress, thereby precipitating civil war and the downfall of a king.

As Paul starts to write tale, the sorceress herself appears to him. He is a liar, she tells him, and always has been. She lays a spell on Paul: from this moment, he will only be able to write the truth.

But what is the truth? All his life he has rearranged his memories to suit his faith. Now, against his will, an entirely different story begins to emerge.

About Award winning author Marie Jakober,

Marie Jakober graduated with honors from Ottawa's Carleton University. She has written nine novels. The Black Chalice was awarded the Independent Publisher Book Award and Only Call Us Faithful received the Michael Shaara Award for Excellence in Civil War Fiction.

Druids
(Part One of the Druids series)

by Barbara Galler-Smith & Josh Langston

The DRUIDS Saga begins…

For over 1000 years, Celts rule Europe. The most revered are the Druids: bards, healers, judges, and seers. A special few protect the secrets of ancient Earth magic, including a healer from Iberia, and a seer from Belgica.

Rhonwen, the healer, keeps the Druidic culture and practises alive in a land ravaged by a Roman civil war. Sworn by her Mother to a blood oath of vengeance, she must choose between fulfilling the promise or following her own heart`s path.

Mallec, the seer, is sent from his warrior tribe to the center of druidic learning to become a scholar. His training does not prepare him for an unexpected discovery of an ancient rite for immortality. Once mastered, Mallec must protect the knowledge from those who thirst for its power and are bent on his destruction.

Seemingly separate paths, entwined by dreams and destiny, the DRUIDS saga unfolds.

By the Light of Camelot

edited by J. R. Campbell and Shannon Allen

Many Were Called. Few Remembered.

Ruled by Arthur, the Once and Future King, these Knights took their place next to those who would become legend.

Lancelot. Galahad. Tristan. Arkin. Tor. Brannon.

Each earned their place at the Round Table. Yet kingdoms are not shaped by myths… but by courage and belief. If they are to fulfill their destiny of glory they must discover the truths within. For no false knight can complete a true quest. Against a landscape of magic, cruelty and destiny, the path to a better future is lit by the Light of Camelot.

An anthology of eleven stories and two poems by:

Jane Yolen, Kurt Unsworth, Fiona Patton, Wendy N. Wagner, Diana L Paxson, William Meikle, Colleen Anderson, J. R. Campbell, M. K. Hume, Lawrence Watt-Evans, Renee Bennett, R. Overwater and Shannon Allen.